Brenna t

distinctive and pale heart shaped g

shadows. She zeroed in on a ghost-like shape in an ancient hickory tree. Peeking out from around one branch, the bird fussed at her with increasing fervor.

"You feel it, don't you?" Brenna said to the bird. "This beautiful place is soiled."

The owl's low, warning hiss sounded in agreement.

Brenna smelled death and sadness with a nasty undertone of evil. She might not be able to conjure the Woman in White at will, but she could reclaim this little sanctuary and clear it of the spirits that disturbed the land's natural inhabitants.

The bird fell silent as she set up her candles at five points. With a flick of her wrist, they flamed to life. Then she shed her clothes and shoes, tucking them near the altar before moving to the center of the ring of fire.

Skyclad, she lifted her hands, palms up, and chanted, "Dirt from the earth, wind through the trees, water to cleanse, salt to set free. Banish the evil, honor my plea. As I will, so mote it be."

With quick, sure motions learned from Sarah, Brenna poured salt and water in a wide circle. She closed her eyes and repeated the cleansing spell aloud. The ache in her heart eased. She felt the calm and beauty of her family's land push against the darkness.

The owl called out another warning. Brenna opened her eyes and locked gazes with a white tiger.

Huge. Predatory. Standing like a statue just beyond her charmed circle. His tongue flicked around his mouth and displayed gleaming, sharp teeth.

Brenna expelled a deep breath. "God, shifter, you scared me."

Praise for Neely Powell

"Neely Powell is a bewitching storyteller. *AWAKENING MAGIC* is *Practical Magic* meets the Sookie Stackhouse series. An engrossing read that brings shifters and witches together for the fight of their lives."

~Lisa Medley, author of The Reaper Series

~*~

"Beautifully written and intriguing, this story will reel you right in. The next one in this series can't come soon enough!"

~Misty Simon, author of Ivy Morris Mysteries

To Christine,
Neely Powell
Leigh Neely
Jan Powell

Awakening Magic

by

Neely Powell

The Witches of New Mourne Series

Awakening Magic

Contact Information: info@thewildrosepress.com

Cover Art by *Debbie Taylor*

The Wild Rose Press, Inc.
PO Box 708
Adams Basin, NY 14410-0708
Visit us at www.thewildrosepress.com

Publishing History
Previously published by Harlequin, 2014
First Black Rose Edition, 2016
Print ISBN 978-1-5092-1159-3
Digital ISBN 978-1-5092-1160-9

The Witches of New Mourne Series
Published in the United States of America

Dedications

Three fellow authors
never stopped believing in me as a writer,
even when I had given up on myself:
Leigh Neely, Erica Spindler, and
the late Beverly Beaver (aka Beverly Barton).
I have unending gratitude to these women
for their impact on my life.

~Jan Hamilton Powell

~*~

For Richard, who never doubted,
for Stephanie, Dale, and Scott,
who made my own story so interesting,
and for Jan Powell,
who was my BFF before it became fashionable.

~Leigh Neely

Chapter 1

Brenna Burns shivered as she watched the storm build outside her family's home. Pines and century-old hardwoods whipped in the wind, bending at impossible angles. Her breath caught as an ancient oak snapped and crashed to the ground just yards from the house. Thunder echoed down the mountains and through the Connelly Valley. Lightning strikes came in a constant stream.

Like fire, Brenna thought, her senses sharpening. A wholly unnatural fire.

This was much more than your usual June thunderstorm in North Georgia. Though clouds boiled overhead, there was no rain, and Brenna's skin prickled. She turned as her younger sister Fiona ran into the room, shouting for help.

"We've got to stop her!"

"Stop who?"

"Eva Grace. She says Garth is in trouble, and she needs to go help him." Eva Grace Connelly was their first cousin, but the three of them grew up together and, as Connelly witches, they shared a bond deeper than sisters. Garth was the man Eva Grace was to marry tomorrow. The women had just arrived home from a bridal luncheon when the storm began to build out of a clear, blue sky.

Brenna gasped as thunder shook the old house,

rattling windows and china in the breakfront. The rumble continued for several seconds before lightning cracked like a giant whip across the sky.

"Come on," Fiona said, and this time Brenna obeyed. She could feel the evil spinning around the house, encircling them.

They ran through the kitchen and found Eva Grace at the door of the screened-in porch, just about to step into the violent storm.

"No," Brenna screamed, reaching for her. "Don't go outside. This isn't just a bad storm. There's darkness in it. It's wasn't produced by the elements."

Eva Grace pulled away. "Garth is in trouble. My moonstone was glowing hot in my pocket. I know he's alone and fighting for his life. I have to get to him. He's at Mulligan Falls." She pushed the door open, and the wind slammed it against the wall. Then she was gone, her long red hair streaming behind her as she ran across the yard.

Brenna's saw her own terror reflected in her sister's eyes. All witches in their coven shared the same green eye color, distinctly Connelly and equally expressive.

"Come on," Brenna said, grabbing Fiona's hand.

They raced into the maelstrom, dodging flying tree limbs and chunks of debris. The physical battle against the wind slowed their steps. Ahead of them, Eva Grace seemed unfazed as the wind ripped at her hair.

They caught up to her just as the lawn gave way to dense forest, and the sisters flanked their cousin, each taking one of her hands. Wind tore at Brenna's clothes, and lightning bolts hit all around them, splitting trees and sending sparks through the dry underbrush. Brenna feared they would never have pushed through the dark force without their magical family link. Three Connelly witches were difficult to stop.

Eva Grace yelled over the thunder and roar of the wind. “Brenna, can you do something to weaken the storm?”

They stopped. Brenna braced her legs and closed her eyes. She raised her free arm and splayed her fingers. While slowly dropping her hand, she repeated an old Celtic incantation.

Nothing happened.

The first drops of rain pelted her face, and the torrent began, a curtain of rain so thick it was difficult to see the path in front of them. “This storm isn’t natural. I can’t faze it.”

For a witch with strong connections to the elements, this was rare. Brenna had a special bond with these North Georgia mountains. Like generations before her, she had often called upon this land’s power for her spells.

“Let’s go,” Eva Grace said, surging forward again. “We have to get to the falls.”

Hands clasped, they bent their heads against the driving rain and pushed forward. Not an inch of this area was unknown to them. They’d grown up and learned their craft surrounded by these tall trees. But today every step of this familiar path was a battle for dominance.

Brenna had always known evil lurked at the edges of their land. They had been warned of the danger all of their lives. She had felt the darkness watching and waiting. Hadn’t their legacy, their curse, been the reason she’d left almost three years ago? She had tried to stay away, coming home for only short visits. But her escape attempt had been a futile effort. She'd moved back from Atlanta just this week, in time for the wedding, ready to reclaim her identity as a Connelly witch.

Was her absence what this was about? The elements were her base. They had always come to the call of her magic. It had been at least a year since she had used them for empowerment. Were the mountains punishing her for trying to make her home elsewhere? Fear squeezed her heart. Had she brought this evil to her family?

This storm felt personal, as if a stalwart evil being was challenging the protections laid regularly by Connelly witches. Her grandmother, Sarah, a particularly strong witch, refreshed those wards every week. Aunts and cousins frequently added their own spells. But the curse had found a way to overcome them.

They emerged in a flat clearing near the edge of the falls. The rush of water joined the cacophony of thunder and rain. The women froze.

"What is it, Brenna?" Fiona gasped. "What's stopping us?"

Darkness fell like a giant curtain. Brenna pulled the three of them into a protective circle. The evil still pushed hard, threatening to tear them apart. If they were forced apart, there would be no hope. That was terrifying.

Brenna reached out and felt the sizzle of dark magic. She jerked back when it arced and sparked above their heads.

"It's like nothing I've ever seen. I don't think we

can get any closer."

"Garth," Eva Grace said, dropping to her knees.

"Get up," Brenna yelled. "I know you're hurting, but if we don't stay connected, it will defeat us."

Fiona helped her get Eva Grace back up, and Brenna heard a growl. She felt hot breath on her neck and had to force herself to keep the circle. A beast hovered at her side. She could feel its need to take her, sense sharp claws raking at their protective magic.

Brenna yelled, "Help me! I'm trying to find nature in this to strengthen my magic."

"This is Connelly land," Fiona said. "We won't let the evil have it."

Fiona and Eva Grace began to chant, and Brenna reached for the world hidden by this unnatural storm. As her sister witches chanted louder, Brenna struggled to concentrate.

Dammit, why haven't I been using my magic?

Brenna felt a surge of strength as Eva Grace and Fiona pushed their own magic into her. Buoyed by pure air and water, she gathered her powers.

Rain pounded, wind roared, and demonic howls joined the din around them.

Searing heat moved up Brenna's legs. Her muscles clenched in protest. The beast screamed in triumph. The evil was using her body against her. She made herself relax and accept the burning pain.

Remembering a phrase her grandmother used often, Brenna said, "*A thabhairt dom neart*!" Give me strength!

Magic pulsed in the center of her body. Joy spread in its wake. Tears of happiness joined the rain on her face. Her magic was awakening.

Raising her cousins' hands with hers, she chanted, "Come to my heart, elements of the earth. Fill my magic, increase my worth. Stop my enemy, give your power to me. As I will, so mote it be." With each word her voice grew stronger until it rang out above the wind.

The blackness in front of them faded, and Brenna saw Garth. His sheriff's uniform intact, gun safely holstered at his hip, he lay at the feet of a beautiful woman. She glowed, her white dress out of another age with a wide collar, long bodice, and a full skirt. Her hair was a mass of long, blonde ringlets around a pale, pale face. Despite the wind and rain that swirled around them, the woman and Garth were untouched by the storm.

Brenna pushed as hard as she could against the magic that blocked them. Here was the evil the Connellys had all had known was coming. As surely as the years passed, this Woman in White always came for a tribute from their coven. Even Sarah's power had been unable to stop her. And Brenna felt helpless in the face of her family's worst enemy and darkest fear.

She felt Eva Grace tremble and put an arm around her. Fiona's arm slid around Eva Grace's waist, pulling their circle of magic tighter.

The woman said clearly, "He is mine."

"No," Eva Grace screamed. "He belongs to me, destined to be my husband. I love him."

Eva Grace's tremors were so strong now, Brenna could hear her teeth chattering. She could also smell rotten eggs, the stench was becoming overwhelming. Why? This was a protected clearing, sacred ground used by the Connelly Coven. How could evil have penetrated it so easily?

The Woman looked down at Garth and knelt to lay a gentle hand on his face. Eva Grace began sobbing, “No, by the goddess, no! Take your hands off him!” She pulled and struggled to get away from Brenna and Fiona.

As Brenna and Fiona held Eva Grace’s arms, Garth drew a deep breath then his chest moved no more.

Eva Grace’s scream echoed through the hills as the maelstrom stopped like someone had turned a switch. The Woman in White stepped over Garth. Her smile was startling, a wickedly beautiful gesture that chilled Brenna’s blood.

“Tell Sarah Connelly I will have the rest of what I’m due and soon,” the woman said and turned. Just before she reached the edge of the cliff, she faded, and only Eva Grace’s sobs broke the silence.

Chapter 2

The temperature was rising again, creating a sauna effect in the thick forest as Jake Tyler swung his Mourne County cruiser to a stop at the side of the narrow country road. When he stepped out of the car, the wind that usually eased the heat was gone. The forest was still and silent.

He felt the familiar heavy dread he experienced when he arrived at a crime scene, only much worse this time. The victim was Garth, his boss and best friend. The dispatcher said Garth was dead. Jake couldn't believe it. Had Garth fallen while hiking? Maybe he was just injured. He couldn't be dead.

He heard the distant roar of Mulligan Falls as he strode toward the head of a little-used path in the woods. Fiona Burns had called 911 from her cell phone just fifteen minutes ago. The dispatcher had immediately contacted Jake, who was deputy sheriff. EMS and other deputies were also in route to this north end of the county, but Jake had been close by and arrived first.

He pushed through the saturated foliage. He had not been raised here, had lived here only three years, but he already knew these mountains well. He spent every free moment roaming this wonderland. For someone of his nature, the remote, sparsely populated part of the county was a dream come true. He thanked

God often that he had met Garth while serving in the military and agreed to come to his friend's hometown. Garth knew what Jake needed. He always understood.

Jake broke into a jog as the sound of the falls intensified. One last turn, and the path gave way to an opening near the cliff. A nightmare scene spread out before him. Eva Grace Connelly stood with her cousins, Brenna and Fiona, their hands joined, chanting softly over Garth's lifeless body. Jake's keen senses smelled death in the air. Garth was truly gone.

Out of respect, Jake stopped a short distance away. Instinctively, he lifted his nose to catalog all the scents of the scene. There was ozone from the recent storm and a darker, unpleasant smell Jake suspected was the evidence of magic. Black magic. Unusual because no one practiced the dark arts in New Mourne.

Magic was in the air everywhere in Mourne County, but generally it was bright and light, like a ribbon of blessing that wound its way through the homes and lives of the special people who lived here.

But this magic tasted nasty, heavy, and oppressive. It had been a long time since Jake had sensed anything this wicked. Something horrible had taken Garth. This wasn't a tragic accident. That knowledge drove like a fist into Jake's belly, and he bent forward in pain, bracing his hands on his knees. Why Garth? Why would Garth be a target for something evil? Jake couldn't stop the rumble of grief that tore out of him.

Brenna's head immediately snapped toward him. The gaze that locked with his was like green fire. She knew, he realized. The witch knew as well as he did that this was the work of an evil force.

Acknowledging Brenna with a nod of his head,

Jake straightened. Then he spoke into the radio on his shoulder. He confirmed he was at the scene and that backup was on the way. The other units were having some difficulty because of trees down across roads due to the storm, but they were coming.

Too late for Garth, Jake thought as he walked toward the women. He'd been around town long enough to know you didn't try to penetrate a magic circle, and that's what the two sisters and their cousin had formed. As soon as they released their hands, he dropped down beside Jake. Already knowing it was useless, he felt for a pulse. There was nothing. Garth's skin was cooling. The man's sightless brown eyes stared up at the blue summer sky. Jake gently closed them.

Eva Grace knelt beside Jake, her tears falling unheeded. She was drenched, and she shivered as if chilled. "I wasn't fast enough," she sobbed. "I couldn't help him."

Jake pulled her against his shoulder. He looked up at Brenna and Fiona and asked, "What happened here?"

Brenna spoke in a clear, certain tone, telling him about the unnatural storm and Garth's murder by an evil spirit. Though Jake had not been around Brenna often, she had always appeared to be cool, distant, and sure of herself. Even now, with Garth dead, she didn't hesitate.

Jake took in the scene. All three of the women's light and colorful summer dresses were soaked. The fabric molded to Brenna's feminine curves. He deliberately turned his thoughts from that distraction, noting instead that her short cap of auburn hair was beginning to dry in the summer heat. They all looked as if they had been through a struggle, just as Brenna had said.

Around them, Jake could see no evidence related to what had happened. Garth's body was clean, the grass in the clearing was wet but held only debris from the forest. There were no obvious signs of anyone else being in the area. It appeared Garth had simply dropped dead.

Fiona's voice was calm as she stated, "There was a malevolent spirit here, Jake, and she was on a mission. She wanted Garth, and she took him. We couldn't do anything about it."

"I didn't get to him in time," Eva Grace said, pushing away from Jake's chest and reaching out to stroke Garth's out flung hand. "I should have come out sooner."

"What do you think you could have done?" Brenna said. "We've always known this could happen. We just didn't know how or when."

Jake frowned at her. "What does that mean?"

Fiona reached Eva Grace and helped her to her feet, "Come on, let's get you back to the house—"

"Sorry," Jake said. "You need to stay here until I can get a statement. This is a crime scene."

Brenna gave him a look that would have melted iron. "We just told you what happened."

"I need details."

"Details," she said and crossed her arms on her chest as if holding herself back. "Let's see. You need a description so you can put out a BOLO? She was tall, willowy, and had blond hair that never seemed to get wet. She wore an old-fashioned white dress and was transparent. She killed Garth with just a touch then she disappeared." Her hands dropped to her hips. "That about covers it."

Jake ignored her and pulled out a notebook. He looked at Eva Grace. "Are you up to this?" He knew he was being tough on them all, but he needed information while it was fresh on their minds. Didn't he owe Garth that much?

Eva Grace raked wet hair away from her face. "I felt a heavy presence. My moonstone was glowing and hot. I knew Garth was in trouble, and I knew where he was, but I have no idea how he got here. What Brenna said is what happened. It was the Woman in White. She killed Garth."

Jake was silent. He had learned long ago not to question the remarkable in New Mourne. He had seen ghosts, been called out to settle disputes involving love potions, and had once taken the report of a resident who was turned into a toad. But this was beyond anything he had encountered thus far, and as a result a good man was dead.

"Can we go now?" Brenna demanded. She put her arm around Eva Grace. "She needs to get inside and get out of her wet clothes."

Jake realized Brenna was right. What was he going to do about a ghost? Except maybe protect the women that Garth had loved so much.

"Go to the house," he said as he stepped toward Eva Grace. "I'm so sorry. I don't know—" His words broke.

The petite redhead took Jake's hand. Jake had so envied the unconditional love between Eva Grace and Garth. She loved Garth enough to let him join the Army and roam the world. She was smart enough to make him court her and earn her trust once he returned. And she tamed the wildness in him. Because Eva Grace accepted both sides of his nature, Garth was confident enough to take her as his mate.

Jake knew, with bleak certainty, he would never be able to trust himself enough to love anyone like that. Harsh lessons, learned in his childhood, had taught him to walk alone.

As his painful memories rose, Eva Grace gripped his hand with hers. "I feel your loss, Jake. You've had too many losses. You didn't deserve to lose Garth. I know what he meant to you."

Emotion clogged his throat. He turned to look at Garth's gray, still features. From Eva Grace's warm touch, Jake felt calm and comfort flood through him. Even in her grief, she used her empathic abilities to help and heal.

"Take care of her," he told Fiona.

Brenna answered him, "We always take care of our own."

"You see to Garth now," Fiona said before he could reply to Brenna's sharp tone. "Do that for Eva Grace then come back to the house to talk to us."

"I need a minute with Garth," Eva Grace said suddenly. "Just a minute alone, please."

Sirens wailed in the distance. The EMS crew would soon be pulling up to the Connelly's home and coming to the falls. Deputies would help Jake cover every inch of the scene with the help of Mourne County's version of a CSI team.

They were local computer geeks who'd taken online classes in crime scene techniques. In between creating programs and building complicated websites for various industries, they helped the sheriff's department on a volunteer basis. They were also avid paranormal researchers, so Jake knew they would look for the elements outside fingerprints and fibers.

Eva Grace deserved a moment of privacy with Garth before that invasion began.

"Take as long as you need," Jake told her and, leaving the grieving woman alone, walked with Brenna and Fiona onto the path that led to the Connelly home.

"Shouldn't we keep an eye on her?" Fiona whispered to Brenna.

"There's nothing here that can harm her now," Brenna said, pausing just inside the forest. "The worst has happened."

"Are you sure it's the worst or the beginning?" Fiona asked. "Garth wasn't a Connelly. Why would the Woman in White take him?"

"She's a ghost," Brenna replied to her sister. "If any of us could sense what she was thinking, it's you, Fiona."

Jake knew Fiona was well known for her ability to communicate with the dead, but she shook her head at Brenna's question. "There was just anger. She didn't communicate anything but anger to me."

Jake interrupted. "Who is this spirit? You talk as if you know who it was."

"The Woman in White," Brenna snapped at him. "She's always been coming for one of us. She comes after all the Connelly women."

"Well, not all—" Fiona broke in.

"At least one of us a generation," Brenna said. "She takes one of us."

"Takes you?" Jake countered. "What do you

mean?”

Brenna regarded him with cold impatience. “She kills one of us, Shifter.”

Jake was startled, but not by what she called him. She was a witch. She was Eva Grace’s close relative. Of course she knew what he was. But why the belligerence? Questions formed in his mind, but a sudden disturbance forestalled any further conversation.

Instinct made Jake step in front of the women, but the source of the noise was not a threat. Sarah Connelly Hayes, the Connelly family matriarch, hurried toward them followed by her husband, Marcus. Sarah’s long gray hair was loose around her shoulders, and for the first time ever, Jake thought she looked old.

“What’s happened?” she demanded. “I was in Eva Grace’s garden, supervising the set-up of the tent for the wedding, and I felt everything change. It went dark.”

“Garth’s dead, Grandmother,” Brenna told her without preamble.

Jake sensed an odd note of triumph in her tone. What was that about?

Sarah turned white and faltered. Her husband stepped up and put his arm around her shoulders.

“Steady, now,” the tall, dark-haired man murmured before he looked at Brenna. “How could Garth be dead?”

“Ask her,” Brenna said, nodding at her grandmother again. Again, Jake felt her anger toward the older woman. “Ask her why her protections failed. She’s had twenty-eight years to prepare for this. So ask her why it happened.”

Sarah’s eyes narrowed, and her frame straightened.

"Yes, blame me, Brenna. I'll gladly take the blame, like all those who went before me. Blame me for this, for all of our losses. Give me the blame, as always."

Brenna's eyes filled with tears, revealing a glimpse of hurt and confusion that surprised Jake. Maybe the beautiful, sexy witch wasn't made of ice, after all.

Sarah stepped up and took Brenna's hands. "I pray you'll be the one who finds the answers, girl. For all of our sakes."

Without another word, Sarah dropped Brenna's hands and pushed past them, calling Eva Grace's name. They followed her to the clearing where she met her grieving granddaughter with a choked cry and an embrace.

Jake noticed that despite the sharp exchange, Brenna linked her hand with Sarah's as they once more formed a circle around Garth.

And as the Connelly witches joined hands, Jake felt evil brush past them as he had earlier. It stirred the trees. All four women looked up and chanted together. A single lightning bolt came out of the clear sky and struck near the edge of the cliff, just next to the falls. Then there was silence.

Marcus murmured, "Holy shit, that's some damn bad mojo."

Jake thought that summed it up well. What was happening to peaceful, magical Mourne County?

Chapter 3

By late afternoon, the home place was filled with Connelly women—cooking, cleaning and guarding the young woman whose heart had been shattered.

Brenna could hear the murmurs of female relatives as she came down the back staircase and into the kitchen. There was a time when she would have been annoyed by their fluttering about. Right now, she was glad to have them close. Eva Grace needed their support.

Brenna and Fiona had been with their cousin upstairs since returning to the house a few hours ago. Eva Grace had been calm as they all changed from damp dresses and into dry jeans and T-shirts that Brenna had supplied. Then a storm of grief had claimed Eva Grace. Brenna knew she would recall her wrenching sobs forever.

Two other female cousins met Brenna at the foot of the narrow staircase. "How is she?" Maggie Connelly Mills asked quietly, nodding toward the second floor.

"Asleep, finally," Brenna replied. "Fiona's with her in case she wakes up."

"I hope she sleeps a good long time," said Lauren Mayfield, the other cousin who was about Brenna and Eva Grace's age. Two aunts in the kitchen agreed with silent nods and tearful sighs.

All of them were struggling with shock and

mourning, emotions this old house had witnessed too much of over the years. Mixed with joy and the family gatherings, there had been plenty of tragedy for the Connellys here.

The kitchen was the heart of the house. The long, log-paneled room had three walls from the first cabin the Connellys had built when they arrived from Ireland in the 1750s. Since then, new generations had added on. The white farmhouse Sarah had inherited was now a three-story, six-bedroom house with a huge great room and a dining room big enough to seat eighteen people.

This was Marcus and Sarah's home. Eva Grace had settled into a cottage in the town of New Mourne, near the shop she ran. Fiona had a small apartment on Main Street. This big house had seldom been empty, however, as there were always Connelly relations in and out. Brenna had moved into the attic suite, so she could have privacy as she adjusted to being home and near her family again.

For a family of witches so strong, Brenna wondered that they couldn't put a stop to the tragedy that haunted them.

Maggie interrupted Brenna's intense thoughts. "Aunt Sarah is in the dining room with the elder aunts."

Brenna hesitated as she glanced toward the front of the house. The elder aunts were her grandmother's two sisters, Doris and Frances. Along with Sarah, they were the last of their generation. Brenna imagined they were talking about what this attack from the Woman in White meant. It certainly didn't follow the pattern set since 1757, when the first Connelly witch had been taken.

Familiar anger surged through Brenna. All these

years, and no one had found a way to break this curse. They weren't even clear on why this had started. It was ridiculous. So many skilled witches should have found a way. She had grown up knowing the legend and knowing that she, Eva Grace and Fiona, along with Maggie and Lauren, stood a good chance of dying young. What she didn't understand is why they had to accept their fate.

The five of them were the Connelly females of their generation. Everyone else in their twenties and thirties were males. Male cousins were never touched. But Maggie and her brother now had daughters. Brenna couldn't bear to think that any of those young girls would face an attack like what had been witnessed today.

Brenna strode into the dining room. Behind her were her two cousins and two aunts. Three older women were seated at one end of the long, oak table. Sarah had changed into her usual flowing tunic and jeans, while her two sisters were conservatively dressed in pastel pantsuits. All of them had thick silvery hair, a common trait among aging Connellys. But unlike Sarah's long tresses, Doris and Frances favored short coifs sprayed into rigid helmets by New Mourne's most revered beauty salon. Brenna often thought her elder aunts resembled pious churchwomen more than witches.

All three women were studying a large open book—*The Connelly Book of Magic*. It included history, spells and magic. At least four inches thick, the book's heavy, old pages were stuffed with loose papers, yellowed photographs and handwritten notes. The book was bound in ancient scrolled leather and laced together with faded ribbons. According to family legend, the cover was cracked from an indiscriminate use of witch water a century ago, and the book itself had been known to speak.

Brenna had tried without success to get a peep out of it over the years. She wished the pages would talk now and explain today's events. "You have to fix this once and for all," Brenna told her grandmother and the elder aunts.

Great-Aunt Doris, who had turned 78 just weeks ago, glared at her. "You don't help anything with your attitude, missy. We're as upset and as mystified by this as you."

"It's no one's fault," added Frances, who was Doris's twin and older by three minutes. "We'll not have you blaming your grandmother."

"She can blame me if she wants," Sarah retorted, her green eyes sharp in her pale face.

Protests and agreements broke out, with elders, aunts and cousins all trying to talk at once.

Sarah pushed to her feet and shushed them all. "I'll not have this," she proclaimed, earning Brenna's grudging respect by the way she took command of the room. "Sit down and talk reasonably or get out."

Though younger than her sisters by eleven years, Sarah had assumed leadership of her family by virtue of her powers. Like Brenna, she drew her strength from nature and had been able to cast spells that controlled wind, rain and fire since early childhood. Doris and Frances were given more to charms and potions and had ceded authority to their younger sister without protest.

At eighteen, Sarah shocked the entire family and

the county by taking up with the son of a group of people known as gypsies. Her young man disappeared when she became pregnant. Though the rest of the Connelly family was married and quite traditional, they had closed protective ranks around Sarah. Her twin daughters, mothers to Brenna, Fiona and Eva Grace, were raised in this very house.

Her grandmother had led an adventurous life without ever leaving her home, Brenna reflected as her relatives settled around the table. In the 1960's Sarah had embraced the concept of communal living, and the Connelly farm had been opened to young people who were seeking peace and enlightenment from living off the land. The commune had folded after a few years, but many of those men and women remained in Mourne County, and they and their families were now pillars of the community, as well as Sarah's staunchest allies and best friends.

While she raised her two daughters, Sarah had discovered a talent for turning natural stone into jewelry and art. Candlesticks she crafted from geodes lined the dining room mantel, and as usual, she wore earrings of her own design that dangled tiny, polished stones. She had taken advantage of the tourist industry that had sprung up in New Mourne and sold her art. Those tourists had spread her work, and she was now a well-known and wealthy artist.

One visitor had an even more lasting effect on her. When Brenna and Eva Grace were about fifteen, Sarah had married Marcus Hayes, seventeen years her junior. He had come to New Mourne to sell his handcrafted furniture, met Sarah, and had never left.

To Brenna, it was never surprising that Sarah had

taken a younger lover; there had been many men in her life. The shocker was that she actually married Marcus. Good-natured and calm enough to settle Sarah's fiery nature, Marcus had endeared himself to the entire family and especially to Sarah's three granddaughters.

Brenna thought of Marcus as a father. Her parents had always traveled the globe, studying magic and mysteries, leaving Brenna and Fiona here with Eva Grace, whose mother was dead. Sarah had raised her granddaughters with more discipline than she had ever applied to herself or her own daughters. Marcus had just loved them all unconditionally.

The only thing that equaled his love was his respect for the power of the Connelly women. He was with the rest of the Connelly men at Eva Grace's house. They were taking down the tent and decorations for the wedding and reception, determined that she have no reminders of the celebration that would never be.

Instead of taking a seat, Brenna remained on her feet, facing her grandmother. Sarah reclaimed her chair at the head of the table, between her two sisters. She met Brenna's gaze calmly, as she always did. This was a scene the two had been playing out since Brenna was a stubborn toddler.

"Say what you need to," Sarah told her.

"This doesn't make sense. Garth shouldn't have been taken."

Frances cackled beside Sarah. "You think we don't know that—"

Sarah silenced her sister with a look. "We agree, Brenna. That's why we're going through the family book. We're trying to find a history of anything like this happening before."

Doris sniffed. "But this book is a mess, of course. It's filled with all sorts of rubbish and nonsense." She pulled a wrinkled and yellowed sheet of paper from the middle of the book. "Here's a spell for easing the pain of kidney stones." She turned the page and clucked again. "And right here is Aunt Delphina's pumpkin pie recipe."

"We've been looking for that for years," said Frances's daughter, Aunt Estelle. "How much nutmeg?"

Once again idle talk broke out in the room. Incensed, Brenna snapped her fingers, and thunder rolled, followed by a shimmering dust that fell onto the chattering group of women, rendering them all silent.

Except her grandmother. Sarah crossed her arms and shook her head at Brenna. "You're going to wake Eva Grace with your parlor tricks."

Brenna gave a guilty start and turned as Fiona came hurrying in from the kitchen, demanding, "What's all the noise down here?"

"I'm trying to get everyone focused on our real problem," Brenna retorted. "All they can talk about is kidney stones and pies."

"Release them," Sarah ordered Brenna.

Muttering a curse under her breath, Brenna snapped her fingers again, and speech was restored to her relatives.

As the tide of voices swelled once more, she became aware of a new presence. In the doorway from the front hall was Deputy Sheriff Jake Tyler. God knew how long he had been there, with his dark brown hat in his hands and his unusual gray-blue eyes taking in the scene. How was it, she wondered, that he made his khaki uniform look like a suit of armor? It had to be the combination of muscular body and absolute confidence that he exuded wherever he went.

He nodded to Brenna. “I knocked, but no one came to the door. I could hear you talking, so I let myself in.”

“I hope you’re not here to interview Eva Grace again,” Brenna said. “She’s asleep.”

He shook his head. “I just came from telling Garth’s aunt the news. She took it hard.”

Sympathetic murmurs sped around the room. In no time at all, Jake was seated at the table with a mug of coffee, one plate heaped with casseroles and salads and another with a giant slice of Aunt Doris’s triple layer German chocolate cake.

Did all of these women keep prepared Southern delicacies on hand just in case of tragedy? Brenna wondered. If she did that, she would have even more trouble keeping her weight in line. Now that she had moved back, would she be expected to have a casserole or a dessert ready for a birth or a death?

Once they were certain that the man in their midst was being fed, everyone gathered around the table except Aunt Diane, Doris’s daughter, who went up to stay with Eva Grace. Brenna sat down opposite Jake and eyed him with wariness.

“What do you need from us?” Sarah asked him.

Jake explained that the crime scene crew was finishing up at the clearing, and that Garth’s body had been taken to the coroner for an autopsy.

“No doubt they’ll discover that his heart stopped,” Brenna said with heavy sarcasm.

The shifter remained cool.

Fiona, seated beside Jake, frowned at her. “It’s

what has to be done. There'll have to be a reason given for the humans in town. Garth was the sheriff, after all."

"What did you tell Carol?" Sarah referred to Garth's aunt who was one of her close friends.

"The truth, of course," Jake replied.

Brenna bit her lip. "How she must hate us right now."

"On the contrary." Jake's eyes narrowed as he studied her. "Carol only wanted to know how she could help all of you. She's frightened for you." He turned to Sarah. "I'd like to know more about the Woman in White."

Silence took over the room as the women glanced uneasily at one another. Their family curse was a topic they didn't like to discuss amongst themselves, much less with outsiders.

"Why is that your concern?" Brenna asked Jake. She felt he was wasting their time.

"Garth would have made it his concern," he countered. "He would want this stopped for Eva Grace's sake."

"I don't know what a shifter can do to help us." The air heated as Brenna glared at Jake.

"Just stop it," Fiona cut in, scowling at Brenna.

"But he—"

"Might have something new to offer," Fiona retorted. "Don't we owe that to Eva Grace? To Garth's memory?"

Chastened, Brenna sat back.

Jake looked to Sarah again. "Why does this spirit take members of your family?"

"We don't know," Fiona volunteered.

"That part of the family history has been lost."

Doris tapped a page of the book. "We know there are pages that are missing. We just don't know where they are or exactly what they said."

Frances sighed. "I'm afraid the book has been ill-used by our family through the years. It became a habit for young witches to take out sections in order to study the spells."

"And somehow part of the family history has been misplaced," Sarah added. "That's one of the reasons I was supposed to keep it in good order, to stop that sort of thing."

"But you didn't." Doris pursed her lips as she flipped pages to the front of the book. "At the start, there is record of the birth of a Maeve Connelly, in Ireland, in 1739."

"She came here with her family," Frances added. "There's record of her death here in Mourne County at age 18, but no reason given."

Doris continued flipping through the book. "At least one woman dead in each succeeding generation—all between eighteen and thirty. The Woman in White took them."

"Just no explanation of why," Brenna inserted.

Jake frowned. "It's not hard to believe that young women died suddenly or tragically back then. Illness, injury, childbirth..."

Sarah said, "We know it's true. This spirit took our sister Rose at age twenty-three. I was only sixteen, but I felt it happen to her. Just as I felt it happen with my own daughter."

Jake's lifted an eyebrow, obviously confused by the all the family connections.

"Eva's Grace's mother was my daughter," Sarah

explained. "Celia died twenty-eight years ago at the falls where Garth died today. The same as today, there was darkness and evil on our property, but no one could stop the Woman in White."

"And was there no warning?" Brenna asked, unable to keep from asking the question that hammered at her each time she had to confront this issue. "Surely you could sense—"

"What did *you* sense today?" Doris asked her, reaching out to enclose Sarah's left hand in her own gnarled fingers.

"Why couldn't *you* stop it?" Frances added with a cold glance for Brenna as she took Sarah's right hand.

The feeling of inadequacy that Brenna had been fighting since the storm had blown up swelled again inside her. The elder aunts were right, of course. She was the Connelly witch with the most power in this generation. *What had she done to stop Garth's murder?*

She pushed to her feet, unwilling to meet her grandmother's tear-filled eyes. Sarah was the only person who had any idea of how responsible Brenna felt, but Brenna would be damned before she would reach out to her for comfort.

Brenna told the assembled group, "I think you can look through the family book, but you're not going to find any account that the Woman in White took someone like Garth—a male and not a blood relative. I studied that book backward and forward when I was growing up—"

"And left it in a mess, it appears," Doris pointed out again.

Sarah squeezed her sister's hand. "The state of the family book rests with me, as its current keeper."

The room seemed suddenly too close for comfort for Brenna. "I need some air," she said, steadfastly avoiding her sister's soft entreaty and the shifter's silvery gaze.

She went through the kitchen and crossed the back porch. Outside, the air was hot, but not untypical for June. Debris littered the yard from the earlier tumult, but otherwise it was clear and beautiful. Tomorrow would have been a gorgeous day for Eva Grace and Garth's wedding.

That thought drove Brenna to the edge of the yard to a small picnic table under a tree. She sat on the crude wooden bench, arms clenched over her belly, aching with the pain of what had happened today. No one deserved this, least of all her gentle cousin.

Wasn't it enough that the Woman in White had taken Eva Grace's mother? Celia Connelly had been murdered just days after Eva Grace and Brenna had been born. Brenna and Eva Grace were practically twins, as well, born at exactly the same time on February 2nd, the festival of Brighid. The family loved to tell of how they were gathered to celebrate when Celia and Delia went into labor. Her and Eva Grace's first cries had sounded at exactly the same time, precisely as the clock struck eleven p.m. in this very house.

And this was where they had grown up, both motherless. Even Fiona's birth when Brenna was six had not prompted Delia to stay home. She had visited only long enough to place her in Sarah's care and join her husband in Russia or France or wherever else he dictated they should go.

But at least she and Fiona had a mother who was

alive, Brenna told herself. Not like poor Aunt Celia, her generation's sacrifice. Brenna had always sworn to herself that she would protect Eva Grace from more tragedy, but she had let her down today.

Could Brenna have stopped this? She had run away from who and what she was years ago. Maybe the spirit took Garth to show her the primitive power of the family legacy. Hurting Eva Grace was a canny move, guaranteed to keep Brenna home.

"You're being stupid."

Brenna looked up. Her sister stood in front of her. Behind her, Brenna could see Jake standing on the back steps. "What do you mean?"

"It's not your fault."

She shrugged that off. Fiona was only twenty-two. She would never understand the responsibility that Brenna felt toward her and Eva Grace. "What does the shifter want?" she asked, jerking her chin in Jake's direction.

"It's really tacky to call him that," Fiona replied. "Garth was a shifter, too. You were never ugly toward him. What's wrong with shifters? There are at least a dozen families with shifters in Mourne County. This is where creatures of all kinds can be what they are. That's why Garth brought Jake here after they left the military."

"Garth was Garth. He belonged to Eva Grace and to us. He was family. Jake is…different." The description was inadequate, but Brenna couldn't find another. She took a deep breath. "So what does he want?"

"Just another couple of questions."

"What does he think he's going to do about all of

this?" Brenna muttered. She knew she was being downright rude to someone who truly cared about Eva Grace, but she didn't want to bother with him right now.

"Just talk to him," Fiona told her and gestured Jake toward them.

Sliding off the table to stand with her sister, Brenna stilled her impatience. "So do you understand our family curse now?"

He turned his hat around in his hands. "I'm a little clearer on the details, but I'm far from understanding it."

"Welcome to the club." Brenna felt bone weary. "What did you want to ask us?"

"Do you really believe today was just the beginning?"

Brenna reached out to clasp her sister's hand. "I've tried not to believe this my whole life, but it is happening."

Fiona added, "I've hunted some pretty bad ghosts. But nothing has ever felt like today. Nothing this dark or evil."

"She's coming for us." Brenna turned toward the woods again. "Listen," she said, shushing her sister and Jake. She cocked her head, puzzled. "It's so quiet. There are no insect or animal sounds."

Brenna felt Fiona shiver. "This is really strange."

Jake took a deep breath. "I can smell animals, but they're silent."

A cat appeared near the picnic table under the trees. Her name was Tasmin, and she was the latest in a family of felines who had called this place home. Gray and white, with sharp green eyes, Tasmin paused and stared at Jake. Then she turned, arched her back, and hissed at the woods.

A growl rumbled from Jake.

Brenna turned to him. "There's no need for that."

"We'll see," he replied. "There's some seriously bad shit about to happen. I wouldn't be Garth's friend if I didn't offer my protection."

Brenna laughed.

"What do you find so funny?" Jake demanded.

"The idea of you protecting us." She kept her head up and let her hips sway as she walked back to the porch. As she had told Fiona earlier, Jake was different. But he shouldn't get big ideas about any of them needing him. Least of all her.

Chapter 4

The air crackled in Brenna's wake, and Jake was left with the lingering scent of honeysuckle.

Fiona remained at his side as her sister slammed the kitchen door. "Please don't mind her. She's not always this way. She's…"

Jake gave Fiona a look. Her fumbling apology halted.

"Oh, hell," she admitted. "Brenna is always this way. She thinks this is a family matter, best handled by the family."

"And how's that working for you?" Jake quipped.

"Obviously not very well."

"I wish that she would realize I'm not an outsider. Garth was the closest I ever had to a brother. He and his aunt…" Jake's jaw clenched with emotion. He shook his head, staring out at the woods, at the spot where the cat had disappeared only moments ago. He longed to join the sleek feline, to break free of the terrible events of this day and run.

He straightened his shoulders and fitted his hat on his head. "I've got to go back to town. The Board of Commissioners has called an emergency meeting to appoint me acting sheriff."

"I'm glad about that."

"I'm not so sure." Jake led the way to the front of the house. He had parked his cruiser behind the cavalcade of Connelly vehicles in the driveway.

"Can we talk again?" Fiona asked him. "Brenna's going to realize that we could use your perspective on this."

"So you're going to convince her to bring me in." Jake gave the younger woman a steady look. No doubt she could do it. He respected her clear-eyed practicality, as well as her gift for speaking to spirits. "Are you sure you didn't pick up on anything more when Garth was being attacked? Something you didn't want to share with Brenna right away?"

Fiona hesitated. She had pulled her dark red hair back into a ponytail, which made her look younger and accentuated her pale skin. "There was a lot of evil. Whatever killed Garth—"

"You said the Woman in White is what killed him," Jake interrupted. "Do you doubt that?"

"No, I just..." Fiona stumbled over her words and frowned. "What took Jake is old and mad, and it's been around for a long time. I was..." She stopped, then plunged ahead, "I was frozen with fear. I've never felt like that before. Talking to dead people most of my life has put me in some pretty bad situations, but this was a whole new level of terrible."

It wasn't just Brenna who felt responsible for what had happened today. Jake could see that Fiona was dealing with her own load of guilt. He started to reassure her when the radio on his shoulder squawked.

He signed on and said to the dispatcher, "What's going on?"

Gladys's familiar nasal twang came over the little speaker. "You've gotta get downtown. There are some teenagers writing graffiti on the side of the Save a

Buck."

"Graffiti? Can't another unit cover this?"

"There's a unit there now. But they're asking for you, Jake. The town's tense after what happened to Garth. I told Commissioner Williams that I'd get you down here."

Jake sighed. He wasn't even officially the acting sheriff, and the heavyweights in the town—like Pastor Fred Williams—were already trying to use their political muscle on him. Much as he loved living here, he wasn't sure how much of that crap he would be able to stand. But he smothered his irritation and replied to Gladys, "Ten-four. Tell 'em I'm on my way."

He turned back to Fiona. "I've got to go. Tell Eva Grace that I'm thinking about her, and we're going to figure this out. Maybe you and Brenna could get some more history on this spirit. Maybe there's something that can help us in that family history book inside."

"I'll also check with some other people in town who know about our curse," Fiona said.

They said goodbye. Jake let his mind wander as he turned his vehicle toward New Mourne. Grief rose again. Garth was gone. He wouldn't see him fixing his gut-burning coffee at the office. He would never get another chance to defeat him at basketball. The goal they'd put up in the parking lot to "stay physically fit" was really to indulge their competitiveness. But that was over.

Jake drove into the picturesque small town. New Mourne had the usual town square, rimmed by small businesses and residential areas. Some chain stores had infiltrated the edges, and a developer had built a mass of large, elegant homes that were occupied by wealthy people fleeing Atlanta's urban sprawl. But for the most part this was a place out of time. Charming for visitors. Peaceful for all who lived here.

He wondered how the humans who pretended to ignore the supernaturals were going to take all of this. The county coroner, an old pro at explaining the inexplicable, would come through with a cause of death that they could put in the newspaper. But what would be the chatter in the diner? What would Pastor Williams be preaching from his pulpit this Sunday?

Garth had explained to Jake early on that Fred Williams knew all about the supers in their community. He railed against evil and wickedness in public, pleasing a certain segment of the population enough that he had built himself a mega church that drew believers from several counties. But he never actually took any action against the supers.

Jake had long wondered what the pastor's real game was. He dreaded having to work closer with him.

Jake pulled into the parking lot between the Save a Buck store and Red Hanson's Food Stop. A crowd had gathered. Everyone looked angry. He hustled out of his vehicle to help the officer on the scene.

At the center of the group, three teenagers were bent double, laughing. Jake let Gladys know he was on scene as he hurried over to Deputy Brian Lamont. First cousin to the Connellys, Brian was a strong man in his late twenties, but he had his hands full trying to hold back the formidable Verna Ryan, manager of the Save a Buck. She was threatening the teenagers with a can of spray paint.

"I don't think you really want to do that," Jake said, grabbing the paint out of Verna's hand. He took a firm grip on her arm and pulled her back. He nodded at Brian. "See if you can disperse this crowd."

The three boys started laughing again. Verna yelled, "Now you're in trouble, you obnoxious twits. Jake'll put your asses in jail!"

"Cool down." Jake held her steady. "Shut those boys up," he called over his shoulder to Brian as Verna continued to struggle. The forty-something woman helped her husband feed and take care of the family's horses before coming to work every day, and she was strong.

"I want them in jail right now with no bail. I already called Pastor Williams, and he said you would take care of this right away."

"Fred got me here." Jake tossed the can of paint aside. He pulled Verna around so that he could clamp hands on both her arms and get her complete attention. "Calm down and then tell me what happened. Start at the beginning."

Verna nodded at the teenagers. "Those three came into the store and each bought a can of spray paint. My cashier told me they were acting strange."

Jake frowned in the boys' direction. Timothy and Jason Hurley and Michael Patrick, all of them under fifteen, were barely managing to control themselves as Brian herded them to his patrol car. Jason, the youngest, couldn't resist one last leer at Verna. The boy's eyes were dilated. These three were normally good kids, but they were high on something.

"You can see what they wrote over here," Verna added.

Jake took in the words on the side of the building for the first time. "See you in the darkness" was scrawled in black across peeling white paint. The letters moved and oozed, dripping downward, bubbling like acid.

"Do you see that?" Jake asked Verna, his eyes focused on the letters.

"See what?" She poked his chest to get his attention. "After the cashier talked to me, I came out the front to see what these boys were up to, but they were gone. I hoped that was the end of it. I had no idea they were over at the side of the building. A customer came in and told me what they were doing. I called y'all's office and went after them myself."

Jake looked back at the wall, but the message was just messy spray paint now, nothing out of the ordinary. Still, an uneasy feeling settled in his gut. Why hadn't the boys run when confronted by Verna? It was almost like they wanted to be caught.

"Have these boys been trouble around here before? Were they mad at you about something?" he asked Verna.

"I don't put up with nonsense from any kids. Everybody knows that." Uncertainty crept into the woman's hardened features. "Up until now these boys have always been real polite."

"You think they bought the paint to huff it?"

"If they were going to do that, why'd they waste it on the building?" Verna folded her arms across her ample bosom. "I don't know why they did it, but I want to press every charge against them I can and you lock 'em up with no bail."

"The courts decide bail." Jake looked at the nasty black scrawl again, eyes narrowing.

"You've got to do something," Verna urged.

"I'll call the boys' parents. If they agree, we'll keep them in jail tonight and bring them out here tomorrow to repaint your wall. Working hard in the summer heat will be punishment for their crime. I'll make sure somebody stays with them all day and that they put two coats on it."

It was obvious Verna was thinking about arguing, but then she nodded. "All right, I'll settle for that, but if this happens again, I'll do everything I can to see those nasty little thugs in jail."

"I'm going to get to the bottom of this. I know both sets of parents. They're going to be more than happy to buy the paint and see this set right."

Verna walked toward the store's entrance without another word.

Hands on his hips, Jake stared at the message again. "See you in the darkness" sounded familiar. Maybe it was from Shakespeare or someone else famous, but he couldn't pull it out of his memory.

Brian stepped to his side. "Are you really gonna keep these boys overnight?"

Jake nodded. "You take them on down to the jail. I'll have Gladys call the parents, and you start the paperwork. Right now I have to go meet with the Board of Commissioners."

"Good luck with that," Brian said with a mournful look in eyes that were as green as his cousin Brenna's. "God help us, Jake. I still can't believe that Garth is dead."

"Me, either." Jake had a cold, bleak feeling inside as he stared once more at the graffiti. Why would three young teens write these words instead of the usual F-U?

He took out his phone and snapped a photograph of

the wall. Then he went to his browser, intending to do a Google search on the phrase. Before he could, his radio squawked again.

Gladys said, "The BOC is waiting on you."

Smothering a curse, Jake hurried back his car.

Chapter 5

Twilight spread over the mountains as Brenna slipped down the path to the falls. The woods were once again alive with the sounds of animals and insects. She thought it could almost be a normal summer evening just before moonrise. Except, Connelly land had been stained by death.

The coven had fortified the wards around their property. Then the house emptied of relatives, leaving enough food to carry the family through a siege. Sandy Murphy, a young woman who worked for Eva Grace at her shop, brought candles, crystals, and herbal potions to soothe her boss. Eva Grace finally escaped into deep sleep. Fiona was tucked into the twin bed near hers. Marcus and Sarah had retreated to their suite on the first floor.

Brenna felt safe in leaving her family to do what needed to be done.

In a small canvas bag, she carried salt and black candles to cleanse the place where Garth had been killed. She was determined to vanquish any trace of dark magic.

As a child, the clearing had been her personal cathedral. The tall pines provided a canopy. During the day, streaks of sunlight would spotlight several large rocks, turning them into natural altars. Even after she was old enough to understand that Eva Grace's mother had died here, Brenna had found peace under these trees. After all, she had never known Aunt Celia. But Garth's cruel death in the spot could mean she would never feel at ease here again.

"You'll not take this from me." Brenna spoke these words as she broke through the trees. She wanted the Woman in White to appear and answer her. She wanted to challenge the spirit's right to inflict misery on her family yet again.

The only response was the sudden, sharp screech of an owl.

A barn owl was out and about, having left the nest in the old barn early on this sad night. These birds were usually seen when it was full dark, their wings spread, carrying them with silent speed. Brenna learned as a child that barn owls didn't hoot. Their call was shrill, almost a scream. Or if threatened, they issued a hiss that could turn your blood cold.

It was fitting that an owl had come out early tonight, as myth and legend associated them with death.

The screeches continued. Brenna turned around, trying to spy the animal's distinctive and pale heart-shaped face in the gathering shadows. She zeroed in on a ghost-like shape in an ancient hickory tree. Peeking out from around one branch, the bird fussed at her with increasing fervor.

"You feel it, don't you?" Brenna said to the bird. "This beautiful place is soiled."

The owl's low warning hiss sounded in agreement.

Brenna smelled death and sadness with a nasty undertone of evil. She might not be able to conjure the Woman in White at will, but she could reclaim this little sanctuary and clear it of the spirits that disturbed the land's natural inhabitants.

The bird fell silent as she set up her candles at five points. With a flick of her wrist they flamed to life. Then she shed her clothes and shoes, tucking them near the altar before moving to the center of the ring of fire.

Skyclad, she lifted her hands, palms up, and chanted, "Dirt from the earth, wind through the trees, water to cleanse, salt to set free. Banish the evil, honor my plea. As I will, so mote it be."

With quick, sure motions learned from Sarah, Brenna poured salt and water in a wide circle. She closed her eyes and repeated the cleansing spell aloud. The ache in her heart eased. She felt the calm and beauty of her family's land push against the darkness.

The owl called out another warning. Brenna opened her eyes and locked gazes with a white tiger.

Huge. Predatory. Standing like a statue just beyond her charmed circle. His tongue flicked around his mouth and displayed gleaming, sharp teeth.

Brenna expelled a deep breath. "God, shifter, you scared me."

He watched her a moment, then turned with slow, deliberate grace.

"No need to look away," Brenna said, straightening her spine. "We're all just as the goddess made us. No shame here."

The tiger turned back. He sat like the majestic cat that he was, his blue eyes moving over Brenna's naked body in a brutal inspection. He stretched, sleek muscles rippling in the twilight and candle glow.

Brenna chuckled. "Preening a bit for me, now, aren't you?"

He growled, low and deep, then showed her his

back again.

"So you want me to get dressed, do you?"

His long, white tail thumped the ground.

Feeling rather satisfied with herself, Brenna closed the circle and doused the candles. The tiger kept a discreet distance while she pulled on her underwear, jeans, and T-shirt. She sat on the stone "altar" to pull on socks and shoes, and was tying her shoestrings when the tiger looked at her again.

Brenna held out her hand. "I didn't expect you to be so big."

He crept into the circle, nose sniffing at the ground, blinking his eyes against the smoke from the candles. He was a massive cat, his head nearly level with Brenna's chest. With some of the shifters she had met in Atlanta, she would have felt fear now. Despite their human nature, they were still wild.

With Jake she felt only curiosity. Or perhaps a bit more, she admitted as he advanced closer. She would like to know how his long, lean body felt beneath his ivory pelt.

He stepped close, his whiskers tickling her skin as he smelled her outstretched hand. He pushed his face against her fingers.

Sighing in delight, she brushed her hand over the soft, supple fur between his ears.

He inched closer and dipped his head against her arm. She stroked down his nose and enjoyed the feel of the velvety fur, wondering how he would react if she laid her cheek against it. A satisfied rumble vibrated through his body. She laughed and scratched him under the chin. His eyes closed in bliss.

Brenna sighed. "You're making me miss my cat.

Her name was Pearl, and she was with me for eighteen years. She died just before I moved to Atlanta. I haven't been able to let another cat claim my heart. I'd use you for my familiar, but I don't think I could afford to feed you."

His eyes lifted, narrowed. Brenna could almost hear his disdainful thoughts.

"Don't worry. I promise not to cast an enslaving spell on you."

She laughed again as he backed away. "Worried, are you?"

In response he disappeared into the undergrowth. Like a dissolving shadow, she thought.

The man in his khaki uniform replaced the big cat. Jake walked toward her. "No spells, please."

"Ah, but you know magic. Else you couldn't change so quickly. And keep your clothes in one piece."

"We shifters learn to adapt." He ran a hand through his dark hair. "Clothes are required in the real world."

"And more's the pity," Brenna retorted, grinning.

His eyes were grayer than the tiger's, Brenna noted, but they had the same knowing gleam as his gaze slid over her again.

"You're beautiful," he said.

Brenna wasn't certain who was more surprised by his words—her or him.

"The spell was beautiful," he amended quickly. "I needed to run, and I was drawn back here to see if I could find anything that could help us understand why your spirit took Garth."

"Did you find anything?"

He shook his head. "I saw you and what you were

doing and stopped looking. You were right to cleanse this place."

She looked around clearing. "I have to admit, that did feel good. I was worried…" She stopped and bit her lip.

"Brenna?"

She shrugged her shoulders. Admitting to a worry didn't make her weak. "I haven't practiced magic like this much over the past few years. I thought I might have lost my touch."

His voice deepened. "From where I was sitting, you looked pretty powerful."

Brenna couldn't help teasing him again. "As a witch or as a woman?"

"Both." His gaze caught hers and held.

The owl sounded. Brenna looked up in surprise, having forgotten the bird with Jake's unexpected appearance. Another call rang out, less fretful this time.

Brenna laughed. "So your woods feel better now?" The answer was low, almost a coo.

"You have a nice touch with animals," Jake said.

With thoughts of touching his fur, Brenna was uncomfortable with the attraction she felt. She turned away. "I need to gather my things and finish this."

While she swept the area with a fallen tree limb, he picked up her candles, salt, and water bottles, storing them in the canvas bag.

They started through the woods toward the house, and Jake's stomach rumbled.

"Hungry?"

"When I shift and come back quickly like that I have to eat."

"There's all kinds of food at our house." She

couldn't quite control her shudder.

"You don't like your family's food?"

"It's funeral food. There's a limit to the chicken casserole and macaroni salad you can eat in one day."

"Let's go to Mary's Diner and grab some cheeseburgers. My treat." He held up his cell phone. "You can call Sarah and let her know where you are."

She hesitated. Every instinct told her to resist this shifter with his silvered gaze and his wild side. But if she was truthful, she didn't want to go home just yet. At home she had to give into the heartache of the day and the worry about what was coming.

"Okay," she agreed.

"We'll walk back up to my car at the head of the other path," Jake said. Darkness had fallen in earnest, and he pulled out his flashlight. They followed the beam through the woods.

Jake took her hand as the path narrowed. Brenna told herself that she didn't enjoy it. But lying to herself wasn't one of her better skills. So she threaded her fingers through his and felt him study her.

Let him try to figure me out, she thought, smiling under cover of night. Other men had tried and failed. She doubted a shifter would have any better luck, but the game could be interesting.

Chapter 6

As usual on Friday night, New Mourne was bustling. Teenagers gathered in groups outside the video arcade. Some of the galleries and shops that lined Main Street closed early, but most stayed open late on Friday. Tourists rocked in chairs on the porch of the Red Oak Tavern and Inn. Lilting notes of Irish folk tunes came from the town square. The Brody family, who entertained on Friday night when weather permitted, sounded in fine form to Brenna.

The familiar noises meant home to her. She was relieved to allow the happy sounds push aside memories of Eva Grace's sobs and the hushed grief of the relatives.

Jake opened the door to Mary's Diner for Brenna. Rich scents of frying burgers and freshly baked bread greeted them. The diner was almost empty. A couple of teenagers talked over an ice cream sundae.

Brenna waved at a baby banging on his high chair tray with a spoon. The eighteen-month-old boy's parents were former classmates of hers, so she stopped to say hello and admire their happy child.

In the back, she saw a neighbor who became wolf at the full moon. He and his wife smiled as Brenna and Jake passed them and took a seat in a booth.

The waitress didn't blink when Jake ordered four burgers without buns. Brenna asked for a cheeseburger, everything on it. Moments later, she also dug into the warm brown bread that the waitress served with their sweet tea.

The bread was the specialty of the house, made by an independent kitchen witch who ran her own bakery up the street. Brenna could taste the magic in the firm crust. She had missed this bread since her last trip home.

"I don't usually like bread very much," Jake said as he slathered a piece with honey butter. "But I love this stuff."

Brenna smiled. Even the shifter hadn't figured out the ingenuity of the two business owners. This special and irresistible bread was the charm that kept customers coming back in a steady stream. And it was too delicious to make her worry about her hips widening. Although Jake hadn't complained about what he had seen of her in the clearing.

Brenna gave herself a stern mental shake.

The teenagers walked by, arms wrapped around each other as they headed for the door. The young man was so caught up in the girl that he tripped over a chair and had to keep himself from falling.

"Teenage love," Brenna said, laughing.

"More like teenage hormones," Jake corrected. "He'll probably have a new love next week."

"Is that the way you treated girls as a teenager?"

He shrugged. "I did my best to stay away from girls altogether."

"Oh, come now."

"Young male tigers are rather unpredictable. It was safer for everyone if I kept to myself."

"Being a teenage witch had its out-of-control

moments as well." Brenna agreed. "When my tenth-grade boyfriend broke up with me, I cast a spell on the girl who stole him. She grew a mustache."

Jake chuckled. "That was mean."

"Eva Grace made me reverse the spell after the poor girl spent a week at home."

"I can see Eva Grace being the good witch."

"And me being the wicked one? You're right. Were you a bad little boy who played tricks as well? Maybe shifting when your parents told you not to?"

His expression sobered. "No tricks from me. I always took being a shifter very seriously."

"So you were good as gold, and your parents adored you?"

"My mother adored me."

"And does she still?"

"She's dead. Both my parents are dead."

The bitterness in his tone struck Brenna as raw. She felt a stab of regret. "I'm sorry. Really sorry."

His silvery eyes gleamed as he drained his tea glass. "It doesn't matter. Some people should never have a family and kids."

Brenna had to agree with him. "My parents certainly shouldn't have bothered. They left me with Sarah right after I was born and did the same with Fiona."

"And you resent them for it."

"Resent?" Brenna shrugged. "That's a simple word for a bunch of complicated feelings." She looked away, not certain why she was sharing so much with this shifter. Maybe the fact that he already knew so much about her family made her feel comfortable with him. That was a mistake.

She turned the conversation back to him. "So where did you grow up?"

"Las Vegas until I was about fifteen."

"I don't know if I've ever met anyone who grew up there. What did your parents do?"

Looking uncomfortable, he said, "My mom was a showgirl until she got pregnant."

"A showgirl? Really? Was she a shifter?"

"No, that gift comes from my father." Jake's eyes had gone cold again. "I don't really like to talk about him."

"Okay, shifter, message received. No talking about your family."

He leaned back, his tousled hair dark against the red vinyl of the booth. "Jake. Call me Jake, please."

"Okay. Jake." Brenna felt a bit ashamed. "I have nothing against shifters."

"That's a relief."

"There are quite a few I like. In Atlanta I have twin friends who change into hawks when the spirit moves them. It's how they get into concerts free in Piedmont Park. They just fly in, land somewhere and enjoy the music."

"Yeah, well, I've never done that. People tend to notice when a white tiger glides into a room."

"I guess you mainly have to worry about hunters."

"That's the beautiful thing about Mourne County. I feel safe most of the time. Garth told me I would, and he was right."

"You've got a place east of our land, right?"

"Northeast. Almost to the North Carolina line. Several acres with a cabin Garth helped me build."

Brenna sighed. "Garth dying isn't what I expected

to happen my first week back home."

"What did you think would happen?"

"The Woman in White would kill me."

He nodded, as if he expected the statement. "Is that why you left here in the first place?"

She shrugged. "As you witnessed today, my grandmother and I don't see eye to eye about how to handle the family curse. She thinks giving up is the way. I think there has to be a way around it."

"No surprise there."

"Sarah is unconventional in most areas of her life. But on this she won't budge. She thinks we just have to accept our fate."

Jake's brows pulled together. "She didn't seem all that accepting today. To me, it's more like she doesn't know what to do."

"That is rare for the wise and powerful Sarah Connelly, coven leader."

"Are you thinking you could do a better job?"

This remark surprised Brenna. How was it that Jake could read her so well when he knew so little about her? Was he a psychic as well as a shifter?

"Why would you think I'd try to take over for Sarah?" she asked.

"Aren't you the next generation's leader?"

"Our generation doesn't really have a leader—"

"Come on," he retorted. "Fiona has no interest in taking over. She's too busy with her blog, her website, her Internet show about ghost hunting, and trying to help lost souls cross over. Eva Grace is very content with her shop. Besides, her spirit is too gentle to lead the charge."

"There's always Aunt Estelle or Aunt Diane."

He shook his head. "If they wanted to be the leader, they would have asserted themselves by now."

Brenna had to agree. "There's also my mother, of course, but she ran away so long ago she's hardly relevant."

"You can't think Maggie or Lauren is destined to be a leader?"

"Well, they're also on the chopping block for the Woman in White this time around. Maybe one of them can break the curse."

Jake shook his head. "Maggie's too sweet to lead anything other than a bake sale. She's totally consumed with her husband and her little girl, decorating her house, and brewing herbal potions and teas to sell at Eva Grace's shop."

"But Lauren…"

Jake smirked. "Lauren has other interests. Many other interests."

Brenna pretended to bristle. "Are you saying that my cousin, my sister witch, likes male company. As in men, plural?"

"Is that what you're saying?"

"I refuse to spread rumors about my family."

"Too late. Lauren is pretty well known."

Brenna wondered if he might have given in to the temptation of Lauren's lush curves and the seduction spells she could weave. A quick jolt of jealousy sparked in her.

Jake didn't notice that emotion, thank goodness. He stayed on subject. "Don't you think it's up to you to change things? Isn't that really why you've come home?"

"I came home because I was tired of working in

advertising. I've signed a contract to illustrate a book, and I decided New Mourne provided a better work atmosphere."

He looked skeptical.

She continued. "I also wanted to get away from Atlanta. I realized I didn't like it there. It's too big. The urban supes are too…" She bit her lip, trying to express herself.

"Competitive?" Jake supplied.

"That's one word for it. There's a reason why they call cities concrete jungles."

"I remember. I lived in a couple of cities before I joined the military."

"After your parents died?"

"Yeah, I tried foster care, but that's not a real good environment for a teenaged shifter. So I hit the road."

Atlanta had been too large for her to feel safe and comfortable as an adult, so Brenna couldn't imagine being alone in the city when she was young.

Jake moved the conversation back to her. "I don't think you came home to be killed, Brenna. You didn't come to escape the city, either. You came home to fight. For yourself and your family."

She didn't like him ferreting out all of her secrets. "That's really not your—"

"Don't tell me again this isn't my concern." The fierceness of his tiger side flashed in his eyes. "Garth's death is my concern. The whole town is my concern. I have to keep the peace."

Brenna resisted the urge to snap at him. "Okay, do you have any bright ideas what we should do about our murderous ghost?"

Jake nodded. "I think your grandmother and your

aunts are on the right track. The answers are probably in your family's past. Maybe in the entire town's past. Weren't the Connellys the first settlers?"

"The Cherokee were here, of course. And there were a few missionaries ahead of us."

"But you're connected to the land. The Woman in White must be as well."

"True, but…" A noise distracted Brenna.

Jake turned and looked toward the back of the diner.

"Do you hear that?" she asked as a muffled noise rumbled from the bathroom at the back of diner.

"Yeah, what do you think is going on in the men's room?" He stood. "I hope nobody's fighting."

"There's barely room to turn around in there," Brenna said, getting to her feet, as well.

Jake's grin was almost teasing. "How do you know what's in the men's room?"

Before Brenna could answer, an animal burst out of the bathroom, leaving the door in splinters. A werewolf, Brenna realized, as the creature raised his head and gave a menacing growl. White fangs gleamed as his drool pooled and his golden eyes scoured the room. Brenna and Jake froze along with the waitress, the cashier and the few other diners.

The beast shook his head and trembled.

Brenna glanced at where she'd seen her werewolf neighbor and his wife moments earlier. The woman was still, her head down, her eyes focused on the table as her husband's wolf howled. He sounded as if he were in pain. Fear shot through Brenna. There wasn't a full moon tonight, so something was wrong—very wrong.

The baby near the front screamed. The wolf

stepped toward the sound.

The mother reached out, no doubt by instinct, but the father stopped her with one quick move. They were both locals, familiar with how to deal with a werewolf, but Brenna could see they were struggling for control as the baby began to sob.

The werewolf, growling low in his throat, took another step forward.

Brenna had to do something. She flung her hand at the child and said, "*Falbh a chadal.*" With her Gaelic command, the baby fell asleep.

The wolf halted. He shook his head and danced in place. He sniffed the air, moving closer to the baby. The mother began to cry, but she didn't move.

Brenna saw Jake raise his hand to his gun, his movement slow and measured. His fingers closed on the grip but didn't pull the gun out.

The wolf planted his feet and shook his head from side to side. He dropped to the floor and trembled like he was having a seizure. A black shadow rose up from the wolf's belly, bounced from wall to wall, and swooped down in front of Jake.

Brenna saw the black energy pass through him. A tiger's roar rose from deep in his chest.

Hair sprouted on his hands. She could see him pushing against the change, his eyes going blue, then silver again as he struggled. Forcing herself to remain calm, she said, "Steady, Jake. Steady."

He leaned down, pressing his palms on the table. Like a bullet, the blackness flung itself out of him, bouncing around the room before disappearing.

Jake's white fur began to disappear, and Brenna put her hand on top of his. "Okay now?"

He let his breath out slowly. “Yeah, I think so. What was that?”

She shivered in apprehension. “Nothing good, that’s for sure.”

They turned back to the wolf, now rolling on the floor in the throes of changing back to human. As his naked body emerged, his wife pulled a red-checked tablecloth off a nearby booth to cover him. Then she eased down on the floor and cradled his head in her lap. He moaned and continued to shake. He was pale and in shock.

Jake headed toward the couple, and Brenna went to her friends with the baby, who was now in his mother’s arms fast asleep. Brenna stroked the little one’s fine, blond hair. “He’ll be fine. All I did was help him fall asleep.”

“Thank you,” the father said earnestly. “You may have saved his life.”

“Are you two all right?”

The mother nodded, though she looked shaken. “This is all so odd. We know that werewolf. He’d never do anything to harm us or the baby. Something made him lose control.”

Brenna agreed, but she didn’t know what had passed through this diner. She plucked a glass of water from a table and took it to the werewolf, who was now sitting up and talking to Jake.

“It grabbed me all of sudden.” He accepted the water from Brenna. “Thanks.”

“He looked sick,” his wife added. “He got up real fast and headed to the bathroom.”

“I was trying to stop it,” the man said. “But whatever was inside me took over my wolf, and I didn’t have enough strength to block the change. It was like I was watching a horror movie. The baby smelled so good. I knew it was wrong, but I almost couldn't keep myself from going for him. It was like I was a monster. I've never felt that way before."

Jake put a hand on the other man's shoulder. "I understand. It almost got me, too. I could see you were fighting it, whatever it was."

"The baby's parents understand too," Brenna assured her neighbors. "They know it wasn't your fault. We all know something strange happened here."

The werewolf pressed his face into his wife's belly and wept.

From the front door, the waitress called, "Jake, I think you're needed outside. Come quick."

Brenna followed Jake to the door. They stepped outside and Jake pulled Brenna behind him. "What in the world…"

She pushed out of his protective grip and was stunned by the scene on Main Street. People up and down the sidewalks were arguing with one another. The music from the park had stopped and was now replaced by angry voices.

Jake barked orders into his radio, calling for backup.

A shoving match started between some men standing nearby, and Jake rushed to intervene. Glass shattered in the distance, and car alarms bleated far and near. Lights snapped on in the inn.

In the midst of this chaos, Brenna caught sight of her cousin Lauren, standing back, grinning like a Cheshire cat. Then she was gone in the crowd. Brenna blinked, wondering if it had been Lauren at all.

But she knew one thing for certain. Black magic had now touched the whole town, not just her family's land.

Chapter 7

The wind through her open window was warm on Brenna's face as she drove her small SUV away from the Connelly home. For the first time in days, her time was her own. She had her art kit with charcoals and colored pencils beside her. She was going to sketch plants that attract caterpillars and butterflies.

Her Aunt Frances had a witch garden with a butterfly garden that was the envy of the local lawn enthusiasts. What better place for Brenna to study a caterpillar's domain for the children's book she was illustrating?

Brenna felt she also needed a break. The past days had blurred into one another.

First there had been the odd disturbances in town. Jake and the rest of the sheriff's department were hard pressed to keep order. Three nights this week, the coven had cast calming spells for the entire countryside. Still not used to exercising her magic so often, Brenna found these group encounters taxing.

The good news was the troubles had subsided, although not disappeared. Brenna could feel an evil presence hovering, but there had been no more incidents like the one with the werewolf in the diner. What was the Woman in White planning next? Brenna couldn't imagine.

Garth's memorial service was held Wednesday,

with an evening wake at Sarah's. Eva Grace and Garth's aunt had spread his ashes in the woods where he had loved to shift and roam.

As Brenna traveled the familiar route to her elder aunt's home, she marveled again at Eva Grace's remarkable strength. The day after Garth's wake, Eva Grace had insisted on going back to her cottage. Brenna and Fiona stayed with her the past two nights, but she asked them to leave this morning. Brenna didn't blame her cousin for wanting some time alone before returning to her shop on Monday.

It felt like they were all getting on each other's nerves. Despite the need to find some answers about the Woman in White and the curse, they had made little headway. Sarah and the elder aunts had turned peevish about *The Connelly Book of Magic*, insisting they needed to study it first. So Brenna and Fiona had learned little new information about the past appearances of the Woman in White and how these might relate to current events.

On top of all of this, Brenna was supposed to be setting her third floor studio/bedroom to rights at Sarah's. She hadn't unpacked before Garth was murdered, and the large room was a jumble of boxes. She knew she should make herself at home in the attic where she, her sister, and cousin had played so often as children. Having her own space was key to being able to live with Sarah and Marcus.

But who could unpack or concentrate on a curse when the mountain roads of her home called on this bright June afternoon?

Better to think about work on the book she was illustrating, Brenna told herself. A friend in Atlanta who was a kindergarten teacher had written a beautiful story about tolerance and acceptance that featured a small bird and a caterpillar. She had submitted a few of Brenna's sketches to the publisher, and now they wanted Brenna to revise and add to the drawings. She was thrilled with this new challenge, not to mention the paycheck. She hoped this opportunity and her savings would launch a new phase of her career.

She pulled to a stop in the driveway of Aunt Frances's sprawling ranch-style home. Red brick was accented with crisp white trim, green shutters, and deep awnings. Both the elder aunts had been given four-acre plots of Connelly land when they had married. Frances's husband, now deceased, had been a successful insurance salesman, and the home they had built reflected their affluence. Her granddaughter Lauren now lived with her.

Lauren was supposed to be helping at Eva Grace's shop today. Brenna had asked Lauren about being in town on Friday night when the fighting in the streets erupted. Her cousin said she had been so surprised by the outbreak of hostility that she had rushed home to make sure her grandmother was safe.

Brenna got out of her car as Aunt Frances came bustling out the front door, waving. Her silvery hairdo was as stiff as ever, and her pink and white pantsuit was immaculate. "I'm so happy to see you," she said and grabbed Brenna in a breath-taking hug. She smelled of lilac and clover, familiar and warm. Despite the elder aunts' irritating stubbornness and the way they defended Sarah, Brenna knew she had their love.

"It's wonderful that you've come home," Frances said. "Atlanta was too far away. Especially with all of this trouble going on."

The older woman took Brenna's arm and chatted about the past days' disturbing activities as she led the way through her well-appointed home to a screened porch.

"Oh my," Brenna said, stepping forward to take in the colorful garden that stretched in every direction. The vast backyard could have been featured in *Home and Garden*. The array of flowers, plants, trees, and bushes was stunning. "I had forgotten how beautiful this is."

Frances hugged her again, laughing in delight. "It just takes care and the right spells, my dear. You could do it all just as well, if you just put your mind to it."

Brenna knew she would never have the patience for gardening on this scale. She followed Frances down the porch steps. "Is Lauren learning all of your secrets?"

"Good heavens no," Frances retorted. Her green eyes twinkled. "You know my granddaughter is a witch with very different talents than mine."

Brenna hadn't realized her elder aunt was so aware of Lauren's activities. But it didn't seem to bother her.

"Your cousin Maggie has always loved working in the garden," Frances continued. "She has many of my plants growing at her own place. I'm just as happy that dear Doris's granddaughter will be the one carrying on my traditions instead of Lauren. Maggie was here working this morning, and I told her you would be coming over."

It was easy to picture Maggie here with Aunt Frances, freckles blooming on her cheeks in the sunshine. What a perfect place for her sweet cousin.

"The butterfly garden is over there," Aunt Frances said, pointing to the left. "This is my herb garden, and over here is the vegetable garden. Cucumbers are ready for pickling. The green beans are about ready to come in, with tomatoes, okra, and corn on the way. Doris and I will be canning the rest of the summer."

They talked awhile longer, strolling through sections. The older woman explained the plants' life cycles and times of planting with pride. All successful gardeners, witch or not, followed nature's signs in planting. The phase of the moon, the appearance of the last frost, and the spacing of spring storms dictated each step. Aunt Frances had it down to a fine art.

She brought Brenna to the butterfly garden and went back to the house. Brenna stood alone and took a deep breath, enjoying the wonderful, earthy smells of summer.

She dropped onto the ground and pulled out her pad and pencils. A rough sketch took shape on paper—yellow sunflowers, lush purple verbena, and the Joe-Pye weed blended artfully with spindly, bright green dill. Though butterflies were not plentiful on this hot afternoon, colorful wings still dipped and glided through the garden.

Brenna knew this would be the perfect magic place for book's little characters. They could walk and talk among the plants in a world she would create with her brush and watercolors.

She moved carefully among the plants, examining many with a magnifying glass to be sure she had the details correct. At one point, she even lay down amid the sunflowers to look up at the stems to get a "caterpillar's eye view" of the world above the ground.

The pages of her sketchpad filled with samples and diagrams and plans to go with the pages of text. Aunt Frances brought her lemonade and some cookies at one point. It wouldn't have been properly Southern of her aunt not to provide refreshments.

Brenna was so absorbed in her task that she worked for another hour before realizing how hot and uncomfortable she was. She closed her sketchbook and was pulling bits of flowers and grass from her hair when a flash of crimson at the base of an oak tree caught her eye.

The beautiful, blood red bloom didn't look familiar. Curious, Brenna walked closer. The flower might not have a place in the book she was working on. But she could imagine a faerie adorning the entrance to its home with such beauty. Drawn to the red plant, Brenna stepped forward. In her mind, she sketched in a pair of eyes peeking out around the flower. The expression in those eyes turned from friendly and welcoming to dark and sinister.

The image was so real that Brenna blinked. Fae of every form and fashion made Mourne County their home. Even the wee folk. However, she couldn't imagine Aunt Frances willingly sharing her garden with any of them, or fae who would live so close to a witch. There was simply too much magical conflict. So those eyes couldn't be real.

"Of course not," Brenna said as she stepped forward, still enthralled with the lush plant. The vivid red petals were like velvet against the green of the plant's leaves. She pulled her magnifying glass out of her pocket to get a closer look. She couldn't resist touching the bloom see if the petals were as soft as they looked.

A vine snaked out and wrapped around her wrist. Brenna dropped the magnifier and pulled back, but she was held fast. When she struggled, her other wrist became more ensnared. She braced herself, hoping her legs would give her leverage enough to release the vine's hold. Instead, she was jerked hard against the oak tree's unyielding trunk. More vines encircled her torso and neck, flattening her face against the tree.

Brenna tried to scream. The vine was compressing her lungs, and she couldn't get out more than a squeak. With her cheek against the rough bark, she couldn't move her head or see much of her surroundings. Her breathing became fast and shallow as her panic grew. The vine continued to enclose her.

Lightheaded, she couldn't move, could not call out, and could not focus her powers to summon help from the Goddess. Surely Aunt Frances would come out soon and could rescue her. Fighting for every breath, she opened her eyes and caught a glimpse of someone near the herb garden. Was it Lauren?

Brenna felt a surge of hope before everything went black.

Chapter 8

Jake was relieved to see Brenna's vehicle in the driveway at her aunt's home. He had tried to call her, but got no answer. Fiona told him it was her sister's habit to turn her phone off when she was sketching.

Since he was already in this part of the county, he figured there was no harm in seeking Brenna out. Just to make sure she was okay. He also wanted to remind her to keep her phone on. Things may have settled down some, but his men had been on five domestic calls today, most of them involving families who were normally quiet and peaceful. That was more domestic cases than the department saw in months. There was too much trouble in Mourne County for Brenna not to be accessible at all times.

Accessible. He smiled at his choice of words. Throughout this long, busy week—full of fourteen-hour days and the final goodbye to his best friend—Jake had thought about Brenna often since last Friday night. Naked in the moonlight, her ivory skin gleaming, auburn hair tousled by the wind while she cleansed her family's land. Since then, he fantasized many erotic scenarios with her curves more than just accessible.

Yeah. He wanted her.

But having her would be complicated. She was a strong witch in the ruling coven of the place he called home. If things went bad…

After the tragedy of his parents' mating, he avoided romantic complications. So why did he swing his cruiser into the driveway next to Brenna's SUV? Easy answer. The memory of full breasts, womanly hips, and Brenna's fiery magic was a powerful draw.

Jake also had news to share with her. This afternoon, he found the source of the phrase that the young troublemakers spray-painted in town last week. According to the internet, the words "See you in the darkness" came from notorious convicted murderer, Gary Gilmore, while he was awaiting his 1977 execution.

Jake still had no idea why the boys had written it on the side of the Save a Buck Store.

Those boys were the reason he was over this way. He had spoken with all of them. Not one could even tell him who Gary Gilmore was. Their drug tests were clean. They were three average boys very ashamed of what they'd done. They couldn't explain their actions, either.

Jake was also frustrated by the store's white wall, which the boys had repainted three times. As soon as every coat of paint dried, the bleak words bled through. He was trying to convince Verna that a deeper color would solve the problem. In truth, he wasn't sure that would work. He wanted to talk to Brenna about it.

A dark cloud loomed over Frances Hutton's house. He wondered if they'd have rain later tonight and watched the troubled sky as he walked to the front porch.

Frances looked startled when she answered the doorbell. "Jake. Oh no, you're not here about more trouble? Is it—"

"I'm just looking for Brenna," he assured her.

She pressed a hand to her chest. "Thank goodness. She's been out back in the garden sketching for hours." She held the door open. "Come on in."

Frances led him to a kitchen bright with late afternoon sunshine. "Let me get you something to drink for Brenna. You look like you need to cool off, too. Can I get you water or lemonade?" She opened the refrigerator door and smiled.

Damn, but these Connelly witches charmed you when their green eyes sparkled, Jake thought as he asked for water. Frances handed him two bottles.

He nodded to the back door. "I just need a minute with her."

Now there was a knowing twinkle in her gaze. "I'm sure you do. Go right on."

It was just as well that Frances knew he was interested in Brenna. The elder witch made no secret in town that she wanted to see her granddaughter, Lauren, married. Lauren had spent plenty of time trying to enchant Jake, but he had never given in. Maybe because he was a shifter, her spells hadn't worked. Of course, he had been forewarned by Garth and knew not to look the tempting beauty in the eyes.

Outside, the color and fragrance of the garden filled his senses. After growing up in a desert where the dominant colors were shades of brown, he had a real appreciation for the colorful plants that grew in the South.

He smacked away a fly buzzing around his face as he crossed the covered kitchen porch. An axe and some saws were leaned against the house, and a fresh tree stump was in the yard just to the left. Logs were stacked nearby, ready for splitting. He remembered Brian telling him that the last storm had knocked a tree down at Frances's house. No doubt one of the many Connelly cousins had been out here working on the clean-up.

No sign of Brenna. A patch of white in the side yard caught his attention, and he walked over. Brenna's sketchpad and pencils were on the ground. Where was she?

Thunder rumbled in the distance, and Jake's attention went back to the cloud. He lifted his head, scenting rain and something more. An acrid smell that sent alarm through him. Where was Brenna? He turned in a circle, looking in each corner of the big yard, from the gardens to the big, ancient oak, to—

At first the nightmare scene didn't register. Then Jake realized Brenna was pressed against the big oak's massive trunk. A bright green vine twisted around her, so thick she was barely visible, pressing her to the tree.

"Brenna!" he shouted.

He saw no movement, no sound, no sign of life. Jake dropped the water bottles, grabbed the axe and ran toward her, fearing she might be dead. Heart pounding, he raced to the side of the tree away from Brenna. He swung the axe with all of his might, cutting into the thick vine. It broke but regenerated in seconds, keeping Brenna wrapped tight.

He shouted for Frances over and over as he fought the vine with his axe. He needed magic to get Brenna out of this. He yelled and battled until the older woman opened the door of the screened porch.

The sensible witch didn't waste time asking for explanations. "Get the flower," Frances screamed at him as she hurried across the yard. "Kill the flower!"

Only then did Jake see the bright red bloom at the tree's base. The flower pulsated, as if pumping energy into the angry vine. The menacing growth was between Brenna's ankles. If he hit too far to the left or right, he could cut off her foot.

"Kill it," Frances shouted as she arrived at his side. Her eyes closed as she chanted, "Guide his hand. Guide him well. Kill this bloom, this vine from Hell. Save this girl. Free the tree. As I will, so mote it be."

Empowered, Jake drew the big axe back, aimed, and brought it down with all his strength. He split the flower exactly in half.

A keening like an animal in pain filled the air as the vine unwrapped. The long tendrils dried up as they hit the ground. Jake was at last able to break the stems. He tossed aside the blade, got Brenna's arms free, and held her as the vicious, living rope fell away and faded to dust. At the same moment, the dark clouds retreated toward the mountains and disappeared.

Jake was laying Brenna in the grass when a shout sounded from the house. Lauren ran toward them, her face white against her fiery auburn hair. "Granny. Granny, are you okay? I came home and heard shouting out here. I thought—"

"It's Brenna," Frances said, grasping her granddaughter's arms. "She's been attacked."

Jake checked Brenna for signs of life. Her breathing was shallow with intermittent shuddering gasps. The damn monster had almost crushed the life out of her. How could he help? He started to speak into the radio on his shoulder.

Frances stopped him. "This was magic-made and will have to be treated with special healing. Get her inside to the front bedroom." She turned to Lauren. "You get on the phone and get Sarah and Eva Grace over here. I'll get something to help Brenna."

While Lauren punched numbers into her phone, Jake picked Brenna up in his arms and followed Frances inside. "That way," she said, pointing him down a hall while she hurried to the kitchen.

In a pale pink bedroom filled with ruffles and lace, Jake laid Brenna on the bed. Her pulse was slow and weak, but she was drawing air in jerky gulps. That had to be a good sign. He checked her body for wounds and found nothing more than purpling bruises. They colored her face, neck and the bare legs revealed by her khaki shorts. Her T-shirt had been ripped and hung in shreds. More bruises and abrasions were visible through the torn knit.

Rage flooded him at the damage to her delicate skin. The wildness he carried inside almost broke free. Despite his efforts at control, he snarled with all the anger of an angry beast.

"Hush now," Frances said as she hurried into the room carrying a teacup. "Eva Grace and the others are on their way. Let's see if we can get Brenna to drink this."

Jake smelled mint. "What is it?"

"Just some hyssop tea. It should give her body a little boost."

Jake slid a hand under Brenna's neck and lifted her so Frances could put the cup to the younger woman's lips. Lauren hovered in the doorway, hands fluttering, murmuring under her breath.

"Come on, Brenna. Drink a little of this. It will make you feel better," Frances crooned. Finally, Jake angled himself behind Brenna, cradling her so that the older woman could force some of the liquid into her. Brenna swallowed automatically.

Frances set aside the cup. She gestured for Lauren. "Get over here and help me. We've got to give her strength."

Lauren linked hands with her grandmother. Both witches chanted as Jake held Brenna in his arms. Her body began to relax. Her breathing evened out and strengthened. He checked her pulse and found it steadier, so he laid her back on the bed. Frances and Lauren stood over her, eyes closed as they spoke low words in a language other than English. A circle of light spread outward, enclosing Brenna and Jake in warmth and comfort.

Within that safe haven, Jake added his will to that of the witches.

The others arrived soon after, and Jake stepped out to let them tend to Brenna. He went to look at the tree again. Other than the discarded axe and Brenna's art supplies, nothing remained of what had happened. The thick grass was free of debris. The tree was solid and strong, with no trace of the sinister darkness that filled its vast limbs only a short while ago.

As he retrieved Brenna's sketchpad and pencils, Jake took a deep breath. All he smelled were flowers, grass, and earth, cut only by the faint stink of a gift a neighborhood dog must have left. He got the art kit Brenna left by the butterfly garden, and then again circled the big tree. He couldn't see anything amiss. He picked up the axe and resisted the urge to drive the sharp edge into the ground.

He looked up as Fiona came out across the yard

looking like a teenager in her ragged T-shirt and torn jeans. "Find anything?" she asked as she neared him.

"Nothing. I hoped I could get some of the vine, but everything's just gone."

Fiona took the art supplies from him. "That's the problem with magic. Once the need for it has passed, it can just disappear."

She closed her eyes. Jake said nothing as she stood still and breathed slowly in and out. He knew she was searching for any supernatural presence. As a medium, she would know if there were visitors from other realms. Maybe one of them could communicate to her about what had happened to Brenna.

Her green eyes popped open, and she took in a deep breath. "It's blank."

"What do you mean?" Jake asked.

"There's nothing here, no spirits, and no ghosts. Everything's gone. Just like the day the Woman in White killed Garth, this spirit drove everything else away. That's very strange. In Mourne County, there are always ghosts. But not right now. I wonder where they've all gone."

From the porch, Eva Grace called to them, and they walked over. "Brenna's going to be all right," she said. "Aunt Frances put some cases washed with a touch of peppermint on the pillows. That will help Brenna rest. And Sarah cast a spell for deep sleep. Brenna will be achy for a few days. But that's all."

"What about all the bruising?" Jake asked.

"We've put on some compresses with St. John's wort. We added arnica salve to absorb some of the blood. I hope that will help."

Jaw clenched, Jake stared into the beautiful garden.

Who would believe this peaceful place had sprouted such evil? How had it grown, right under Frances's watchful eye? Had it been waiting for Brenna or would any of the family have done just as well?

Whatever was chasing the Connellys was fierce. But that was too damn bad. He was a tiger, and there were few foes that could defeat as animal as big and mean as he. He was sure he could take down and destroy whatever was after Brenna.

"Don't be thinking you can go after it," Eva Grace told him.

"Don't you take up that old song about this being a family matter."

"I'm not saying that," the redhead replied. "But it won't do Brenna any good for you to go chasing off in the woods. We're dealing with something that is ancient and powerful."

Fiona agreed. "We've got to get into the *Book of Magic* and find out more about the other times the Woman in White has claimed one of our family. Maybe now that this has happened to Brenna, Sarah will see reason and release the book."

"Maybe," Eva Grace murmured. "Sarah's very disturbed. I've never seen her like this. Almost powerless."

The shocked look on Fiona's face told Jake just how unnatural it was for the leader of their coven to be in such a state.

"There's work to do here," Eva Grace said after an uncomfortable silence. "Sarah and the rest of the coven are on the way over. We'll strengthen the protections around the house."

"I'll take the first shift with Brenna tonight," Fiona

said. "Someone should be with her until she wakes up."

"No need," Jake said. "I'll be staying with Brenna all night. You all go home and rest. I've got this."

Fiona started to protest, but Eva Grace laid a hand on the younger woman's arm. Her gaze was steady on Jake's. "You think you can handle whatever comes calling?"

"I'll take care of her," Jake said, surprised by the gruffness in his voice. He was in deep with this complicated bunch of females. He had to stay here tonight. Even if they made him stay outside, he couldn't leave Brenna. He had sworn never to get himself in this position, but there was more than one kind of magic afoot here.

He strode back into the house, still gripping the axe, ready to defend Brenna against any foe.

Chapter 9

The antique grandfather clock in Frances's living room struck midnight as Jake watched Brenna sleep.

He had been at her side most of the night, writing notes about everything that had happened since Garth was killed. Working things out on paper always helped him. But as the clock's last chime sounded, he felt only frustration.

They had brought an ottoman and an easy chair into the bedroom. The worn leather was soft, and the chair's size fit his long frame. Frances said it had been her husband's favorite chair. Jake found it a comfortable place keep watch over the woman whose sleep appeared dreamless.

Frances checked on Brenna often. Lauren made delicious soup and cornbread for dinner, and both of them insisted that he take a couple of breaks from his vigil. However, Jake was relieved when they went to bed.

He sighed as he looked back at the legal pad in his lap. None of what had happened in the past week made any sense. Fiona was right. They needed some fresh input on the Woman in White's previous appearances in Mourne County. He made a note to look up the sheriff's reports from the time when Eva Grace's mother had been taken by the Woman. Was the whole town in an uproar back then, as well?

Brenna made a sound, and he sat forward. But she just curled a fist against her cheek and slept on.

Perhaps he could have left her to Frances and Lauren's protection. New wards had been laid. The Connelly magic was powerful here. But how could he leave? What if the evil in that vine snaked into the house and tried to take Brenna again?

He was still puzzled by how the plant had grown here. Sarah and Frances, despite their years of experience with protecting their home and land, said they didn't have a clue. Frances swore that the flower had not even been there when she and Brenna toured the garden and the yard. She had grown indignant when Sarah suggested that she might have forgotten some strategic spells for protection. The two older women had argued, with the younger generation, looking on, very disturbed.

A creak from the hallway brought Jake out of his reverie. He stood.

Lauren appeared in the doorway. "Hey," she whispered. "I wanted to look in on Brenna before I went to bed. You need anything?"

"I'm fine," he replied, averting his gaze from hers.

"You sure?" Her voice dropped to a husky drawl as she stepped forward.

In the dim light from the bedside lamp, Jake could see that the witch wore a thin, gauzy nightgown that outlined her ripe figure. Tall like Brenna, with the typical green eyes of the Connellys, Lauren had more red in her long, curly hair. The tendrils around her pretty face looked damp.

"I just had a shower." She brushed a hand through her hair, the movement thrusting her large, firm breasts upward.

Those breasts were enticing, Jake thought, as his eyes were drawn back to them. As was her silky skin. Her plump lips. She had doused herself in a musky perfume that twisted through the air and filled his head. Steadfast, however, he resisted her offer of enchantment.

Lauren's sultry grin told him she was aware of his struggle against her feminine wiles. "Wouldn't you like to get a shower?"

The image of naked flesh, pressed again his in a cascade of water, was almost more than Jake could bear. He couldn't believe she was hitting on him with Brenna inches away and her grandmother sleeping in a bedroom nearby. Even for blatantly sexual Lauren, this was very bold.

"I don't need anything," he reiterated, his voice gruff. "You should go to bed."

Instead, Lauren sat down on the side of the bed so that her knee touched his. She laid a hand on his thigh. "I know this must have been very upsetting for you."

He froze.

"I just want to help," she said leaning forward, which put her erect nipple just a couple of inches from his arm. "Why don't you go lie down in my bed for a couple of hours, and I'll stay with Brenna. I'll call you if she wakes up. I promise."

Jake got to his feet. He had to stop this right now.

"Go to bed," he told Lauren in a flat, even tone. "I don't need anything from you. I'm here for Brenna."

Lauren stood and took a deep breath, unruffled by his rejection. "I was just trying to be helpful. Goodnight, Jake."

He followed her to the door and closed it in her face when she turned to smile at him one last time.

What in the hell was wrong with everyone?

He waited until he heard a door close down the hallway. Then he paced like a tiger in a cage, casting guilty looks at Brenna. He wanted to shed his human form and run in the woods to rid himself of Lauren's cloying scent.

He couldn't stand the smell another minute. He opened the door and stalked across the hall to the bathroom. With quick jerky movements, he scrubbed his hands, arms, and face and roughly dried them with the plush guest towel he found on a decorative stand. He felt like a bull in a china shop amid the feminine décor of the little room.

Under the sink, however, he found what he needed and took it back to the bedroom. Hoping it didn't disturb Brenna, he sprayed the disinfectant. It drove the last trace of Lauren from the air.

And woke Brenna up.

She sat up, choking, and glared at him. "What in the hell are you doing?"

He moved to her side. "Are you okay?"

"Other than almost being murdered by that spray, yes, I'm okay."

"I'm sorry." He poured her some water from the pitcher Frances had placed on the dresser. Brenna seemed strong and alert as she drank it down. She demanded to get up to visit the bathroom and winced only a few times while he escorted her across the hall. As he helped her back to bed, she gave no indication that it was strange for him to be with her. She also knew she was in her aunt's front bedroom and that her grandmother had been there and put her under a spell.

"Sarah's magic is familiar," Brenna explained. "But once upon a time, it would have made me sleep all night." The statement seemed to worry her.

Jake sat down and took her hand. "Do you know what happened? "

"A vine tried to kill me." She looked surprised by her own words. "I remember the plant. It twisted around me. I couldn't breathe." For the first time, panic edged her voice.

"You're safe now." Careful not to be too rough with her bruised body, he drew her against his chest. He inhaled the honeysuckle scent in her hair. The natural, fresh smell was more potent than Lauren's nauseating attempt at allure.

"You saved me." She turned her head so that her face was against his neck. Her arms crept around him.

"Me and Frances." He pulled away to explain what had happened. "Your aunt is one tough witch. Quick on her feet and in her mind."

"Where was Lauren?"

"We had you out of the vine before she got there."

"But she was…" Brenna frowned as she looked up at him. She shook her head and sighed. "I guess I don't remember everything."

"No, think about it," he said. As an investigator, he couldn't resist pressing for her first recall of the incident. "What did you see?"

"I thought I saw Lauren." She studied him, her eyes narrowing. "I just heard her voice, too. Just a minute ago."

"She was just here," he admitted. God, he hoped Brenna had not taken in all of his exchange with

Lauren.

Brenna chuckled. “She tried to seduce you.”

He drew away, none too pleased by her nonchalance. “Doesn’t that bother you a little?”

She shrugged. “We’ve always been competitive. She probably figured out that I’m attracted to you, so she made her move.”

“It was more than that,” Jake insisted. “She acted weird.”

“That’s Lauren.”

“No, it’s…” His brain circled back to her words. “Wait a second. You said you’re attracted to me?”

She lifted a hand to his face. “Surely a big cat like you can scent a female’s interest.”

He drew in a breath then stroked a hand down her hair. Her mouth lifted to his. As if they had kissed a thousand times, he thought as his lips claimed hers. So new, but so right.

An older shifter had once told him it could be like this with a mate. Like it was planned. Jake had never believed it was possible. Could he trust himself with Brenna?

He broke away before the kiss could deepen. “You move me, witch.”

“I second that emotion, shifter.”

If he followed his most primitive instincts, he would take her now. Claim her as his own.

But Brenna’s almond-shaped, green eyes were drifting shut again. Green as the mists of Ireland, Jake thought as she slid back into sleep in his arms. She barely stirred as he settled her back under the fragrant linens of Frances’s bed. Carefully, he curved his body around hers.

He allowed himself to sleep, knowing no evil could touch either of them tonight.

Chapter 10

Brenna felt a soft touch on her lips, a sweet, tentative kiss. Then the lips pressed firmly and released. She pulled back and opened her eyes.

Jake's gaze was steady on hers in the faint light sliding past the mini blinds and pink ruffled curtains at the bedroom window. "Hey, sleeping beauty."

"Hello," she said and kissed him again. He had held her all night. Each time she had awakened, his warm, strong presence had soothed her back to sleep.

"It's still early," Jake said, making no move to leave her side. "We could keep sleeping."

"And pretend like nothing happened yesterday." She sighed and snuggled closer to him. "I love that idea."

On the bedside table, his cell phone chirped. Footsteps sounded in the hallway. Frances or Lauren was already up and getting ready for the day.

Brenna groaned. "No one's going to let us alone."

With obvious reluctance, Jake turned on his back and picked up his phone. He squinted at the display but didn't answer the call right away. "It's not quite seven on a Sunday morning, and the office is calling. Sometimes it's two or three in the afternoon before we even have a speeding car on Sundays in New Mourne. I hope nothing else has happened."

Brenna agreed and pushed herself up. She winced

as muscles protested. Various points on her body throbbed and complained. Jake put extra pillows behind her back as she sat up.

He got out of bed, shoulders rippling under his plain white T-shirt as he stood and stretched. At some point during the night he had shed his khaki uniform shirt and made himself a little more comfortable.

Brenna felt a pang of guilt. “You didn’t have to stay with me all night. I would have been fine with Frances and Lauren.”

“I couldn’t leave you.” It was a statement of fact, a blunt and bold declaration that Brenna would have protested once upon a time.

She was jolted into silence by how little it bothered her now.

“I doubt the owl would have let me leave,” Jake continued. “Did you hear him last night?”

“Did an owl wake us up earlier?”

“Just before sunrise. I can’t say for sure that it was the same owl we ran across last week in the woods, but it was right outside this window.”

“He hissed several times,” Brenna said, only now remembering one of the occasions she had awakened during the night. “That’s the sound barn owls make when they’re warning you away from their nest or their territory.”

“I’ve had plenty of them hiss at me in the woods at night. The sound is eerie.” Jake lifted one of the blinds covering the window to peek outside. “I wonder what was happening out there that he wanted to tell us about.”

“Or warn us against.” Brenna shivered.

Jake studied her. “Do you remember anything else

about the plant attacking you?"

"The flower was beautiful, and I had to touch it. I was drawn to it." Brenna recalled the perfect symmetry of the blossom, its blood red color, and intoxicating smell. She also remembered the eyes she thought she saw glimmering at her from behind the bloom and the leaves.

"So your immediate thought was this was fae," Jake asked after she had described the moment for him.

"I just saw what I thought were eyes. There was nothing distinctly fae. We're not exactly friendly with the fae, but there have been few conflicts. Why would they want to hurt me?"

"Maybe this is a visitor."

Brenna laughed. "I'm sure you know that Willow Scanlan is the oldest and most powerful faerie in Mourne. It's not likely that some renegade faeries would be running wild without her knowledge. She would have asked for our help to send them to eternal damnation. If it had been faerie magic that killed Garth, Willow would already have claimed vengeance."

"But something unusual is happening here," Jake said.

"It's all tied to the Woman in White."

"And perhaps it is more than Willow Scanlan and Sarah can…" He stopped, shook his head and held up his phone, which was buzzing again. "I'd better see what the office wants. They were going to try to give me the morning off if there were no new incidents. So this must be something bad."

Faintly Brenna heard Jake's terse conversation. Before the phone rang again, he had been about to voice her own fears. What if the magical leaders of this area were losing their powers? Brenna had been concerned last night when Sarah's sleeping spell had worn off after only a few hours. That was unlike Sarah. But it was also unlike Aunt Frances to allow a killer plant to grow in her garden.

The Connellys had kept the peace among all creatures in this region for centuries. But if Sarah was no longer strong enough to hold off evil, if their coven was weak…

Brenna bit her lip. Her own absence these past three years could have caused the current crisis. Like a family, a coven was a delicate balance. It wasn't that every Connelly witch had to stay here. There were Connelly witches in many places who could trace their ancestry to the original family who had moved from Ireland in the 1700s. But the central trunk of the family tree, where the most power dwelled, remained in Mourne County. That same trunk always bore the sacrifice to the Woman in White.

"And I deserted them," Brenna muttered to herself. "Shame on me."

"What did you say?"

Brenna looked up to find Jake was off the phone.

"I was just thinking out loud about the balance of power in our little county."

He grunted as he stuffed his phone in his pocket. "Speaking of power, there's been an incident at Fred Williams' church."

"Is anyone hurt?"

"Some minor vandalism, but he's demanding me on scene."

"I've never liked that man."

"Garth didn't trust him, but he kept him mollified

somehow. I need to do the same." Jake shrugged into his uniform shirt and sat down on the recliner next to the bed to put on his shoes. "So I need to get over there and check this out. I hope it's not related to what happened here yesterday."

"It's all related." Brenna was silent as she watched Jake gather his notebook and other belongings.

He reached out and touched her cheek. "Stay in the house."

Brenna bristled at the instruction. "No, thank you. I will not be staying in this or any other house. And you staying with me last night doesn't give you any right to say that."

"Okay, okay." Jake held up his hands in surrender. "Just be careful, witch. Use your magic to guard yourself."

"That I can do," she agreed. "Watch yourself, too."

The air sizzled around them, alive with a connection that both puzzled and pleased Brenna. What was happening between her and this shifter? She didn't have time for this kind of entanglement now. Even though she'd appreciated his long body curved around hers all night long. Even though, right now, she wanted to kiss him goodbye…

"I'll call you later," he said, saving her from her impulse.

When he opened the door, Lauren fell into his arms, caught in the act of eavesdropping.

The voluptuous witch laughed as her arms circled Jake's waist. "I was just about to knock."

Jake set her away from him. "I'm glad you're here, Lauren, because I have to run. Take care of your cousin. " He directed a devilish grin at Brenna before he left.

Lauren looked at Brenna. "You look fine to me. Do you need looking after?"

"I feel sore and achy, but that's about it."

"You got yourself in a bit of a squeeze, no pun intended." Lauren chuckled. The wicked humor was as predictable as her throwing herself at Jake. Lauren never changed.

"Jake was really frightened," Lauren added.

"Imagine how I felt," Brenna said ruefully. A sudden memory tugged at her as she studied her cousin. "I saw you yesterday. You were standing near the butterfly garden. I was hoping you would help me."

"I came running in when I realized what was happening," Lauren said, sitting down in the leather recliner. "I was so scared I didn't know what to do. After I got home from the shop, I went into the woods to the side of the house looking for partridgeberries for poor Christine Forest. She's had three miscarriages in seven years and, now that she's pregnant again, I wanted to help her.

"When I heard Granny and Jake yelling, I froze for a minute. Then I ran to help. But I was scared when I saw what was happening. You were white, just white and still on the ground. There was that axe lying there, too. I thought you could be dead, that the Woman in White had…" Lauren looked stricken. Silent understanding flowed between the two women. No matter how different they were, their common fear of the family curse bound them on a deep level.

Lauren took a deep breath. "Thank the goddess, Granny took control. Jake carried you inside, so brave and strong." Tears filled her green eyes. "It all just terrified me."

"You're lucky you weren't seeing it from my angle."

"I don't know if I'll ever forget how frightened I was," Lauren said, tears overflowing.

Brenna sighed as she offered Lauren a tissue from the box beside the bed. As always, her cousin had made the entire event about her own feelings. But in the end, Brenna was willing to admit that in the confusion of events yesterday she might not have seen Lauren in the garden. Perhaps she had glimpsed her in the woods searching for partridgeberries. It wasn't like Brenna had been able to scream out at that point. There had been no reason for Lauren to look her way.

Brenna soothed and comforted Lauren, assuring her that she had been brave and helpful. When the crying jag was over, however, she looked her cousin in the eye and said, "You need to back off the shifter. He's mine."

"All yours?" Lauren looked disappointed.

"Yes," Brenna said. She had been telling Lauren to back off from toys, dolls, clothes, and males for as long as the other witch had been alive. The only thing different about Brenna being in charge right now was how much she meant this. She really wanted her beautiful cousin to stop trying to tempt Jake.

"All right," Lauren said. Brenna was pleased that her younger cousin was still so easily led.

"Now I need to get up," Brenna announced. "I want a shower."

Her cousin helped her hobble to the bathroom, where the warm cascade of water eased some of her aches. Aunt Frances fixed them all a breakfast of rosemary scrambled eggs, toast, and ginger tea. Feeling much better, Brenna refused to go back to bed, content to drink tea in a cozy nook overlooking the garden. She kept thinking she'd see something in the flowers that would give her more hints about yesterday's attack.

Lauren hovered, bringing Brenna citrine, green moss agate, and lepidolite to soothe and strengthen. Aunt Frances filled the room with vases of colorful blooms, eager to erase Brenna's memories from yesterday. The scents were fragrant but somewhat overwhelming. Brenna's two relatives were slowly driving her insane.

When she asked to borrow some of Lauren's clothes and leave, her elder aunt put up a fierce protest. Sarah had said Brenna was not to be alone today, Frances proclaimed. Brenna gave in, but she was ready to scream by midmorning when Fiona walked in.

"Sarah wants us all at the house for a coven meeting," her sister announced.

"Does she have a plan to go after the Woman in White?" Brenna asked.

Fiona's gaze slid sideways from Brenna's. Not a good sign.

Her sister told Lauren and Frances, "You two go on to Sarah's. I brought Brenna some clothes, and she and I will be along as soon as she is ready."

Brenna knew Fiona had orders not to tell her anything more about the meeting. Most likely she was to delay Brenna's arrival too. What was Sarah discussing with everyone else that Brenna didn't need to know just yet? Though Brenna had pretty much ruled her cousins and her sister their entire lives, she would never be able to get Fiona to break a direct promise to

Sarah, and she didn't try now.

Brenna dressed as quickly as her aching body would allow. She didn't fight when Fiona told her to leave her car at Frances's. Without protest, she rode to the Connelly farmhouse in Fiona's rattletrap old van, filled with camera, audio, and ghost-hunting equipment.

Female voices filled the house when they opened the front door. The entire coven gathered around the dining room table with Sarah at the head chair. Frances was at her right hand. Next to Frances was her daughter, Estelle, flanked by her own daughter, Lauren. Eva Grace sat beside Lauren. To Sarah's left was Doris with her daughter, Diane. Next was Maggie, whose grandfather had been the elder witches' brother. Three chairs were empty.

"I think you should have discussed it with her," Frances was saying to Sarah as Brenna and Fiona paused in the doorway.

Doris soothed, "Now, Frances, you know Sarah only does what she feels is right."

"Sarah needs to try a little harder to get along with her," Frances said with a huff.

"Who are you talking about?" Brenna asked, breaking into the conversation.

The room fell silent. All eyes turned to Sarah.

"Please sit down," Sarah said with her usual command.

Fiona slipped into her place next to Maggie. Brenna took the chair at the end, opposite Sarah. She looked long and hard at the empty chair that was still available next to Eva Grace. "Who are we expecting?"

Instead of answering her, Sarah said, "I've given the events of the past week a lot of thought. I believe the best thing we can do is get some outside help."

"Who do you think can help us?" Brenna asked.

To her credit, Sarah didn't delay. "I've called Delia and Aiden, and they'll be here day after tomorrow. So they're not really outsiders."

Brenna sat silent, trading unblinking stares with Sarah as the cacophony of voices rose around them. She leaned forward, her hoarse whisper cutting through the din. "Why the hell would you want to bring *them* here?"

Sarah sat still, eyes narrowed and hands flat against the ancient wooden table. The coven again fell silent as she answered, "Your mother belongs here."

"You've never thought she was needed before."

"That was different."

"When I fell out of the barn loft and broke my arm and my leg, you told her to stay in France."

"You were taken care of by all of us," Sarah retorted. "Your mother and father couldn't have done anything."

Except maybe comfort me, Brenna thought, *soothe me, love me*. Instead, she had been with Sarah who told her everything would be fine and expected that, somehow, it would. Because she always expected Brenna to be fine, to be strong, not to cry or to be afraid.

Brenna's thoughts turned to another memory. "Why didn't you call them when I won the art prize my senior year and got the scholarship?"

"We couldn't interrupt your father's studies in Russia. They sent you a beautiful gift."

A bracelet Brenna had thrown over the cliff. Sarah had tried grounding her for that but Brenna was eighteen. It seemed pointless. Brenna was contented with the frustration Sarah felt when her strongest spells couldn't locate the lost jewelry. The younger witch had cloaked the bracelet well. It still lay buried under a rock at the bottom of the waterfall.

Memories of anger and hurt and missing her parents bubbled inside Brenna. It was one thing that they had ignored her from the moment she was born—Brenna was strong and capable of enduring their absence. But what about Fiona?

She demanded of Sarah, "Remember when the voices came at Fiona so hard and heavy when she was twelve? She was growing up, learning to be a woman and a witch, and trying to deal with half the dead people in Mourne County. Why didn't that warrant a summons for the mighty Delia and Aiden Burns?"

"Don't, Brenna," Fiona said, leaning forward to touch her arm. "It doesn't matter."

"Yes, it does," Brenna claimed. "It matters to me why Sarah thinks now is suddenly the time to bring Delia and Aiden here. We're facing the crisis of our generation. One of us is going to die unless we find a way around it. And who knows how many people are going to go with us first? What can Delia and Aiden do about that? The only thing they do well is running around the globe chasing their own dreams. And it's not like Delia decided to come home. Sarah probably had to beg her."

"That's not true," Sarah claimed. "She wants to be here. She was here when Celia was taken, so she remembers this terrible time. She's faced what you're facing."

"No doubt Aiden wants to write a paper about the

phenomenon," Brenna said with derision.

"His academic career supported you." Sarah's tone remained calm and steady, but her sisters took her hands as she faced Brenna. "Your mother and father always made sure that you, Fiona, and Eva Grace were taken care of."

"You're applauding them for sending us money?" Brenna almost spat out the words. "They dumped me and Fiona here right after we were born and ignored Eva Grace, and you're telling me I should be grateful because they sent money?" Anger cycled inside her like a storm rising. The china in the old breakfront rattled. The iron light fixture above the table swayed as she pushed to her feet.

"Hold on," Eva Grace murmured, getting up and taking Brenna's hand. "Be cool."

Fiona joined them, clasping Brenna's other hand. "Don't blow, Brenna. Please don't blow."

Taking strength from the two people closest to her, Brenna grasped hold of her fury. She glared at Sarah. "I hope you don't regret giving Delia a seat here again."

Sarah's eyes narrowed. "Her seat has always been here, waiting. We need her now. We need some positive energy. Not anger."

"Maybe I'm the one you don't want at the table." Hurt nearly broke Brenna's thinning control. "Maybe I should leave for good this time." She turned to her cousin Maggie, "Maybe in twenty years when it's your girl who is facing the Woman in White, you can beg me to come back and help."

Maggie broke down into sobs, and the tension in the room crumbled. Brenna dropped Fiona and Eva Grace's hands and stalked up the stairs to her attic studio. Like a teenager, she took great satisfaction in slamming her door. She hoped it infuriated Sarah and the rest of them. She couldn't be with her family right now.

Funny, how earlier today she had thought her being here could help them find a way through the current nightmare. Now all it meant was that she was going to have to confront her absent mother and father, along with the family curse.

Chapter 11

"I remember when this church had just one building. And was just a church."

Deputy Brian Lamont's comment made Jake look around as he pulled his cruiser into the parking lot of the Circle of Faith Church. The church campus included a large sanctuary, a smaller chapel, an administration building, gymnasium and sports complex, and a school. "It's definitely more like a community center now."

"A center for certain Mourne County residents." Brian's laugh was dry. "According to my grandmother, this was just a little country church when Fred's father preached here. About twenty years ago, when the economy was really booming, we got lots of people moving in from Atlanta. Fred decided to offer them what they wanted."

"Fred's a lot of things but not dumb."

"Now he draws a huge crowd from counties all around. They say there's a waiting list for admission to the school."

"I guess a lot of those rich people living in their McMansions want a good, conservative education for their children."

Brian laughed again. "And the regular Mourne County schools are full of God-only-knows what kind of people."

Jake grinned, knowing Brian had pegged the situation. The people who escaped Atlanta's metropolitan sprawl of traffic and crime were happy to keep to themselves for the most part. They had a country club and a golf course as part of The Enclave, the gated community where they lived. Other exclusive developments in surrounding counties provided a large base of similarly-minded individuals for socializing. They adopted Fred's church and school as their own. Of course, they had to shop and do other business in New Mourne. But a real divide existed.

Last year, Rash Anderson, the chief developer, had come to Garth, wanting to turn The Enclave's security guards into a bona fide police force. The county charter didn't support such a move and getting it changed was not simple. Garth resisted. Fred sided with the developer, but the move didn't pass. The Mourne County Sheriff had always been the lead law enforcement official. How would the power shift if there was a separate force for The Enclave?

Jake suspected the issue would come up again. The newest wrinkle was that in April The Enclave had put one of their own on the County Board of Commissioners. The vote could go another way next time.

The recent troubles had touched The Enclave. Brian and another deputy had broken up a teenage party turned raunchy and rowdy at one of the mini estates on Friday night. Fred called immediately, anxious to smooth over the difficulties for the kids involved who attended his school. He blamed everything on a couple of county kids at the party. Now his complaint was the vandalism.

"Let's get this over," Jake said to Brian. The parking lot was almost empty. Fred wanted to ensure the investigation wouldn't interfere with a church service. That's why he set this meeting for one o'clock.

Some investigation, Jake thought wryly. What was there to see?

He probably should have come out here right away when Fred called, but he needed to go home, get some breakfast, and take a shower after his long night with Brenna. Brian took the initial call this morning, so Jake knew he collected evidence while it was fresh. That's why Brian was along for the follow-up chat with Fred.

Jake and Brian walked over to the brick sign that faced the road. Fred had the sign covered in canvas before services, but Brian pulled it off. The sign usually contained a verse or pithy message. Today all the plastic letters were on the ground. Someone had used black paint to write, "From the world of darkness I did loose demons and devils."

Once again the quote sounded familiar to Jake.

"Charles Manson," Brian said.

"Huh?"

"Those are Manson's words. I looked it up when I got back to the office."

"Just like that other graffiti on the Save a Buck was Gary Gilmore. Another killer." A shiver ran through Jake as he studied the words on the church sign. He expected them to start running and bubbling, like those on the store. He was relieved when the letters didn't move. They were still ominous, however.

"There's something bad wrong in this town, Brian."

"I know," the younger man responded.

"Supernaturally wrong."

Jake heard footsteps and turned to see Fred coming toward him. Handsome and muscular at fifty, the pastor had the perfect amount of gray at the temples and filled out his tailored slate-gray suit with broad shoulders. His face held just the right amount of concern.

At his side was his wife, Ginny. Thin and blonde, Ginny was beautiful in a remote way achieved through careful grooming and exquisite makeup. She wore an ice-blue dress that matched the coldness in her blue eyes.

Jake took off his hat and nodded to both of them. "Afternoon."

"This is a travesty," Ginny said. "Deputy Tyler, you have to do something about what's going on around here."

Fred put an arm around her. "Ginny, it's Sheriff Tyler now, not deputy."

"Sorry," she murmured with an expression that was anything but apologetic. "*Sheriff* Tyler, what are you going to do about all of this?"

Jake did his best to ignore the couple as he walked around the sign. Just as Brian had reported, there was little to see. Someone had broken the locked glass panel to get at the sign and write their message.

"You know it's most likely the same boys who messed up that wall downtown," Fred said. "Now they've moved their pranks to my church."

"I checked on those boys first thing this morning," Brian said. "They left yesterday afternoon for a weekend trip to Atlanta, right after the sheriff talked to them again about the other graffiti." The young deputy tried, but he couldn't quite keep the satisfaction out of his tone. Jake sent him a warning frown.

Fred sputtered, “Then who is it? Who in the…” He caught himself, straightened, and calmed his voice. “How about some of their friends? This kind of activity has infected the entire county this summer, so I’m sure there are plenty of other little imps out there.”

“We’re talking to the known troublemakers,” Jake assured him. “If we can find evidence, we’ll deal with whoever did this.”

“You might want to talk to the Connellys,” Ginny said.

Brian’s expression turned stony. “Excuse me?”

Jake raised his hand to silence the deputy. “What do you think the Connellys have to do with this?”

Ignoring her husband’s frown, Ginny touched manicured fingers to her stylish blonde hairdo. “Sheriff Tyler, I’ve lived here my entire life. When trouble happens in Mourne County, you can always trace it back to the Connellys.”

“Which Connellys?” Brian asked. The green in his eyes flashed temper.

“They’re all the same.” Ginny shrugged, then her gaze latched with laser intensity onto Brian. “You’re one of them, aren’t you?”

“Yes, ma’am. Doris Connelly is my grandmother.” His voice deepened. “You think my grandmother had something to do with this sign?”

“Brian,” Jake said quietly. “I’m sure that’s not what Mrs. Williams is saying.”

Ginny’s reply was an arched eyebrow.

Fred stepped in. “Now, let’s not go getting all riled up. Ginny is just frustrated and worried. She didn’t mean any disrespect to Doris.” He sent his wife a sharp glance. “Did you, Ginny?”

“Of course not,” she declared, though Jake would bet his life that she was lying. “I’m sorry if I upset you, but I’m very disturbed by what is happening to our county. I don’t want the law to overlook any possibilities.”

“I can assure you, we won’t,” Jake said with elaborate politeness. “I think we have all of the photos and evidence we need on the sign.” He turned to survey the front of the church. “You guys don’t have any security cameras set up out here, do you?”

“That may have to be our next step if something isn’t done about the troubles soon.” Ginny turned without another word and stalked back toward the sanctuary.

Fred sighed and said to Jake and Brian. “Please excuse Ginny. She’s distraught.”

“Of course,” Jake said before Brian could speak. He shot another warning look at the younger man. “Fred, you might as well report this damage to your insurance company and get it fixed.”

“I have a maintenance man waiting to do that right now,” Fred said. “We don’t want this blasphemy on display any longer than necessary. “ He gave Jake a hard look. “You better take this seriously, Tyler. You’re sheriff for now, but that’s only temporary.” Fred could be subtle, but not today.

“I’m taking all of this very seriously. We’ve stepped up patrols. We have officers working overtime. We’re doing all we can with the manpower and budget we have.”

The pastor kicked at a couple of the sign’s letters on the ground. “I’m going to get a digital sign installed so there's no chance of anything like this happening again. The congregation has been slow to approve it. I'm sure they'll want it now, too."

"Probably a good idea."

"I hope you find the miscreants who did this and make the punishment fit the crime."

He grabbed the canvas and began putting it back over the sign. Jake reached to help him.

"It's graffiti, Fred, not breaking and entering."

"Nevertheless, this is God's house, and I expect it to be respected as such," Fred said. "If you don't make an example of these delinquents, it could happen again."

Resting his hands on his hips, Jake said, "I'm sure you're just like me and want to do what's right. I'll call you later, Fred."

Brian said little during the ride back into town. Behind the courthouse, Jake parked in his space. He turned to the deputy before they went into headquarters on the second floor. "Please don't take what Ginny Williams said too personally."

"I know better, but it's hard to take that shit when you know your family has done nothing but try to protect this county."

"Garth's death stirred up a lot of worry. Then, with the other troubles—"

"Which could be from the new people moving into the county," Brian interjected. "But of course, Mrs. Williams would never think her friends in their big houses with their big checkbooks could have anyone who wanted to stir things up. This could all be political, you know. Everything planned to prove how much we need a private police force out at The Enclave."

Jake nodded. “It could, but that explanation doesn’t cover everything. You know what happened yesterday to Brenna at your Great-Aunt Frances’s place?”

“My cousin, Maggie, says it’s the Woman in White. Maggie’s really scared. The whole family is.”

“It could be the Woman.” Jake wasn’t sure how the Connelly family’s curse fit into everything else that was happening in his county, but he was sure it did.

“What else could it be?”

“Does the Woman in White always create this much chaos before she comes for one of the witches?”

Brian shrugged. “I don’t know.”

Beside them another cruiser slid into place. The county’s lone female deputy, Kathy Harrigan, stepped out. Jake could see her passenger in the back seat. He and Brian got out of their vehicle.

“What’s up?” Jake said.

“Bill Riley,” she replied, shaking her head, naming a farmer who lived not far from the Connellys. “He wrung the necks of his wife’s eight prized laying hens. His wife said he went out to the barn right after church to check on an ailing mule. He was washing off at the water hose beside the back door and he threw the hose down, went to the chicken coop, and started killing chickens. Fayrene was real upset. Those were her hens, and she uses the money for her yarn so she can knit baby blankets for all the newborns at the hospital.”

“What did Bill say?”

“He said he felt like he had to kill something, and he figured the hens were better targets than Fayrene and the boys. He scared Fayrene plenty and was shook up himself, so I decided to bring him in.” Kathy shook her head again. “It just doesn’t make sense what’s happening here."

Jake agreed. The incidents all over the county had run the gamut. From the egging of the front door of a gay couple who ran a small retreat, to the number of church-going people who had walked out of the local convenience store with pockets full of stolen candy bars. A hunter who'd never broken any rules had killed three deer and the ducks in the park pond in the past week. People who never caused a problem before were locked up for assault. Most everyone was confused about what they'd done and why they did it.

"You get Bill processed," Jake instructed Kathy. "I think we can just keep him overnight to make sure he's put all thoughts of killing things out of his mind."

"I don't think he poses a real threat," Kathy agreed, turning back to her car.

Jake looked at Brian. "I want you to put together a report for me. Beginning with Garth's death, I want a summary of every call we've been on, every incident that's been reported."

"I can do that."

"And I'm going to go through the old records and see what was happening around here the last few times the Woman in White was due."

Brian grimaced. "You know, of course, that the old records are buried in the basement of the courthouse in about an inch of dust and cobwebs."

"I'm not afraid of spiders."

"But you'll need some help."

With his deputies already stretched to the max, Jake felt he couldn't ask one of them. There was someone, however, who had the same interest he did in getting to bottom of all of this.

He pulled out his cell. Brenna's number was already on speed dial. He wasn't sure if that was a good or bad thing. He only knew that he felt instant warmth when she answered.

"I need you," he said.

There was a short pause. "I've had some interesting offers in my time, but this is a little abrupt."

He laughed. "I didn't mean that the way it sounded." *But he did, of course.*

A teasing note in her voice, she said, "Then what can I do for you?"

"Can you get into town to the courthouse? We need to do some research."

"You know, I would love to get out of the house this afternoon. I'll have Fiona take me to my car at Frances's house, and then I'll be right there."

Jake was grinning as he ended the call. He looked up to find Brian studying him. "Something you need, Deputy?"

Brian just smiled and walked up the steps to the department entrance.

Hours later, Jake stared at Brenna across the table they had set up in a far corner of the dusty courthouse basement. "Your Woman in White is apparently one mean bitch."

Brenna swiped at a streak of dirt on her cheek. Her green eyes were somber. "Every time she's come for one of us, she has punished the town, as well."

Around them on the table and floor were incident logs, dispatch records, and arrest files. She and Jake had started with files dated in the months leading up to her Aunt Celia's death more than twenty-eight years ago. Then they had moved twenty-two years before that to the death of Rose Connelly. So far, they had been able to locate archives from four generations of deaths the Connelly family attributed to the Woman in White. This was all the history Brenna knew since she wasn't allowed to study the *Book of Magic* yet. But it was enough evidence to tell them that the Connelly's generational tragedy was always accompanied with a sharp spike in crime.

"It's the same kind of thing we're dealing with now." Jake was careful as he stacked some fragile papers from early in the twentieth century back into a box. "People who had no criminal record were suddenly shooting each other."

"Or stabbing their mothers to death," Brenna said with a shudder.

Jake nodded. One crime from near the time of Rose's death had disturbed them both. A young man named Rufus Kelly had killed his mother with a butcher knife. Kelly never denied the murder. He just said he couldn't remember what happened. He didn't know why he had stabbed his mother to death. Declared insane, he was sent to the state hospital for the criminally insane in Milledgeville, Georgia.

The next time Kelly's name came up in the files was over twenty years later. His doctors and a crusading attorney managed to have him released. In his forties, he came home to Mourne County and lived for several years with his sister's family, working on his brother-in-law's dairy farm.

Just days before Celia Connelly had been claimed by the Woman in White, Kelly hung himself from a tree in the New Mourne town park.

"The officer who wrote up the report said he had

been living a quiet life since his release from the hospital. He was never any trouble."

"And he sang like an angel in the church choir." Jake ran a hand through his hair. "There was no reason for him to kill himself."

"Just like there was no reason for Bill Riley to kill his wife's prize hens today," Brenna added. Jake had told her about the incident.

Other similarities between the two men chilled Jake. Bill had just come from attending the Methodist church where he sang baritone in the choir. "I guess it's a good thing Bill was able to get his murderous impulse out on just the chickens."

"You know what's weird?" Brenna frowned down at the files in front of her. "We don't talk much about these kinds of things happening in New Mourne. I never heard about Rufus Kelly."

"You'd think a known murderer hanging himself in public would be something the town kids would tell around the campfire forever," Jake agreed.

"We all like to pretend that this is just a peaceful, wonderful place to live."

"That's how Garth described it to me when we met. He said it was a place where everyone was accepted. And that's how it's been for me."

"But once a generation, there's violence and death. No one really warns you. It's like no one wants to face it until it's upon us again."

"But you Connellys know about the Woman in White. You're all warned."

"But we aren't prepared to fight it. Neither is the town. I mean, maybe we should warn Bill Riley's family that she's not done messing with him."

Jake frowned. He didn't have room in the jail for everyone who had acted out this past week.

"And Sarah's only answer is to call my parents in to help. What a joke." Brenna stood with a huff, hurriedly stacking files and shoving them into boxes.

Jake watched her for a minute. "From the way you're acting, I'd guess you don't want your mother and father here?"

"We have not seen them since a surprise visit for Eva Grace's and my birthday about four years ago."

"What keeps them away?"

Brenna snapped the lid shut on a box and reached for another. "Surely you know that my father is a bestselling author of books on magic. He's studied sorcerers, witches, and wizards from all corners of the world. He was Mother's professor in college. They married when she was nineteen, had me when she was twenty, and left me here for Sarah to raise so they could travel the world for his research. His work and each other. That's all they care about. I understand that I was an accident, but I've never understood why they had Fiona."

"Hard to say why people have children sometimes." Jake could identify with Brenna about unplanned pregnancy. But at least he had known his mother wanted him. She loved him right up until the moment her life ended in blood and torment.

"You're lucky you had family who cared," Jake muttered. He had fended for himself on the streets.

Brenna looked like she might protest. Then she sat down and pushed her hair away from her face. "I guess it's better that Fiona came into our lives. She's always given me something to focus on other than my resentment toward my parents. Fiona and Eva Grace are my touchstones."

"I used to think it would have been easier if I'd had a brother." The thought reminded Jake so sharply of Garth that he pushed himself to his feet. "Let's get out of here," he told Brenna. "I'll put all of this back tomorrow."

Her gaze was steady on his. "You need to shift."

He shrugged, unsettled by how well she read him.

"How long's it been?" she asked. "Two days? More?" Her laugh was deep and throaty when he held up four fingers. "Now you know you can't do that. Magic demands that it be used, or you lose it"

"Fine words from a witch who ran away from her heritage for several years."

"You're right. I've realized I need to practice." Brenna snapped her fingers at the stacks of papers still on the table. "As you were," she said with a flick of her wrists.

The papers flew back into their boxes. Lids closed. Dust settled.

Jake was impressed by her economy of words and motion. Brenna had some serious power. "You didn't put anything back on the shelves," he pointed out.

"You should have to do something," she teased.

He laughed and gestured for her to precede him out of the basement. He snapped off lights behind them, and they emerged into the June twilight. "Whoa. I didn't realize it was so late. Can I buy you something to eat?"

Brenna shook her head. "You need something more than food."

The sparkle of her eyes and the curve of her lips set

off a serious ache inside him. He stepped forward, his hand cupping her face. "Is that an invitation?"

"You need to shift," she said again, with a firmness that belied the hunger in her gaze. She made no protest when his arms curved around her, and his lips settled on hers. He hardened as her breasts pressed against his chest. Round and ripe, only a motion away from his touch. He pictured her as she'd been in the moonlight last weekend. Proud and naked. Glowing with her power. How would it feel to be inside that magic?

"Not tonight," she told him as she drew away.

"Soon, though?" He wasn't sure if it was a promise or question.

"Run tonight. You'll feel better."

"Only one thing could really make me feel better," he murmured as he claimed her mouth again.

She was laughing as she pushed him back and stepped toward her car. "Do white tigers howl at the moon?"

"Sometimes."

"Then I'll be listening for you."

Jake chuckled as he watched her drive away.

Later, when he was chasing deer through the woods near the Connelly home place, he roared.

He knew Brenna heard him.

Chapter 12

Brenna slept fitfully Sunday night and woke late to full sunshine and Tasmin who was purring in her face. Stroking the gray feline, Brenna said, "Well, you're not the cat I wish I was waking up with, but I guess you'll have to do."

Intelligent feline green eyes held a trace of disdain as Tasmin flipped her tail and jumped out of bed. The cat, spayed after her first litter of kittens, had no use for males.

Clearly reading the cat's thoughts, Brenna replied, "But I do."

Tasmin left the room, and Brenna sat up to survey her tumbled sheets. She blamed her uneasy night on the many fantasies she had entertained about Jake. In her dreams, his smooth skin kept morphing into warm, white fur. Late in the night, she thought she heard him roar outside her window.

She was tense with sexual frustration and wished she had given in to his kisses last night. Then at least she'd be exhausted for all of the right reasons. A shifter who hadn't shifted in four days would likely have kept her—and himself—up all night. She felt a bit wistful about the missed opportunity.

Sarah and Marcus were gone when she finally padded downstairs to get coffee and refill Tasmin's food bowl. A note on the dining room table said her grandparents were spending the day in Chattanooga, about two and half hours away. Sarah's jewelry was to be part of an exhibit featuring artists from all over the country at the Hunter Museum of Art on the Tennessee River.

Which meant the house was free and clear for Brenna to search for *The Connelly Book of Magic.* She knew she needed help to break the guards Sarah and the elder aunts had placed on the book. Grinning at Tasmin, Brenna called Eva Grace and Fiona.

An hour later, her cousin's convertible pulled into the driveway. Brenna opened the front screened door with Tasmin at her side.

Eva Grace walked up the steps of the broad front porch and frowned at Brenna. "You look like hell warmed over. You should treat yourself to a beauty spell."

"It was a bad night." Brenna pushed at her unruly hair and wished she had done a little more than take a shower while waiting for her co-conspirators. Eva Grace was stylish as ever in soft gray pants and a crisp pink shirt. The color and her flowing red hair shouldn't work together, but they did. After all Eva Grace had been through these past two weeks, she still managed to look serene and beautiful. Brenna gave her a hug. "I hope you never change."

Eva Grace returned her embrace with warmth and affection.

"What's she doing?" Brenna asked, nodding toward Fiona who stood beside the car. Her dark-haired sister looked hip as usual in her faded jeans and a vintage Rolling Stones T-shirt. Fiona appeared to be in earnest conversation, although there was no one nearby.

Eva Grace stepped inside and set her big purse—by some designer Brenna didn't know—on the table in the foyer. "Fiona's being bothered by Edward Harkins. He's afraid his wife is getting married too soon after his death. He wants Fiona to tell her it's a mistake. Fiona's trying to get him to realize that Lena has to keep living her own life, and Edward needs to move on to the other side."

"Hasn't he been dead for a while?"

"At least five years."

"And that's too soon for Lena to get married?" Brenna sighed as she gazed through the screened door at Fiona who was looking a bit agitated. "That's kind of selfish, don't you think?"

Eva Grace stood beside Brenna. "He's been watching over Lena. Before he died, she didn't even know how to drive. Now she's become self-reliant and is planning to marry Kirk Harper. Lena's doing just fine, but Edward can't move on."

While they watched, Fiona stopped talking and pointed to a spot in the distance. The air around an aging pine tree shimmered for a moment with an incandescent light, and when it faded, Fiona came up the sidewalk.

"Hallelujah! That man has been pestering me for two years, and he's finally gone." Fiona pulled open the door and came into the broad, central hall.

"Why did he leave you alone for three years after he died?" Brenna asked

"He couldn't figure out how to communicate, but once he did, he has talked to me almost every day." Hands on her hips, Fiona looked at Brenna. "Okay, what are we doing here?"

"We have to find *The Connelly Book of Magic*."

"I know that," Fiona retorted. "What I don't know is how."

"With us and her." Brenna pointed to the doorway of the dining room, where Tasmin sat licking a paw.

"Oh, no." Eva Grace shook her head. "You're not involving me with Sarah's cat."

"You know she's not Sarah's," Brenna retorted. "Tasmin is almost five years old, and she hasn't been claimed by anyone in the family. To be honest, she's rather pissed off about it."

The cat paused in her grooming to issue a plaintive meow.

Fiona and Eva Grace exchanged startled glances. "She almost never makes a sound," Fiona said.

"She's been talking to me quite a bit." Brenna stooped to stroke Tasmin, earning a soft purr of approval. "When her great-great grandmother died, Tasmin was the natural choice to replace her in Sarah's affections. I was in Atlanta and still grieving the loss of my cat, Pearl. The two of you moved out of here and didn't take Tasmin or any of her siblings or her kittens with you. But she and Sarah did not have a connection. The poor thing's been waiting for someone."

"So now she's yours?" Fiona said.

"Not entirely." Brenna studied the gray and white tabby as she stood. Tasmin stretched, preened and pretended she didn't care she was the subject of their conversation. Having had a familiar, Brenna knew that she and Tasmin had yet to be linked in the deepest possible way. But she had a feeling that was coming.

Fiona's expression was still doubtful. "So how does Tasmin help us find the book?"

"We ask her," Brenna replied.

"If it's that simple, why did you need us?" Fiona asked.

"She's needs our power," Eva Grace explained.

Fiona still was not convinced. "Sarah will know what we're doing. She'll feel it and come and stop us."

Brenna sighed. Just like in childhood, Fiona and Eva Grace needed to be coaxed into misbehaving. "Sarah has been known to fly, but even she can't get here from Chattanooga in time to stop us." She held out her hands to her sister and cousin. "What do you say?"

They still hesitated.

"I'm sure the book is rigged with some additional guards," Eva Grace pointed out. "It would be just like Sarah to have a trap set for whoever finds it. I don't really want to be bitten or shocked by anything this morning."

"Remember all the times she set itch spells around our hidden Christmas gifts?" Fiona said.

"Every year Brenna would convince us to go snooping for our presents, and every year we itched almost to death as punishment."

Ready to cast a torture spell of her own on both of them, Brenna exclaimed, "We've got to look in that book. I told you on the phone everything Jake and I discovered yesterday. We've seen the human records of what was going on in the town the last few times the Woman in White came. We also need to see if there's record of supernatural activity."

Fiona frowned. "No one has said anything about that kind of activity going on when Aunt Celia passed away."

"Haven't you figured it out?" Brenna said, rolling

her eyes. "It's like a case of collective amnesia with Sarah and the elders. Each time the Woman comes and takes someone they love, they try their best to forget it. No doubt they've used magic to ease the pain. How else would they be able to live year in and year out, knowing what was going to happen to someone in their families? How could they have had children, knowing one of them would die?"

Muscles worked in Eva Grace's throat. Fiona's eyes filled with tears. Without further ado, they each clasped one of Brenna's hands and linked together as well.

"Thank the goddess," Brenna murmured. She glanced over at the cat. "Tasmin? Won't you join us?"

The tabby slunk toward them, wound herself around their legs several times, sniffing at Fiona's high-topped sneakers and Eva Grace's elegant, high-heeled sandals before she settled in the middle of their circle like a gray sphinx.

Brenna, Fiona, and Eva Grace looked at each other, down at Tasmin, then up at the hall ceiling. Brenna felt her mind falling, blending into the familiar rhythms of the other two women's thoughts. Eva Grace was open and accepting, but Fiona still held some fear.

Brenna squeezed her sister's hand. "Let go now. It's just us. Just as we've always been."

With that, Fiona released her anxieties. The craftsman-style chandelier overhead began to sway. The front screen door banged open as a breeze blew into the hall. The three of them united as only family witches could.

Locking her gaze with Tasmin's, Brenna said, "Cats do roam and cats do know, all the secrets houses show. Cat, use your powers, and search every nook. Find our family's magic book."

Tasmin blinked. For a moment, Brenna feared the spell hadn't worked. Maybe she was wrong about this feline's abilities. Then the cat meowed, a surly and demanding sound.

As if on cue, books flew off the long, low shelf outside the dining room, making Fiona jump and Eva Grace gasp. But their circle held and at the rear of the top shelf sat the bulging, untidy mess that was *The Connelly Book of Magic*.

"Oh good grief," Brenna muttered. "Only Sarah would hide a book in a bookcase near the front door."

"She knows us too well," Eva Grace added. "We always overlook the obvious."

Tasmin meowed again. The wind in the hallway died, and the front door banged shut. The witches dropped hands.

"You're a good cat," Brenna praised Tasmin. "Tuna for you for lunch." She turned to pick up the book.

"Watch out," Fiona warned. "Remember there could be traps."

But Brenna knew there were none. She was right, because she picked up the book without a problem. This was bad. Sarah was too complacent. The book held magic and secrets that no one but Connelly witches should see. The guards hadn't held against the three of them and Tasmin. What if an outsider had found it?

"Let's get lunch and study this," Brenna said, leading the way to the kitchen.

An hour later, Tasmin was asleep in a patch of sunshine on the dining room window seat, her belly full of tuna juice. Eva Grace, Fiona, and Brenna were at the dining room table, staring at each other, aghast.

"The book is in worse shape than we thought," Brenna said, shaking her head over the collection of yellowing pages spread out on the table. "What could Sarah have been thinking?" What had once been a powerful book was now little more than a large pile of loose papers.

Fiona sighed. "There's so much missing from the history."

"Maybe this is why Sarah called your parents," Eva Grace added. "With their knowledge, their skill with history and fables, perhaps they can fit the pieces of this back together so that it tells a complete story."

Brenna shook her head. "I realize all they do is research magic, but they've made it a point to stay away from New Mourne all these years. Why does Sarah think they can do anything now?"

Fiona and Eva Grace exchanged a look.

"What?" Brenna demanded.

Her sister laid her hand over Brenna's. "It couldn't have been easy for Sarah to call Mom and Dad. She's never called them. Don't you think they're worth a try? Our lives are on the line here. Sarah does understand that, and she was willing to ask our parents to come back to a place where they obviously don't want to be. Sarah doesn't do that to any of us unless she needs us."

"She never asked you to come home from Atlanta." Eva Grace's almond-shaped eyes were luminous as she looked at Brenna.

"Maybe she should have." Brenna bit her lip as she looked back at the book. "She should have asked me to help with this."

Eva Grace agreed, but she added, “We don’t need your father the Rhodes scholar to tell us to get these things organized.” She picked up scraps of paper and clippings, haphazardly stuck between pages, and began sorting them into piles. “Let’s put what history we can find together. We’ll sort the spells and charms, the recipes, and gardening tips. Going through it all may help us find what we’re looking for.”

“I’ll get my laptop.” Brenna said, rising. “We can index everything.” And not need our parents’ help when they get here, she added to herself.

Before she could go more than a step, she heard a car rumbling up the drive.

“I hope that’s not Sarah,” Fiona said.

Tasmin rose from her perch, ears at alert, whiskers bristling. Then she shot out of the room like a gray streak.

“Surely that’s not Sarah.” Eva Grace looked nervous as she headed to the window.

“Oh, for heaven’s sake,” Brenna said. “Y’all need to chill. We have just as much right to this book as Sarah does, maybe more. We’re the ones the Woman in White is after.”

Eva Grace peered out the window. “It’s Willow Scanlan.”

“I was hoping we would see her soon.” Brenna waved a hand over the book’s contents on the table, setting guards in place before she went to greet the old woman. “I want to make sure the fae are not involved in what’s happening here.”

“Don’t insult Willow by suggesting that,” Eva Grace admonished as she and Fiona trailed Brenna to the front door.

"I'm not stupid," Brenna told her.

Fiona whispered, "They say Willow has buried sixteen husbands."

"They also say she's been here since the first settlers," Eva Grace added.

"And probably knows everything we need to find out." Brenna opened the front door and went outside to greet the old lady who was mounting the front steps with a spryness that belied her reportedly ancient age. Her facc was lined, and her hair was white against the vivid purple of the heavy suit she wore. Despite the heat of the day, she looked cold.

"Hello, Willow," Brenna said. "It's so nice to see you. Won't you come in?"

"I'll just stay out here." Willow sat heavily in one of the porch's many rattan chairs. She looked tiny and frail, but her eyes snapped with life as she studied the three witches. A smile touched her lips, revealing sharp, white teeth. "My, but you're all healthy looking."

As was always the case when confronting a fae, Brenna had the uneasy feeling she was being considered as a meal. She turned from that thought, and Willow's teeth, by looking out at the woman's long, dark Cadillac, where an old man sat straight-backed in the driver's seat.

"Doesn't your friend want to come in?"

"He's just there to drive me. He'll wait," the old woman said.

"Can we get you some sweet tea and Sarah's ginger cookies?" Eva Grace offered.

"No," Willow said with typical fae bluntness. "I've come to give you information. Isn't that what you want from me?"

"Yes," Brenna responded, just as directly. She started to ask a question, but Willow cut her off with a sharp look.

"First of all, this mess is none of my kind's making," Willow told them, her eyes narrowing.

Fiona began, "I was just sure none of you—"

Her words halted with scathing glare from Willow. Fiona fell back a step. It always amazed Brenna that her sister talked to the dead but was easily frightened, otherwise.

Willow looked at Brenna. "What you're seeking will be difficult to find. You need to keep your search focused. Don't give up, and take the easy way out."

Brenna was puzzled. "There isn't anything easy about this."

"It's always easier to give in. That's what most Connellys have done in the past. There are only a few of you who have truly wanted to fight."

Suddenly, Fiona waved her hand as though she was fighting off a gnat attack. "Not now, please," she said, her voice laced with frustration.

Willow raised a hand crippled with arthritis and addressed the empty space beside Fiona. "Liam Young, leave the girl alone and be on your way. We need to talk."

Eva Grace and Brenna's heads moved like spectators at Wimbledon as they gazed between Fiona and the ancient fae.

"Are you a medium, Willow?" Fiona ventured.

"I have good sight, but I'm not here to discuss my gifts. You girls have to ferret out this evilness and banish it from our town."

"What do you think it is?" Eva Grace asked.

"That's not my problem," Willow snapped. "I'm just here to tell you it's time to go to work and save our town just as the first Sarah Connelly had to do in her day. She was a powerful woman. I hope one of you inherited that."

Brenna dared another question, "Did you know the first Sarah, Willow?"

The old woman cackled as she pushed herself to her feet. "Now how in the world would that be possible?"

Without another word, Willow crossed the porch, went down the steps and out to the car. The old man got out and helped her into the backseat. They drove away while the witches watched in silence.

Eva Grace murmured, "I haven't seen her in a while. She's so old she looks like she could dry up and blow away any minute."

"She terrifies me," Fiona said unnecessarily. "I had no idea she talked to the dead, too."

"I should have known she wouldn't just tell us what we need to know." Brenna's disappointment was keen. "We have to get some answers on who the Woman in White is. What gave her the right to make demands of our ancestors? If the first Sarah Connelly was so strong, how was this evil spirit able to get the best of her in a bargain?"

"Willow said we have to save our town," Eva Grace added. "So this isn't the first time Mourne County has been hit by evil forces. Will it end when the Woman in White takes one of us?" She shivered, despite the heat, and looked frightened. "Or will someone else have to die like Garth did?"

Fiona put her arm around her cousin. "Surely if this

is all just hopeless, she would tell us."

"Fae don't give advice that simple." Brenna sighed. "But I do think she was trying to encourage us. Let's get back to straightening out the book."

Before they could move, another vehicle came up the driveway. "Kind of busy around here today," Brenna said as she recognized her Aunt Doris's pickup.

The pickup was just one of the many differences between Doris and Frances. Although they looked identical and dressed alike, Doris had been married to a carpenter and assisted her son-in-law in the family business by making supply runs. She had driven the truck for more than fifteen years, while Frances rarely went three years without a new Chevrolet sedan.

"I wonder what she's doing here." Brenna waved to her elder aunt, who got out of the truck clutching a large, white envelope.

Doris came up the front walkway, looking grim despite the cheerful mint green pantsuit she wore. "I know what you're up to."

"Busted," Fiona murmured.

"Just keep quiet," Brenna whispered to her sister.

"I knew the minute you found the book," Doris continued as she mounted the front steps. "Frances called me right away, and we talked about what we needed to do since Sarah was out of town."

Brenna stood her ground. "We need to get that book in order."

"Well, that's what Frances said." Doris thrust out the envelope she was holding. "Here, take this. It's the part of the book that I found at my house."

"Why did you have part of it?" Brenna took the envelope.

"We told you that we used to take parts of the book to study," Doris retorted. "I thought I had brought all my sections back, but I started going through my house after Garth was killed. I found these."

The envelope was thick. A significant portion of the book, Brenna thought.

Doris shifted from foot to foot and avoided Brenna's gaze. "Frances has a few parts she's trying to chase down. I'd imagine there are other parts strewn here and there all over this house. Maybe even in other places. I've asked Diane, and Frances is talking to Estelle. I don't believe Maggie's family has anything since there were no girls in her family before her."

Eva Grace stepped forward, her expression disapproving. "I wish you had told us this instead of just trying to hide the book from us."

"We were ashamed," Doris retorted. "And Sarah's not going to be happy that I talked to you about it. She was trying to get the book in order before Celia was taken. Then we were so…" She shook her head. "We were just beaten down. And there were you girls to take care of and other business to attend to. We had all the pages we needed to teach you young ones the craft, just as we taught our daughters. We decided that's all we needed."

Opening the envelope, Brenna found brittle old pages and saw old-fashioned handwriting. She knew just enough Gaelic to make out the first words. "This is Sarah Connelly's writing," she said. "The answers to all of our questions could be right here."

Eva Grace and Fiona crowded around her, anxious to see the pages.

"Our family had the complete book for a long, long

time," Doris said, her tone defensive. "They never stopped the Woman before."

"Is that why you and Sarah and Frances think we shouldn't try?" Brenna asked.

Doris drew herself up. "I've brought you what I had. Frances will too. And we'll take your side against Sarah about your locating the book against her wishes. As for the other pages…" She swept a hand toward the house. "See if you can locate them magically, the same way you found the book today. Sarah, Frances, and I never could. But maybe you have power that we didn't. Maybe if we had tried before Rose died, when we were all together…"

Kind and forgiving as always, Eva Grace stepped toward her. "Don't worry, Doris. We know you tried to save the next generation, and you want to save us."

"Do you?" Doris accepted the redhead's embrace, but her gaze was on Brenna. "Do you really understand the guilt we bear for bringing you all into the world? At one time or another, every single one of us thought we had the answer. It's been twenty-eight years since Celia died. We even hoped it was over, that it wouldn't happen again. Then poor Garth…"

"It's all right," Eva Grace said, patting her back.

Doris's voice trembled as she hugged Eva Grace again. "Oh, my dear girl. You've borne the worst of all of this, losing first your mother and then your true love. It's just not fair. We're all just sick. But we've never let the worry or the fear keep us from living and loving and sticking together as a family. We can't turn on each other."

"Of course not," Fiona said, moving to hug the older woman, too. "We will always stand together."

She turned to Brenna. "Won't we?"

"Of course," Brenna said, but she made no move to join the group hug. All she knew was she held magic in her hands, the writings of a witch who had crossed the ocean to start a new life for her family. She wasn't sure if there could be any forgiveness for allowing these precious words to become separated from *The Connelly Book of Magic*.

Maybe that's why the book was no longer able to speak, as family legend said it could. Or that was why the guards Sarah had set up hadn't held. Because the book wasn't whole. It was weak, as she feared her family had become.

Eva Grace drew away from Doris and looked at Brenna. "What do you think we should do?"

"Let's find the rest of the book," Brenna murmured. "Let's make it as it should be."

She turned her back on her family members and went into the house, more determined than ever to fit all the pieces of the puzzle together and end the curse.

Chapter 13

Jake made it until almost three that afternoon before calling Brenna. He considered that a major achievement in restraint. Though he stayed busy all day on paperwork for the large number of citizens arrested during the weekend, he thought of her at odd moments. He remembered her sleeping in his arms. The scent of honeysuckle in her hair when they kissed. How right she had been about his needing to shift and run.

She answered her phone on first ring and was eager to talk about the sections of the family magic book that she, Eva Grace, and Fiona had received from Aunt Doris and Aunt Frances. Brenna related the correlations between family history and what they discovered in the sheriff's records at the courthouse. She said she wanted to see him and explain what the missing pages revealed and get his perspective, but she needed to work with her cousin and sister as well.

He'd ended up inviting three Connelly witches to dinner at his place. It was two more than he wanted, but it felt like the right thing to do.

He was putting together a fresh salad when Eva Grace and Fiona arrived. They crowded into his small kitchen. Fiona opened the bottle of Cabernet he had waiting on the counter. Eva Grace pushed him aside to add some seasoning to his salad. Aware of her culinary skills, Jake allowed her to take over.

Fiona took wineglasses down from a shelf and filled three. "What's that wonderful smell?"

"Lasagna," Jake answered.

"You made lasagna for us?" Eva Grace said.

"I made extra last time, and I just pulled it out of the freezer for tonight." Jake didn't want to be rude, but they were missing the most important person in this group. "Where's Brenna?"

Fiona looked at Eva Grace and giggled. Jake decided he wasn't fooling anyone.

The redhead gave her younger cousin a reproachful glance as she explained, "Brenna decided to drive so we wouldn't have to go out of our way taking her home tonight."

"At least that was her story," Fiona murmured into her wine.

"What's up?" Jake looked from woman to woman.

"Ignore Fiona." Eva Grace turned toward the oven. "Is the lasagna ready? We can get the bread warming while we wait for Brenna. I brought bread from the bakery, of course. I need butter and garlic—"

Her words were interrupted by the sound of a crash. Jake took off before he could think, racing out of the kitchen, through the living room, and outside.

His stomach clenched as he saw Brenna's SUV wedged alongside a pine tree next to the house. Her head was against the window, what looked like blood smeared the glass. Jake's breathing slowed. He felt like he was running in quicksand as he rushed across the yard.

Overhead, wings beat against the hot still air. A shrill scream cut through the woods. Jake saw the flash of a bird's whiteface and recognized the eerie sound.

The owl. Brenna's owl was here and calling for Jake.

He wasn't sure how he knew the bird was calling for him. But Jake got to the vehicle as quickly as he could, wrenched the driver's door open, and braced to catch Brenna. She swayed as she looked up at him with glazed eyes. Blood trickled from a cut on her forehead.

"I hit my head." She struggled against the seatbelt.

Jake knelt beside her. "Don't move now. Take it easy." He undid the seatbelt that pressed her against the seat and eased her out of the car.

Brenna showed him her bloody fingers. "I hit my head," she mumbled again. "And I'm bleeding."

"Oh my god," Fiona said as she and Eva Grace arrived. "Is she all right?"

"She's got a cut on her head," Jake said. "Let's get her in the house and see if there are any other injuries."

Brenna looked up at him again and frowned. "Damn it, shifter, I don't like how you're always coming to my rescue. I can take care of myself."

Relieved by the humor in her voice, he helped her stand. "Much more taking care of yourself, and you're going to kill me, witch."

Eva Grace took one arm and Jake the other. They walked Brenna onto the porch and through the door that Fiona held open. Jake insisted Brenna lie down on his sofa while he got the first aid kit, towels, and a washcloth. Fiona hurried off to rescue the lasagna and get ice.

With the sure, capable hands of a healer, Eva Grace cleaned the blood from Brenna's forehead and checked her from head to toe. Aside from the cut, Brenna had only a raw, red mark on her neck where the seatbelt had tightened to hold her in place. Best of all, Brenna looked more alert by the moment. Wincing at the alcohol Eva Grace used and rolling her eyes at Jake as her cousin fussed over her, she said, “I think I’ll live.”

Eva Grace told Jake to hold a washcloth over the cut and apply some gentle pressure. She took Brenna’s hand and murmured softly. Jake imagined her words were laced with magic, and he breathed easier. Brenna was okay, really okay.

Still, his heart pounded. He took a look at the gash, wondering if they should call the paramedics. It was a small abrasion but there was a nice little goose egg under it.

“It’s nothing major,” Eva Grace assured him before he could say a word.

“Shouldn’t we cover her up?”

“Good idea.” Eva Grace unfolded a comforter from the end of the sofa and draped it over Brenna. “There, now, she should be—”

“I’m right here.” Brenna pushed Jake’s hand away with a grumpy sigh. “You’re hurting my head.”

“Here’s some ice.” Fiona handed Brenna a bag of ice wrapped in a kitchen towel.

Jake lowered himself to his whiskey barrel coffee table and took a deep breath. He was coming down from his adrenalin rush. “What caused you to go off the road?” he asked.

“The owl,” She said and pushed the blanket off. “Did you see it? It swooped down at my windshield. I jerked the wheel. Next thing I know, I’m parked against your tree.”

“Is it the same owl you’ve seen before?” Eva Grace asked.

Brenna rubbed her face, and Eva Grace tucked the blanket back around her legs. “I don’t know. It looked the same. But it seemed huge as it flew at my windshield. I swear the wings completely covered the glass and blocked the light. It was incredible.”

“I saw it, too,” Jake added, “when I ran outside. It was…” He started to say it had been calling to him, but he decided that might sound weird even to a group of witches. “It made that noise. That hiss we heard from outside the window at Frances’s house.”

“He’s warning you, maybe,” Fiona murmured.

“How do you know it’s a male?” Brenna retorted. “It could be a very wise, old female.”

“It’s a male,” Jake said, not certain how he knew, but he did.

“Depending on where you live, owls can be a sign of good or evil,” Fiona continued. “In India, they’re always seen as bad omens, bringers of ill will, and servants of the dead. With Native Americas, they’re considered wise and aid in helping humans see in the dark. Native Americans believe owls reveal deception.”

“They’re also perceived to be spirit guides and can bring healing to a situation,” Eva Grace added.

Brenna once again shoved aside the comforter and waved Jake and Eva Grace away as she sat up. “I don’t know why the owl was chasing me. We’re here to discuss something much more serious than a crazy bird.”

“You sound like your usual self,” Eva Grace told her and headed for the kitchen. “I’m going to make tea.”

Jake took the ice pack and held it back to Brenna’s head. “I don’t have any tea,” he called after her cousin.

Eva Grace laughed. “I have tea in my purse. You have your first-aid kit, and I have mine. I’ll get the bread in the oven, too. I think our patient will be ready to eat soon.”

Brenna took control of the ice and held it in place herself. She looked from Jake to her sister and back again. “Do both of you think the owl has something to do with the Woman in White?”

Fiona shrugged. “Is there anything happening these days that doesn’t have to do with her?”

“Of course it does,” Jake said. “The bird’s trying to tell you something, Brenna. I’d advise you to listen.”

‘I don’t speak owl,” she said with a grumpy sigh. She leaned her head back against dark leather cushions of his sofa. Bruises from Saturday’s attack were fading, but the new marks stood out against the white skin of her neck.

Only then did Jake take full notice of how Brenna looked in a fitted sundress of scarlet, slender gold hoops at her ears echoed by a gold disc on a chain at her throat. She wore makeup, too, a dusting of peach across her cheekbones and her lashes a dark sweep over emerald eyes.

She had dressed up for him, he realized. And while Brenna in her usual jeans and T-shirt attire was just fine with him, he was pleased she had taken the extra effort.

He wished she could use some of her magic to make her sister and cousin disappear.

As if she read his mind, Fiona cleared her throat. “If the two of you are just going to sit here making eyes at each other, I’m going to help Eva Grace.”

Brenna ignored Fiona, smiled, and held out her hand to clasp Jake’s. “Thanks.”

"I didn't do anything."

"You left that tree growing right next to your house. Otherwise, my car would be sitting in your living room. My insurance company would not be happy."

"I'm sure the tree was just waiting for you to hit it." His fingers curved around hers.

"Dinner's ready," Fiona called from the kitchen.

Jake did his best not to groan.

"Easy, tiger," Brenna murmured to him. "The night is young."

He helped her up, and they went to have dinner and discuss what the three women had learned from *The Connelly Book of Magic.*

As they enjoyed the meal around his oak table, Jake found himself caught up in the story of the Connellys who founded Mourne County. In the papers from Frances they had found an English translation of the first Sarah Connelly's story of their flight from Ireland.

"They were running from absolute devastation," Brenna said. "The problems started in the 1700s with a fungal infection in potatoes. Then it got so cold that no crops could grow."

"I confirmed it all on the Internet," Fiona added. "It was part of what's called the 'Little Ice Age' in Europe, their last big freeze."

"So the Connelly witches came to America," Jake said.

Eva Grace served herself a second helping of salad. "According to the pages we put back in the book today, there were more than a hundred people in the Connelly party. But only forty-nine of them were alive when they reached Charleston. After that, they packed up their belongings and traveled in wagons over the mountains to get here."

"It was late spring when they arrived," Brenna said, sipping her wine. "They planted a good crop, and were creating a new home. But a terrible fever went through the settlement in October."

"It snowed before Samhain." Fiona frowned. "Even back then that was extreme weather. Many of their cattle disappeared into the mountains during the storm. They were convinced the bad luck had followed them."

"The Connellys were the leaders and well-known for their magic," Brenna explained to Jake. "Everyone in the village looked to Sarah to do something. Not knowing what else to do, she appealed to the spirit of the land to help them."

Eva Grace shivered. "Her journal said she knew the magic here was black, and she feared it. But she had no other choice."

The table fell silent. Jake looked from woman to woman. "What happened then?" he asked. "Does she tell us what happened with the Woman in White?"

"There are pages missing from the story after Sarah recorded that she was going to the cliff above the waterfall," Brenna told him. "The next entry is the record of her daughter's death. Sarah said her Maeve was 'given in tribute' to 'the Woman who dwelt at the falls.'"

Jake sat back, not quite understanding. "Does it say why Sarah made such a terrible sacrifice? Wasn't there another way?"

The witches shook their heads.

"We can't find another word that Sarah wrote," Eva Grace said, sighing. "Before her daughter's passing, she wrote spells and charms and detailed daily life in the settlement. Afterward, there was nothing."

"Until the next Connelly witch took up the story, decades later." Brenna bit her lip. "She wrote about her younger sister falling over the cliff. And she mentioned demons were loose in the town."

"We found tales of devils and evil spirits throughout the book," Fiona said. "Every fifteen to thirty years, there were plagues of insects, murders, and cases of unexplained madness. Just as we've been setting wards throughout the county this past week, the Connelly witches back then were busy, too. In the 1880's, three of the coven drove out a demon that possessed a local hermit. The guy started killing everything in sight—livestock, horses, and finally people."

"Like Bill Riley and his wife's prize hens." Jake was shaken by the information the women had gleaned. It confirmed his worst fears. None of this was random. They were under siege from a sinister force.

"One thing is very strange," Brenna said, leaning forward. "There's no mention of the Woman in White killing anyone the way she killed Garth. As far as we could see, she has only been seen when she takes a Connelly."

"Maybe she's just in another form when she wreaks havoc on the rest of the community," Eva Grace suggested. "Plenty of people close to the family have lost their lives through the years."

"But never by her hand." Brenna's eyes were bright as she considered this possibility. Jake could tell her thoughts were whirling in a million directions. "We have to find out who the Woman was. That's the key."

"There's still some of the book to go through," Fiona said.

"The answer won't be there." Brenna looked certain, and her sister and cousin didn't disagree. "But we have to keep looking. Remember what Willow told us today."

"You talked to Willow?"

The women told him about the puzzling visit from the faerie as they cleared the table. Their quick teamwork amazed Jake. Like magic, leftovers were stowed in the fridge and the dishwasher loaded in half the time it would have taken him. Maybe it *was* magic, he thought, grinning as he watched them from his seat at the table. He could get used to witches in his kitchen.

"You cook, we clean," Fiona said, as she smiled back. "When you come over for dinner at my place, you'll be doing dishes."

Eva Grace sighed as she crossed the kitchen. "I'm really tired, guys. Aren't you?"

Jake looked at her in concern. Eva Grace was pale and drawn. He got to his feet, reaching for her arm. "You need to sit down. You're worn out."

"And you took all of my pain." Realization breaking across her face, Brenna crossed the room to her cousin's side. "No wonder I'm not feeling like I was punched in the face. For the second time in three days, you took my hurt away. Eva Grace, you can't do that—"

"It's what I do," Eva Grace said, though she looked a little shaky as she took the chair Jake had vacated. "I'm not going to let you suffer, Brenna. I couldn't do that. And something terrible is after you. The same thing that took Garth." She put her head in her hands.

The rest of them stood in awkward silence, looking at her. For once neither Brenna nor Fiona seemed to know what to do or say as their cousin fought for control of her emotions.

But Eva Grace didn't give into tears, Jake observed with admiration. She drew in a deep breath, and then looked up at them. A brave smile played about her lips. "I think I'm done for this day, folks."

"You were going to go to the shop today," Brenna said with even more guilt. "And I made you spend the day on all of this, instead."

"All of this is life or death," Eva Grace replied with firmness. "Because we were together, we have valuable information that we didn't have before."

"And we got the book in good working shape for Mom and Dad to look at it," Fiona added.

Brenna's frown didn't escape Jake's notice. She really wasn't keen on her parents coming, but from other things mentioned tonight, he knew Fiona and Eva Grace didn't share her feelings. Wisely, he thought, she didn't pursue the sore subject now.

Jake was able to get Brenna's SUV out of his yard and assessed the damage as minor. He assured Fiona and Eva Grace that he would be certain it was safe to drive. The two of them departed in Eva Grace's smart little convertible.

Night sounds closed in around Jake and Brenna as they stood together on his front porch. Moonlight slanted through the trees. The scent of pine was heavy in the moist summer air.

"I imagine you're as tired as Eva Grace," he said

when the quiet had stretched a little too long. “Let’s not bother with your car. I don’t want anything else happening to you on the way home.”

Brenna put her arms around his waist. “How about I ease your mind by staying here tonight?”

Chapter 14

Jake stepped back, his face showing his surprise. “Stay here tonight?”

“Sure, it seems logical to me. We’ve had a nice dinner, some wine, and now it’s time for dessert.”

To her amusement, he didn’t move. “What’s the matter? Never had a woman come on to you before?”

Jake appeared to be searching for the right words. Brenna’s smile faded. Where was the man who had kissed her with such passion last night? The man whose hungry gaze she had enjoyed over dinner. She had no doubt Jake had been eager for her sister and cousin to leave the two of them alone. So why the hesitation?

“What’s the matter?” she asked, stepping closer. “Are you not so sure you can handle a witch?”

With a groan, Jake settled his hands on her shoulders. “That’s not it. Not at all.” His fingers trailed up and down her arms, making her shiver.

She pressed her body to his. “Mmmmm. You’re so warm. I’ve heard that about shifters, that they run a little hotter than the rest of us. Does that mean you’re hotter in every area?”

He held her away again, his breathing hard. “Are you sure this is a good idea?”

“Why not?” She framed his face with her hands, intrigued by the way his eyes turned silvery in the moonlight. “We’re both well beyond the age of consent, and we've got no other commitments." That made her pause. She had assumed there was no one else. "Are you seeing someone?"

"No, it's not that—" he started.

"Then I see no problem."

"With everything that's going on with the town and your family, do we need to complicate things?"

"I want you, and you want me. It seems pretty simple to me." Her arms wound around his neck. His lips were close and tantalizing.

"You know that entanglements are never simple," Jake replied, still holding back from her. "And I'm the sheriff now—"

She threw back her head and laughed. "Are you standing here, trying to tell me that you're worried about your reputation?"

"That's not what I meant." He sighed, his arms closing around her, pulling her close. "There's so much happening, and your family is at the center of most of it. I need to keep my perspective."

She laughed again, and he smothered the sound with his kiss. He could claim reluctance all he wanted, but Brenna knew there was nothing tentative about the way his mouth claimed hers. From the heat of his body, she thought he had only one perspective on his mind at the moment.

She broke away, her laughter teasing. "If you think I'm trying to bribe a public official with sex, you can be assured that I don't expect any special treatment. Except maybe in bed. Unless you'd rather I go."

She turned, and he pulled her back, his touch not so gentle now. "Don't tease me, Brenna." A deep growl rumbled from him.

Brenna molded her body to his. "Are you angry with me? I've been reading about tigers, and I understand they like a little snarling and scratching before they have sex. I'm up for some play."

Jake jerked away. "Of course I'm not angry. I'd never hurt you, Brenna. I don't hurt women."

Recognizing that she had touched a nerve, Brenna became serious. "I didn't mean to imply that you would. You're not that sort, Jake. I could tell that the moment I bothered to look beneath the remote, lawman front you put up most of the time."

"I'm a shifter, Brenna."

"And last week, when we met in the woods, you could have ripped my throat out," Brenna reminded him. "But you didn't." She placed a hand on his chest, feeling his heart racing. "You stood still and let me stroke you."

"Your magic would protect you," he said. He looked uncertain. "Wouldn't it?"

Brenna shrugged. "In Atlanta I didn't practice my craft the way I should. I'm getting better now, being back with the coven, setting wards to guard the town, renewing my memory of the spells I learned when the elders trained me. But I'm not sure I could hold off a white tiger."

"You'll never have to find out." Jake pulled her to him again. "No one's going to get hurt, Brenna. I'm talking about more than the physical. I'm a loner. I'm not looking—"

"For love?" Brenna's gaze was steady on his. "I'm not looking for that, either. How could I, with the threat that's hanging over my head? The previous generations of my family may have been able just to live their lives, but no matter how this next encounter with the Woman in White turns out, I'm not going to forget and settle down and raise a family. I'm not looking to add another generation of Connelly witches to this curse."

When he was silent, Brenna continued, "I don't want to get involved. I just want a little jungle sex with my friendly, neighborhood tiger. It's no big deal."

"Sex *is* a big deal," he said with frustration. "It changes everything."

"Hopefully for the better," she said. "I guarantee I can leave you well satisfied. Do you want references?"

His eyes flashed sapphire. "Don't be crude."

"Sometimes I like being crude," she said, reaching for his belt buckle. "It makes for edgy sex, which is pretty exciting."

Jake tried to back up, but Brenna had a firm hold on his waistband. She pulled him toward her and planted her lips firmly on his before he could protest again. By the time her tongue slipped between his lips, she was pressed against his obvious arousal.

He pulled back and tried one more time. "Brenna, I think—"

"That's the problem." She reached behind her and unzipped her sexy little red dress. "You're thinking way too much."

As her dress slipped from her shoulders, his eyes widened. She thanked the goddess for the sheer red bra she had dug out of her still unpacked boxes. And she laughed out loud at Jake's expression when the dress fell from her hips to reveal the matching red thong panties.

He actually swayed on his feet. His growl was full of blatant need, a demand for satisfaction.

Brenna opened the front door and tossed her dress inside. Framed in Jake's doorway, she posed in her revealing underwear and black, strappy sandals. "Are you going to take me to bed, or what?"

"Ah, god," he moaned and pulled her to him. "I give up."

Brenna laughed as he lifted her, his big hands closing on her soft behind. She wrapped her legs around his waist. "Can we get on with this, tiger?"

Jake kissed her all the way to the bedroom, not struggling in the least to carry her. Brenna wasn't sure how he walked with the erection that nudged against her cleft. Somehow he managed. At his bed, he dropped to his knees with Brenna's legs still wrapped around his waist. He kissed her as they gently fell down on the pillows.

When they finally broke apart, he looked at her with a touch of sadness in his eyes. "I didn't mean for this to happen."

"Oh, come now," she murmured as she began pushing his T-shirt up. "You know you've been picturing this since that first night in the woods."

He pulled the shirt over his head and threw it aside. "Are you psychic as well as a witch, the way Eva Grace is also an empath and Fiona is also a medium?"

"Why do men always think they're not being obvious when they want you? You've wanted me since we met when I came home for Christmas two years ago."

"We first met at a party at Eva Grace's house." His eyes claimed hers as he finished undoing his jeans. "You were wearing tight black pants and this white, see-through blouse with a black lacy bra underneath. I thought about your breasts for a long time after that. I thought about them every time I saw you. I thought about them at other times, too."

She grinned, pleased that she had been the object of his sexual fantasies. "Sarah told me I looked like a trollop that night. I was so pleased that she was displeased. I wanted people to comment on me to her."

"You're not very nice to your grandmother." Jake stood to strip off his jeans.

Brenna unhooked her bra and was rewarded by his sigh of appreciation as her generous breasts tumbled free. For a moment, his eyes gleamed liked the tiger's eyes in the woods, when she stood skyclad for his study.

"You are amazing," Jake told her. "I can imagine how worried your grandmother must have been when you started turning into the woman you are now."

"She didn't like it," Brenna admitted. "Which is ridiculous. Sarah was a wild and free woman in her prime. She never gave a damn what anyone said about her. She let my mother and my aunt do as they wanted most of the time. For god's sake, my mother had a torrid affair with her professor, and Sarah blessed the union. So I couldn't understand why she was so hard on me and Fiona and Eva Grace. She wanted us to be different, somehow. I guess that's why I was so determined to be what I wanted to be."

Jake shed his underwear. This time Brenna sighed in appreciation. She kneeled on the bed and wrapped her hand around his penis. He grew even more rigid at her touch, and she grinned at his indrawn breath. She liked the power of arousing him.

With a growl, Jake kissed her until they were both

breathless. His hands were on her breasts, a gentle stroke of fingertips against nipples that strained to his touch.

Brenna broke away to move her kisses down his neck to his chest. She kept going down until she took him in her mouth and went still. With abandon and enthusiasm she pleasured him until he yanked her up and devoured her mouth.

He peeled her thong down her thighs then slipped a hand between them. She jerked in response to the easy pressure of his stroke, her release trembling just beyond her reach. She pushed the thong the rest of the way off. Jake slid his fingers inside her. Deeper. With more confidence. Her hands fell to her sides as she closed her eyes and gave herself up to the sensations his movements created.

"God," she said on a gasp. "You'll have me purring in a minute."

She melted against his hand, her breath stopping as her body bowed and an orgasm washed through her. Her hands fisted on his shoulders. Hands on her bottom, Jake lifted her again. He entered her and began moving, a steady rhythm.

She pulled him back on the bed, and he filled her. She met his thrusts with eagerness. Warm, familiar magic began at her throat and traveled out to her fingers as she pulled his hips against hers. His release was a blast of heat and color. Their cries filled the room as her magic rose up and sparkled above them.

Brenna was startled. She'd had her share of lovers, but her magic had never had anything to do with them. What was it about this shifter?

They lay on the bed with chests heaving for several

moments. Brenna ran a hand down Jake's arm and grinned at him. "Any regrets?" she teased.

He moved like lightning, pushing her back on the bed with an ease that was all cat. His weight covered her from head to toe with a pleasant, male heaviness. He growled against the base of her throat. "How about you?"

"No regrets," she murmured as she pulled a hand through his damp, dark hair. "No complaints, either."

"So you don't think we just ruined a nice friendship?"

"Sex doesn't have to spoil a friendship. It can make it better."

"Although I've known sex to ruin a good thing before, I'm not in any position to argue that right now," he said and kissed her.

She was opening herself to him and wondering if they were really going to make love again when Jake's phone rang.

"Damn," he muttered. "I want to ignore that, but I can't." He got up and scrambled through the pile of clothes to get the phone out of the pocket of his jeans. She curled onto her side and admired his taut buttocks and strong torso.

"Tyler," he said into the phone, his gaze traveling in equal appreciation over her.

As Brenna smiled at him, his face grew serious. "We'll be right there."

She sat up. "What is it?"

"There's been a break in at Eva Grace's shop," he said pulling on his jeans. "Brian said it's bad. He found it during routine patrol. The alarm didn't go off, but he said somebody really messed up the place."

Brenna got up and retrieved her underwear from the side of the bed. “This is terrible. Eva Grace doesn’t need more trouble right now.”

“Well, there’s going to be a lot more,” Jake said.

His grim tone startled Brenna. “What do you mean?”

“Brian says there’s a body in the shop. Somebody else is dead.”

Chapter 15

The parking lot at Siren's Call was bright with the flashing lights of two patrol cars. Jake pulled his cruiser to a halt in front of the renovated old house at the edge of downtown. Brenna was out of the car and racing toward the shop before he could stop her.

"Dammit, Brenna, wait a minute," he yelled as he wrenched open his door. Thankfully, Brian stopped her at the shop's entrance.

Fiona's van pulled in with a screech of tires. She flew out of the vehicle in a flash, but Jake caught her as she started after Brenna. "Slow down. You're going to hurt yourself or someone else."

Fiona pulled away. "Is Eva Grace okay? Brian called me and told me what happened."

Jake followed her to the door where Brian was holding Brenna back. The younger deputy looked shaken. "I couldn't stop Eva Grace," he told Jake. "She did something magic to me, made me let her in."

"Smart witch," Brenna said as she snapped her fingers in front of her male cousin's eyes. Brian released her and stumbled backward.

"Hold it." Jake reached for the sisters, but they were in the shop faster than he could react. "This is a crime scene," he called after them. He traded frustrated glances with Brian and trailed after them.

Glittering sparkles topped everything in the store's

front room. Every crystal and piece of glass and pottery appeared to be in shards covering the floor and all of the merchandise. The devastation was thorough. The work of countless local artisans had been destroyed. Candles were melted into colorful blobs. Ritual athames were driven into the walls and the ceiling.

Jake pointed to the knives and told Brian, "None of those should have been sharp enough to stick like that in the plaster. What happened here?"

Herbs that had been dumped from bins and baskets crunched underfoot as Jake and the younger man made their way deeper into the shop. Essential oils leaked from broken glass vessels. The combination of aromas was pungent.

In the corner where Eva Grace kept a display of local Native American art and totems, Jake saw only splintered wood and stone with shredded feathers on top. Like a pile of broken dreams, he thought.

He could apply the same description to Eva Grace. With Fiona and Brenna on either side of her, she knelt beside a body near the shop's counter. He shook off how familiar the scene looked.

As Brian had said when he called Jake, the dead person was Sandy Murphy, one of Eva Grace's shop assistants. Her unblinking eyes stared up at the ceiling. Her arms and legs were spread like she lay on a pentagram. Her long, dark hair was a velvet blanket under her head. There was blood on her arms and face from small nicks. The cuts looked as if they could have been made by flying glass. Jake couldn't see any other obvious wounds or any other blood. But she was unmoving, pale, and very clearly dead.

Eyes glassy with shock, Eva Grace looked up at

Jake. "She was only twenty," she whispered. "She was working here to learn more about Wicca. She was helping her parents pay for her college. Since we stay open until nine during the tourist season, I made her the night manager."

Eva Grace drew in a deep, shuddering breath. "I relied on Sandy more than anyone. More than Lauren or Maggie, even. She had an eye for display and a way of upselling that was so natural. She's been working so much since Garth died, taking up slack for me."

Fiona took Eva Grace's hand in her own. Brenna's arm went around her shoulders.

"I killed her," Eva Grace said as tears slid down her cheeks.

"You did not," Fiona said.

Brenna added, "You couldn't have known this was going to happen. The only person at fault is the one who killed her."

"No, it's me that put her here," Eva Grace said. "I put Sandy in the path of death. Everyone around me dies."

Eva Grace crumpled between her cousins. Jake stepped forward and caught her. He pulled her gently to her feet and wrapped his arms around her. "Stop it, now," he said. "This isn't your fault. This isn't about you."

The redhead pushed him away. "Of course it is. It's about all of us. We saw today in our family book how people have died in this town for over two centuries because of us, because of something our ancestor did. If the Woman wasn't coming for me, why would she come here and destroy my shop. Sandy died in my place."

"We don't know that this was the Woman in White." Brenna put her arm around Eva Grace again. She looked at Jake, as if asking him to show them that this couldn't have been their family's enemy in action.

He couldn't do that, of course. The inside of the shop looked like a bomb had detonated. But Sandy's body would have been blown to bits if that had happened. There would have been an explosion felt by half the town. The windows would have been shattered, the roof possibly blown off. Instead, the alarm in the shop hadn't even activated. If Brian had not driven by and seen lights on where there should have been none, no one would have discovered this until tomorrow morning.

"There's been evil here." Fiona's gaze traveled around the shop. "It's black. Can't you feel it, Brenna?"

Brenna nodded. "There's heat, too. And a charred smell. Like there's been a fire."

"Damn," Jake muttered, turning to Brian. "Get Harrigan in here and go through the place. Make sure we don't have anything smoldering in here."

"That's not necessary," Brenna said, countering Jake's command. "It's not smoke in the normal sense. It's unnatural."

Fiona agreed. "It's so bad that even the ghost who lives in the shop is gone. She's been in this old house for nearly a century. Only something terrible would force her away from her home. It's the only place she's ever wanted to be."

"Are you sure she's gone?" Jake's gaze drifted toward the staircase that split the shop in two. He had heard about the resident ghost from many people, including Garth and Eva Grace. They said she often glided down that staircase as if coming down to receive guests. He had never seen her himself, but he didn't doubt for moment that she existed.

"She's gone," Fiona insisted. "I'm going to need to find the ghost, help her come back."

"Is Sandy here?" Eva Grace asked Fiona through tears. "Can you feel her?"

Fiona once more looked around the shop, and then closed her eyes. The only sound was Eva Grace's quiet sobs. Finally, Fiona looked at Eva Grace and shook her head. "She's not available to me. She may have simply crossed over."

"I need to get to her parents before they hear this from someone else," Eva Grace said.

"We'll tell them," Jake assured her. "You can call them tomorrow."

"Don't put that on yourself tonight," Brenna agreed.

A voice called from the front of the store. In silent agreement, Brian, the Connelly witches and Jake worked their way with care to the entrance again.

Deputy Harrigan greeted them at the door. The female deputy nodded in sympathy to Eva Grace, then said to Jake, "The coroner's here with the crime scene guys. The state lab's already got somebody in route, as well."

Jake wasn't surprised. He had put a call into the state as he was driving with Brenna to the scene. Two murders in his little county in under two weeks were too much for his team to process.

"We need to clear the scene," he told the others.

"They're not going to find anything useful to us," Brenna murmured to him.

Though he agreed, he had to do what was right. “On the off chance that this wasn’t connected to your family’s curse, we have to go through the motions of an investigation.”

“I don’t want to leave Sandy alone,” Eva Grace protested.

Harrigan patted her on the shoulder. “We’ll take care of her for you. We promise you that.” With a jerk of her chin, she gestured for Brian to follow her back into the shop.

As Jake herded Brenna and her family out of the store, the county’s amateur crime scene techs began collecting evidence and taking photos at the door. Red ambulance lights had joined the blue strobes of the sheriff’s cruisers in the parking lot.

The county’s coroner greeted them all as he slipped white booties over his shoes with EMTs at the ambulance. “This is a damn shame,” he told Eva Grace. “Your beautiful shop ruined and that young woman dead.”

“There’s no obvious cause of death,” Jake murmured to the doctor. “If you and the state guys could get that for me soon, I’d appreciate it.”

The doctor nodded. Jake turned back to Brenna, her sister and their cousin. “You should all go home now. Leave this to us for now, and we’ll talk tomorrow.”

“I want to stay,” Eva Grace said. “Maybe we can start cleaning up as soon as the doctor is finished.”

“That’s going to take a little while,” Jake demurred, looking to Brenna for help. The best thing they could all do for Eva Grace was get her out of here. She didn’t need to be here when they brought Sandy’s body out.

Brenna nodded as if she understood. "Let's go now," she suggested to Eva Grace. "Tomorrow is soon enough to start sorting through the mess."

"I need to put up the closed sign. Sandy hadn't done that yet."

"Which may help us fix a time of death. The front door was open, so this must have happened before she closed." If this murder had not been a supernatural act, the evidence would help. Jake patted Eva Grace's arm. "We'll put the sign in place. Where are your keys, so I can lock up?"

"Use mine." Fiona pulled a key off her key ring and gave it to Jake.

Eva Grace sighed as she pushed her hair back from her pale features. "How did any human or super get through the wards I had set on the store?"

"They don't work when it's time for the Woman in White to come," Brenna said. "That much is obvious."

A large SUV pulled into the parking lot before anyone could comment. Sarah and Marcus got out of the front, but the two people who came from the passenger seats were unfamiliar to Jake.

He heard a sharp intake of breath and looked at Brenna. Anger had replaced her expression of concern for her cousin.

"What's wrong?" he asked her.

"They're here."

Who "they" were was instantly apparent as Fiona darted forward. "Mom. Dad," Fiona cried, opening her arms to the couple who trailed Sarah and Marcus.

A slender redhead who looked remarkably like Eva Grace grabbed Fiona in a fierce hug.

"Your parents." Jake turned again to Brenna. "Looks like they got on a plane right after Sarah called them."

"Sarah and Marcus must have picked them up in Atlanta." Brenna's expression went blank as Eva Grace also moved forward and was wrapped in a hearty embrace by a tall, handsome man with dark hair.

Jake stayed in step with Brenna as she moved slowly forward.

Her mother, Delia Connelly Burns, was now greeting Eva Grace. "Oh my girl," she said, wrapping her niece close in her arms. "My sweet, dear girl. What a terrible time you're going through."

"We came straight here," said the man who was clearly Brenna's father. He was looking toward Brenna now, over Fiona's head.

Brenna stopped a couple of feet in front of her parents. Everyone fell silent. To Jake, the locking of Brenna and Delia's gazes was more a dominance standoff than a mother/daughter reunion.

Aiden Burns slipped around his wife and went to his oldest daughter. He gave her a one-armed hug and left his arm draped around her shoulders. He looked awkward, but Jake noted that he made an effort. On the other hand, Brenna's mother made no move toward her.

"Do you have any idea what happened here tonight?" her father asked.

Still glaring at her mother, Brenna said, "Not yet."

Since Brenna made no move to introduce him, Jake stepped forward and put out his hand. "Sheriff Jake Tyler."

"Aiden Burns," Brenna's father said. "And this is my wife."

Delia broke away from Brenna's regard long enough to greet Jake.

Sarah said, "We were on our way from the airport when Doris called to tell us about the break-in." She clasped Eva Grace to her side. "We'll clean it up, dear. I promise we'll fix it."

"We'll all help," Aiden said.

"Right," Brenna said with sarcasm. "That's what family is for, isn't it, to be there when they're needed?"

She stepped away from Aiden's hold, moving closer to Jake. It was the first time she had ever looked at him like she truly needed his help.

"Can we get Eva Grace home?" she said.

"The entire coven is gathering at the home place," Sarah replied before Jake could answer her.

Brenna frowned. "It's after midnight, and Eva Grace is exhausted."

"And a woman is dead," Sarah snapped. "We have to make a plan."

Jake could feel the fury simmering just underneath the surface in Brenna.

She said to Sarah, "I guess now that our two saviors are here, you feel somehow empowered. Are you expecting them to put our family book back together? We already started on that without you or them."

"I knew when you found the book this morning," Sarah replied. "I could have stopped you, but I didn't."

"You could have done a lot of things," Brenna said. "Like spending the last twenty-eight years trying to stop this madness from happening again. Isn't it a little late to be calling in the expert help?"

Delia stepped in between her mother and her oldest

daughter.

"Aren't we beyond this kind of adolescent bickering?" Delia sent Sarah a reproving look as she turned to Brenna. "We're here to help end the 'madness' as you call it. We're so happy that your grandmother has asked for our help."

Brenna stepped back and said, "And as long as you're happy that's all that matters, right?" Then she walked to Fiona's van, got in the passenger side, and slammed the door.

Jake looked from her to her family, feeling helpless. He thought Brenna had good reason for the disdain she had for her parents. However, this family needed to unite if they were going to defeat the sinister forces that had just claimed another life in their town.

Or would the next death be one of the Connelly witches?

Chapter 16

Though it was nearly one in the morning, Brenna wasn't surprised that the rest of the coven waited for them at the home place. The house was lit up like All Hallow's Eve.

Brenna noted that elders, aunts, and cousins were all in attendance as she followed her sister, parents, and grandparents into the house. Tears were shed and embraces exchanged as Delia and Aiden were welcomed back into the fold.

So simple for them all to laugh and cry and pretend like there's nothing amiss, Brenna thought as she paused in the doorway to the dining room. She had never been able to understand how the whole family overlooked that her parents had abandoned their children. Though she knew there was little to achieve by fighting with anyone about it tonight, she still resented how everyone welcomed Delia home like a heroine.

"Please try."

Brenna turned at the sound of Fiona's voice. Her younger sister threaded her arm through Brenna's, clasped her hand, and leaned close. "Please just let it go for tonight."

When they were young and Brenna had been arguing with Sarah, this was the tactic Fiona always used to get Brenna to back down. A simple plea. Naked entreaty in her green eyes. And as had been the case for much of her life, if Fiona asked, Brenna found it tough to resist. “I’ll try,” she told her.

“Let’s help them get the food together.”

“Because, of course, we have to have a table full of food before we do anything else.” Brenna shook her head at the bounty spread in front of them. The relatives had arrived with a truckload of Southern “comfort.”

From the elder aunts there was homemade bread and strawberry jam, cinnamon rolls, and sliced ham. Lauren’s mother, Aunt Estelle, was carrying in a blackberry cobbler, hot from the oven. Maggie had retrieved peaches from Sarah’s canning cellar and was emptying them into a large glass bowl, while Aunt Diane sliced a pound cake that Brenna knew contained a pound of butter and almost as much sugar. Lauren set out cups, plates, and silverware.

“I brought you a couple of dozen eggs,” Aunt Estelle said to Marcus from the open kitchen door. “Get in here and do what you do best.”

Marcus was famous for his scrambled eggs with cheese, fresh basil, and sour cream. He turned to Brenna. “Come help me crack some eggs. Next to me, you do it best.”

Brenna smiled for the first time since the phone call had summoned her to Eva Grace’s shop. Trust Marcus to pull her close to the family again, to give her something to do. Content to let the rest of the coven buzz around them, she broke eggs, tore basil leaves, and shredded cheese at his direction.

By the time two huge skillets of eggs were ready, an urn of coffee had been made. The family gathered around the table, passed platters of food, and ate.

Sarah sat at the head with Aiden and Delia on either side. Frances and Doris were next, with Estelle, Diane, and Brenna's sister and three cousins filling in next to them. Marcus took the chair opposite Sarah, and Brenna sat down beside him.

For a little while, they behaved as they always did with a family feast, complimenting each other's culinary skills and asking for seconds.

Brenna was glad, however, that the elders didn't let the business at hand wait very long.

Doris spoke first, unusual for someone who rarely took the lead. "Tonight has shown us that we're facing a terrible time, one that we hoped would never be repeated."

Sarah nodded. "We're all devastated by what's happened tonight, what's been happening since Garth was killed."

"We don't like to think about the worst of the past," Frances added. "But this is as bad as when Rose was taken."

"What exactly does that mean?" Brenna kept her question mild in tone. If she came on too strong, the elders would pull back. "What happened when Rose died?"

"Several innocent people were hurt," Sarah replied. "You three read a lot of history today, and I know you and Jake went through the records in the courthouse. There was a lot of trouble in town when Rose died."

Frances said, "I remember one of Scissom boys beat a man from Calhoun nearly to death."

"He did time for that," Doris said. "But he came home and became a respected business man."

"And old lady Bobbitt threw a meat cleaver at her

son-in-law," Sarah said, shaking her head.

"Did she hit him?" Fiona asked. "I talk all the time to Mrs. Bobbitt, who hasn't been able to pass over. I've always wondered what was holding her back, but she's never mentioned a murder in her past."

"Her son-in-law ducked when she threw the cleaver," Frances said, smiling. "She never could say why she did it, and she felt so guilty that she bought him a farm."

"Too bad he was a worthless farmer." A grin flashed from Sarah. "The Bobbitt daughter would have been better off if the cleaver had connected."

Brenna was amazed at the flow of memories. Right after Garth died, Sarah and the elders could have talked this way and told them more about their history. She started to ask a question but caught herself as the aunts continued reminiscing.

"No doubt Edna Bobbitt's guilt over trying to kill her son-in-law is what's holding her to this world." Doris sighed and sat back in her chair, looking tired and old. "There was so much that happened that spring. Remember that boy who was sweet on Rose who was killed up on Bear Mountain?"

"Larry Blackburn was his name," Sarah said. "He was running moonshine. Mother and Father didn't like him."

"That's right," Frances agreed. "Everyone said that he was just acting out the night he died."

"Rose sent him away that very night," Doris pointed out. "She had strung him along for quite a while. Then she told him there was no hope."

"Rose said she was in love with someone else." Sarah frowned. "I never knew who it was."

“But Larry was very upset. Rose told me he went tearing off like hell on wheels,” Doris continued. “Later that night his car went off the road. They say he burned to death when it exploded.”

“Funny thing was there were no skid marks.” Frances sniffed. “We decided it was the Woman in White.”

“But why would she do something like that?” Eva Grace asked, frowning. “I don’t understand.”

“Neither did we,” Sarah retorted. “But later on, after Rose was gone, we looked at everything that had happened, and we saw it was all connected to the Woman. Rose felt so bad about Larry’s death. She was weak by the time the Woman came for her.”

Brenna couldn’t stop her question this time. “Why have you never told us any of this?”

Sarah and her sisters exchanged glances that didn’t quite hold. Brenna noted that they didn’t answer her.

“And now the Woman has killed poor, sweet Sandy.” Frances suddenly looked as old and tired as Doris. “What are we to do?”

Maggie burst into tears. Brenna fought her frustration with the whole lot of them, while Lauren and Fiona soothed the coven’s most sensitive witch.

Eva Grace looked agitated. “Everything is pointing to me as the next tribute. First, I lose Garth and now Sandy. I’m under attack from all sides. It’s obvious the Woman in White wants me.”

A babble of protests broke out around the table, but Eva Grace was insistent. She really believed she was the next target. Most of all, she told them, she hated thinking that others were being taken because of her. Brenna couldn’t stand seeing her in so much pain.

Before she could say anything, her father spoke up, "Have any of you considered that tonight wasn't the Woman in White's work?"

"Why do you say that?"

He frowned, studying the peaches and pound cake on his plate. "I'm just thinking. Other than what all of you saw when Garth died, have any of the accounts of troubles in the past mentioned the Woman actually manifesting herself?"

Brenna had already noted that there were no reports of anyone seeing the Woman away from Mulligan Falls.

"Tell me about what it was like in Eva Grace's shop tonight," Aiden continued. "How did it feel?"

Fiona frowned. "Evil."

"No, that's not what I mean," Aiden responded. "What did you feel, smell, and taste?"

Fiona said, "It was kind of warm."

Brenna nodded. "Very warm, actually. I figured the attack had somehow damaged the AC Unit."

"We thought we smelled smoke," Eva Grace added.

"That's not good," Delia said.

Aiden dug into his cake, still looking thoughtful. "You should call your sheriff," he told his oldest daughter.

Brenna frowned at the way he referred to Jake as hers. "Why?"

"Tell him to have his crime scene techs check for remaining pockets of overheated air throughout the building."

"I'm on it," Fiona said, digging out her ever-present cell. She headed out of the room, phone to her ear

"But what does hot air tell us?" Brenna pressed her father.

"Could be a demon." Aiden speared an errant peach slice with his fork. Brenna noticed that her studious father looked more than a little excited about his theory.

"A demon?" Maggie wiped her tears and blew her nose into her napkin. "That's nonsense."

"Demons and witches are natural enemies," Doris stated. "They've come to our town before. One I remember in particular. Such a handsome devil."

"Yes, very handsome," Sarah agreed with a look that had Brenna wondering just how well she had gotten to know this demon. "But he was a new demon with limited powers."

Doris's green eyes twinkled. "We made quick work of him."

"That we did, sisters," Frances said.

Sarah sat forward, resting her chin on her clasped hands as she thought. "We've crafted our protective spells especially to ward off demons. New Mourne is such an accepting place that we've had them sneak in now and again, but we learned our lesson." She seemed confident in the guards the coven had put in place.

Too confident, Brenna surmised, thinking again of how easily the *Book of Magic* had been found earlier.

Multiple conversations once again started around the table. Maggie took up Sarah's claim that a demon couldn't cross the Connelly wards. Lauren agreed. Rather vehemently, Brenna thought.

Doris argued that demons could come in disguise, taking over a human's body, and sneaking past even powerful magic.

Aunt Diane and Aunt Estelle said that they had always felt Fred Williams was possessed by something evil.

Delia agreed with them, adding, “I once turned him into a rat when we were in high school. He looked very natural like that. He gritted his little rodent teeth at me and hissed like a snake. Celia made me turn him back. She always liked him.”

Brenna could see the discussion was getting out of hand and called a time-out. “Okay, so maybe we have a demon and the Woman in White. Doesn’t that mean we’re in twice as much trouble?”

The room fell silent. Once again, Aiden nodded.

“We need more information on who the Woman is,” Brenna said. “We’ve got to find the rest of the *Connelly Book of Magic*. Fiona, Eva Grace, and I tried to locate more pages in the house today with magic, but we didn’t have any luck.”

“I can look again at home,” Frances said, though she seemed doubtful.

“I turned all my pages in.” Doris looked pleased with herself.

Fiona cocked her head to the side. “You know, I’ve heard the best historian in town is one of our distant relatives, Inez Connelly.”

“She was married to Craig Connelly” Doris said. “She was thirty years younger than him.”

“Which is why she’s still alive,” Frances said. “Craig was of our parents’ generation.”

“She might know something that would explain some of this.” Sarah seemed doubtful, and Brenna felt her impatience returning. She didn’t like the negativity

Sarah kept bringing to their efforts. Didn't she want them to find a solution?

"Inez always dreamed of being a writer," Doris said. "She researched all sorts of local history and wrote a lot of it in her journals. Remember, Sarah, she was so interested that we let her keep The Dead Box."

"The Dead Box?" Fiona asked.

Sarah explained, "It's the record of all the deaths in the Connelly family. These days it's mostly obituaries clipped from the newspaper."

The chime of the doorbell interrupted, and Maggie cried out.

"Oh for heaven's sake," Brenna admonished her. "Do you think a demon is going to just ring the doorbell?"

"He might." Lauren's very serious answer made Maggie chirp in fear again.

"I'll get it," Brenna said as the bell peeled again.

But Marcus was already rising. "I've got it."

No one spoke as they waited for him to return. When he did, Willow Scanlan was on his arm.

Aiden immediately stood.

Brenna, startled to see the old fae again so soon, got up, as well. "Willow, please join us." She expected Sarah to stand and greet the older woman. But Sarah glared at the fae in a way that was rude. Brenna saw that Delia regarded Sarah with the same surprise she felt herself.

Marcus grabbed his chair and sat it beside Brenna's. The old woman sat down, keeping a hand on her cane.

"I'll not be staying, but I do have news," Willow said. "It's good that you're all assembled. You've got to gather your resources."

"We already know that," Sarah said. "What do you have that can help us?"

Willow regarded Sarah with an uplifted eyebrow. "New Mourne has moved to the dark side of The Mirror." She turned to Brenna. "You must bring it back to the light."

Once again Maggie began to cry. But no one bothered to comfort her.

"Can you explain your meaning?" Aiden's manner toward Willow was differential. Brenna could see he was fascinated by the old crone.

"It means the time for talking is finished." Willow's gaze swept from one end of the table to the other. "You must all take action, or New Mourne will no longer be under the control of the Connelly family." She scowled at Sarah. "You keep thinking you'll just pay your tribute and go on with your lives. You've become complacent and think you're just like the humans. Your coven has fallen out of practice. That's foolish. There's too much at stake to forget who forged this town and who made it a haven for people like us who can't exist in an everyday world."

"Who has brought this darkness to New Mourne?" Sarah asked.

"That's what you've got to find out. All the answers are in your family's book, but they won't just appear because you need them. You need a strong person to take the lead and dig out the truth."

"I'm the strongest witch in the Connelly clan. You know that." Sarah's voice was tight with anger. "I've led this coven for many years."

"Your magic will be needed, but it's time for you

to start delegating tasks to these younger ones. They've got the skills and the desire to find an answer to the plague that visits your family and this town every generation." She pointed a crooked, sharp-nailed finger at Sarah. "You have been a strong leader, but you need to be stronger. This is pure evil you'll be dealing with, and you'll need everyone's gifts to get it out of our town."

No one spoke as the old woman rose and headed back to the door. She brushed aside the hand that Marcus offered in aid. She took a step toward the hall then turned back to the group at the table.

"New Mourne has moved to the dark side of The Mirror, and Brenna must bring it back to the light," she repeated.

She was gone so fast that Brenna thought she had disappeared. Only the sound of the front door closing gave proof that she had even been there.

Marcus gazed from the hall to his wife. "What did all that mean, Sarah?"

Brenna thought it was obvious. "I think she just said I'm to be the tribute for the Woman in White."

Fiona's voice rose in protest. Eva Grace got to her feet, shaking her head.

Sarah cut them off. "All it means is that Willow is sticking her nose in our business. And I won't have that."

"I think she's got a point," Delia said quietly.

Surprise flickered across Sarah's features. "And what would that be, Delia?"

"It's time for the younger witches to take a more active part in regular rituals and ceremonies," Delia said. "How else will they carry on the traditions?"

“Makes sense to me,” Frances said. “And as mad as you are, Sarah, you know we’d be foolish not to heed what Willow is saying. She has access to what’s behind The Mirror. She has walked in that world. Her magic is great.”

“She is powerful,” Aiden offered. “Centuries old and far-seeing. She didn’t have to come and tell us anything.”

Sarah rose and picked up her son-in-law’s plate along with her own. “Willow’s power doesn’t mean she knows what best for us.”

“No,” Delia said. “But you’ve never been one to believe you had all the answers.”

Sarah didn’t respond as she exited into the kitchen.

Defending Sarah was an unnatural role for Brenna, but she found herself angry that Delia would criticize the coven leader. “Since when have you participated in rituals here?”

“Not since I left, but that doesn’t mean I don’t know how important it is,” Delia replied. “Besides, rituals and magic are what your father and I research. We know what they mean for keeping balance in the world.”

“And we all know how important your research is,” Brenna said, “so important you’re never here for any of the Sabbats.”

Delia studied her with cool disdain. “You’ve missed quite a few yourself, Brenna. I guess we’re cut from the same mold.”

Brenna’s face heated. “Don’t lump me into anything you’re involved with. I’m home to stay. How about you?”

Her mother didn’t answer, and Brenna frowned as

her father reached across the table for Delia's hand. They were so caring with each other, but nobody penetrated that little circle.

She turned as Sarah came back into the dining room. Brenna thought her grandmother's shoulders looked weighed down as she leaned against the buffet.

Feeling an unexpected surge of affection, Brenna spoke quietly. "Give us a chance to help. Fiona, Eva Grace, and I can get the book organized and do some research."

"First we have to cleanse Eva Grace's shop." Sarah straightened as she spoke to the group. "In fact, we'll put it all back together. Everything the Woman destroyed. I think all of us will be needed."

A collective gasp issued from the group.

"That's not a good idea," Delia said.

"Of course it is." Sarah moved to gather more dirty dishes. "Eva Grace has borne enough. We'll clean this up for her, and she'll have the shop back to normal in a day or two."

Delia argued, "But you heard what Aiden said. This could be a demon. Even if it isn't, we know there's residual black magic around. It could affect the spell or one of us."

Sarah passed the dishes to Marcus and turned back to Delia. "When all of us gather, our magic is stronger than any other."

Aiden traded a concerned look with Delia. He shook his head.

"We should not do this," Delia said with force. "Demons are unpredictable. According to our research—"

"There's that word again," Brenna muttered,

though she was amazed to see her mother and grandmother argue. They had never raised their voices to each other in her presence.

"I think you need to reconsider, Mother."

Brenna was astonished. Delia always called Sarah by her given name. This was a red-letter day.

"We'll be gathering just after moonrise tonight, Delia, to give Eva Grace our help," Sarah said blandly. "If you can't make it, we'll understand. You missed other events, and we were still successful."

Brenna's eyes widened as Sarah's barb hit home. Delia looked like she'd been smacked. Aiden rose and walked over to put his arm across his wife's shoulders.

Sarah sailed out of the room, dirty dishes in hand and head held high.

"How do we kill demons?" Lauren murmured in the silence that followed.

Once again Maggie began to sob.

Brenna groaned. She had a terrible feeling her mother was right about the folly of Sarah's plan. What's worse, she knew Willow had spoken the truth to all of them. Brenna held the future of her family in her hands. From where she sat, with no clue of how to stop the curse, that was more frightening than an army of demons.

Chapter 17

On Tuesday, as night fell over New Mourne, Jake waited for all of the Connelly witches to gather at Eva Grace's shop.

"I'm definitely not sure about this." He and Brenna stood at the front window watching for Maggie. She was the only witch who had not arrived.

Brenna had told him about Willow's visit and the argument between Sarah and Delia last night. "I'm not even sure Maggie will show up," she murmured. "She and Lauren have taken my mother's side in the argument against this ritual tonight. They're scared to death by all of the demon talk."

"How is everyone else aligning?" Jake glanced over his shoulder. Lauren was talking with Delia and Dr. Burns. Sarah, Doris, and Frances were discussing an athame Frances held. The other women huddled in the middle, looking like a bunch of jittery hens.

"This is really getting to Fiona." Brenna nodded toward her sister, who was staring down at her cell, her eyes red-rimmed and glazed, as if she had not slept at all. "She desperately wants to believe in our parents, but she's also so loyal to Sarah. She spent most of the day trying to find the ghost who used to live in this shop."

"So she's still missing?"

"Fiona says all the town's ghosts are very quiet."

Brenna shivered. "That's not normal."

"Eva Grace seems calm." Jake frowned. He wasn't sure the redhead's cool demeanor was a good thing.

Brenna echoed his thoughts with her troubled sigh. "She thinks the Woman in White is coming for her. She's so resigned to that she won't even discuss it with me and Fiona. She says there's no point in more research because the inevitable is going to happen."

Anger flashed in Brenna's eyes. "It infuriates me that she's being worn down by this. The elder aunts and Sarah told us last night that their sister Rose was like that before the Woman took her. Just hopeless and lost."

"Was Eva Grace's mother like that before she died, too?" Jake was concerned as he studied Eva Grace's serene features. She didn't look quite like herself.

Shrugging, Brenna looked back out the window. "They wouldn't discuss Aunt Celia today. Sarah was holed up in her room with *The Connelly Book of Magic*. I offered to help her with tonight's spell, but she told me she was still the one in power."

"She feels threatened by what Willow told you all last night." Jake ran a hand through his hair, weary to the bone. He wished this nightmare were over, that the demon or the Woman, or both, were defeated. He wanted to take Brenna home, keep her in bed for several days, and then allow his tiger to run free in the woods.

Sandy's death had shaken him badly. She'd been young and innocent. Notifying her parents early this morning had been awful. Why kill her or Garth? Why torture the entire town? He wanted all of this to end.

But if history was borne out, the only possible end

was the death of one of the Connellys.

Brenna could be the one chosen to die.

Fear rose in Jake, tightening his chest. After the way he had grown up, after all he had done and seen as a man and as a tiger, he wasn't often afraid. The thought of losing Brenna shook him, however. He didn't expect that emotion and was glad to see Maggie coming up the walk.

The young witch seemed distracted as Jake opened the door for her. Her auburn hair, long like Lauren's, was usually arranged in a conservative style. Tonight, she had drawn it back in a severe bun.

Her clothes were all wrong, too, Jake realized. The thermometer had topped out in the nineties today, but she wore a black turtleneck and dark jeans that molded her generous curves. He guessed Maggie might be dressing for dramatic effect. Lauren certainly had, in a form-fitting dark purple dress with sparkles on the bodice. He thought the rest of the witches, in their sensible pantsuits, jeans, and T-shirts were attired more suitably for the mess that surrounded them.

"I was afraid you had decided not to come," Brenna said to Maggie as she and Jake followed her to the center of the store where the others were gathered.

"I thought about it," Maggie replied. "But I realized that Sarah is right. We have to put Eva Grace's shop back in order. It's the first step in getting all of this over and done with."

Brenna studied her younger cousin with surprise.

Sarah greeted Maggie with a smile and kiss on the cheek. "Thank you for believing in me, my dear."

Jake stepped back, and Dr. Burns and Marcus joined him.

“Are we ready?” Sarah stood at the bottom of the shop’s staircase, her long, gray hair loose around her shoulders. She seemed to glow, her skin and eyes luminous. At her signal, one of Brenna’s aunts turned out the lights. In the twilight gloom, the faces of all of the women were shadowed as they formed a loose circle around Sarah.

Jake believed in the Connellys’ magic, but he doubted they could affect the mess here with a little abracadabra. He had been in the store most of the night and day, helping process the scene. The place was a ruin of shattered glass, pottery, stone, and wood.

The state’s crime scene investigators were finished; although Jake didn’t believe what they had gathered would prove useful. The local guys thought Sandy’s death was just like Garth’s—a supernatural murder. Hours after the young woman died, they had recorded a number of the “hot spots” Brenna’s father suggested they look for.

Dr. Burns was more convinced than ever that a demon was involved with what was happening in the town. Earlier today, he had studied the graffiti on the Save a Buck store’s wall, as well as Mary’s Diner where the incident had occurred with the werewolf. The researcher called both places, “proof of demonic malevolence.”

Jake called it damn scary.

Now, the man cleared his throat. “I wish you would think about this a little more, Sarah. Consider the level of evil that is still in this shop.”

Sarah made an impatient gesture.

Delia took up the argument. “You can smell the sulfur in the air. Surely you know what that means.”

"Is that the rotten egg smell?" Brenna asked. "That stink has overtaken the herbs and oils that were spilled everywhere last night."

"Sulphur is the classic demonic calling card," Dr. Burns said. "Again, Sarah, I caution you—"

"Be still," the coven leader said with a sharpness Jake had never seen from her. "All of you men need to step back."

Jake caught Brenna's gaze and tried to nod in encouragement as he, Marcus, and Dr. Burns moved to the entrance.

Sarah leaned down and lifted a thin wooden box.

"What's that?" Jake murmured to Marcus.

"The family wand." His voice held a note of awe. "It's made of Irish bog oak and was crafted more than three centuries ago. A Connelly witch went out after lightning struck the tree and took a broken limb while it was still warm. To understand that fully you have to know that thunderstorms are rare in Ireland so this was a significant event. It took her months to craft the wand and imbue it with power."

Sarah carefully lifted the wand out of the box and gripped it firmly.

"I can smell the magic from here, kind of hot and sweet," Jake said. "Amazing."

The wood in the wand was black with a beautiful grain and tapered like a candle. When Sarah clutched it and did a sweep through the air, it began to pulsate. She stepped into the center of the circle.

"Join hands." Her shoulders straight, Sarah reminded Jake of one of his colonels. Like her, the man had worn the mantle of leadership well.

The women twittered. That was the only word Jake

could put to the soft sound of their excitement. He could feel their exhilaration and something else, something that smelled just a little off, like cold, wet ashes. The hot spots the forensic techs discovered had cooled but were still warmer than the rest of the room. He thought Dr. Burns was right to have warned Sarah to stop, but it was too late now.

Sarah's wand slashed through the darkened air. The women's murmurs faded. Jake watched as each witch centered herself. Brenna closed her eyes, and he could see she gripped Doris and Maggie's hands.

Sarah let her head drop to her chest. When there was silence, she raised her head and looked at each witch in turn, her gaze steady and strong.

Jake felt power stir the air.

Sarah's voice rang clear as a bell. "What once was whole now is shattered; what once was organized is now scattered."

She raised the wand. The end glowed in a small circle that grew with each word she spoke. "We gather our power, full and free, to bring back together piles of debris."

She swept the wand in a wide arc and light bloomed from its tip.

"As we will, so mote it be."

A whoosh of light swept out of the wand and around the room. Glass began to rise in small circles and pieces began to assemble into crystals, candelabras, mortars and pestles. Soon items were lining the shelves and filling various racks. Jake watched in stunned silence as the store reassembled itself.

He glanced at Brenna, and his heart skipped a beat. She was breathtaking, her arms raised as she clasped the hands of the witches on either side of her. Her body glistened, much like the magic that had fallen like silver dust over his bed when they made love last night. His body responded to her with a primal heat that tightened his jeans. When she smiled, he thought he would explode with wanting her.

The women continued to chant, and Sarah held the wand up as light poured out of it like liquid fire. As the chant rose, the room worked to right itself and the store began to look again like the homey, welcoming place it had been. The floor cleared of trash, and crystals sparkled from the strings that once more tied them to the ceiling.

Jake was enthralled by the sight of Brenna and the power of the Connellys. He'd known New Mourne was a magical town; he'd just never seen that magic quite so alive. The sight was dazzling, he thought. It could enchant a man…

Fighting a wave of dizziness, Jake heard Dr. Burns groan. Marcus murmured his wife's name. Jake struggled to move, but like the men beside him, he was plastered to the wall. He felt like he was on the Tilt-A-Whirl at the county fair, and gravity was chaining him.

Darkness fell like a curtain. Someone screamed. In a flash of light, Jake saw Brenna on her knees beside one of the older women. Doris, he thought.

Calling on his tiger for strength, Jake broke free of whatever held him. He raced to Brenna's side. Her hands were covered with blood as she applied pressure to Doris's neck.

"Get help," she screamed at Jake. "She's dying."

He grabbed the radio off his hip and called for an ambulance.

Eva Grace knelt on Doris's other side. She put her hand on top of Brenna's and closed her eyes. Jake could see her lips moving. Brenna began to murmur in rhythm with her cousin. The bleeding slowed, at least the pool of blood under the older witch stopped growing. Delia dropped down beside Brenna and took over the pressure on Doris's neck. Brenna sagged back, her shirt wet with perspiration.

Jake pulled her to her feet and into his arms. "Are you okay?" he whispered.

Brenna shook her head. "She can't die. She just can't."

A siren sounded in the distance, and Maggie ran outside. The rest of the coven joined hands, voices rising in a chant that Jake couldn't understand. Ancient words. Healing magic.

A wave of power rippled through the room. Frances fell to her knees, clutching her chest.

Beside her a woman dressed in white rose up from the wooden floor. She was blonde and pale. Her features were beautiful, and yet terrifying. Exactly as Brenna had described her to him.

The Woman in White.

She pointed at Sarah.

Sarah raised the wand. "Not now."

"I will have my tribute," the ghost roared. "I will have what is mine."

Before Jake could grab her, Brenna wrenched away from him and took Sarah's hand. A streak of fire pushed out of the wand.

The ghost flitted back. "Damn you, Sarah Connelly, I will have what is mine!"

Sarah pulled the wand back against her chest. With

one hand still joined with Brenna's she again swept the wand forward. Small balls of magic pelted the ghost.

The Woman shrieked in pain, an awful sound that pierced Jake's skull. He winced and saw Brenna stagger.

But she didn't fall. She held tight to Sarah. When the wand flashed again, there was a loud pop. The ghost was gone.

Brenna and Sarah fell against each other, gasping. The wand's light disappeared.

Paramedics burst through the doors before Jake could reach Brenna's side. He made sure they were taking care of Doris and directed them to take a look at Frances as well.

As he turned, looking for Brenna, he saw Fiona behind the counter. She was backed up in the corner, holding a pair of ritual knives in front of her, like weapons. He strode toward her. "What is it? Are you all right?"

Brenna pushed past him and reached out to her sister. "Give me the knives, Fiona. You're okay."

"No, I'm not." Fiona surrendered the knives without protest, but her teeth were chattering as she stared at Brenna. "Aunt Celia just appeared to me. She said there is a traitor among us."

Brenna's terror was palpable. Like Fiona, she began to shudder. "No," she whispered. "It can't be."

Jake wrapped both of them in his arms.

Chapter 18

The ambulance took Doris to three-year-old Mourne County Hospital. The medical facility's land and building had been donated by Rash Anderson, developer of The Enclave. A coalition of new and old residents had joined together to raise funds for equipment and other necessities. The hospital was a private enterprise, but there was an agreement with the county about providing necessary care for all citizens.

Though she had mixed feelings about The Enclave, tonight Brenna welcomed the hospital built because of the residents who lived in the "exclusive gated community nestled in the serenity of the mountains." She wasn't sure Doris would have survived the trip to hospitals in nearby communities or a medical helicopter flight to the trauma center in Chattanooga.

Brenna had heard the hospital had an excellent surgeon. Board certified as a surgeon and a plastic surgeon, he had moved his practice from the city a couple of years ago. He made a good living with women from Atlanta and The Enclave who liked the privacy they found in New Mourne for their face-lifts and breast augmentations. The town was blessed because he and the associates in his practice were also willing to address traumas such as what had happened to Doris tonight.

After Fiona had been calmed down at Siren's Call,

Jake learned from his dispatcher that Doris was in surgery. He drove Brenna and Fiona to join the rest of the coven at the hospital in a small waiting room. Their despair hung so heavy it felt alive. Brenna had never heard of an injury happening when the coven was joined together working their magic with one goal in mind.

Sarah looked grim and was huddled with Frances. Marcus sat on the elder aunt's other side, holding her hand. Frances had been shaken up by her fall after the Woman in White appeared, but the paramedics had found no injuries. Besides, Brenna knew it would take a lot to keep Frances from her family while they waited for news of Doris.

Though she had tried to clean up a little before they left the shop, Brenna's clothing was soaked in Doris's blood. Crimson stained under her nails, and she had missed a smear of blood on one forearm. So much blood, she remembered, as she closed her eyes and murmured a blessing for Doris. She had been terrified the older woman would die before help arrived. If Eva Grace had not been there the outcome would have been much different.

Brenna noted that her cousin was also still bloody, but as could be expected, she had done a much better job cleaning herself than Brenna had. The redhead was sitting with Diane and Estelle, their hands joined as they chanted in low voices.

Delia's jeans and peasant top were less bloody than her daughter's or her niece's, but the bleeding had been slowed when she had taken over for Brenna with Doris.

Her mother had surprised Brenna tonight with her quick and calm action. *I don't know her well enough to expect anything from her.* The thought made Brenna frown. It wasn't her fault that she didn't know Delia.

Right now, Delia was talking in a low, angry voice to Aiden. She kept glaring at Sarah, while Aiden touched her arm and obviously tried to calm her. Fiona joined them and sat down, turning easily to her father for comfort. How did that come so naturally for her sister? Brenna never felt that easy around their mother and father.

"What are you thinking?" Jake leaned close to her.

She sighed and allowed herself to brace against his warmth. Despite the close confines of this room, she was chilled, especially when she thought about what Fiona had told them.

"I'm wondering who the traitor is," Brenna whispered.

"So you believe Fiona?"

"She would never lie, especially about something like that." But her sister had begged Brenna and Jake not to say anything to anyone else, to allow her time to think about what had happened. Brenna had promised with reluctance. But she knew this had to be confronted.

"Do you think she will tell your mother and father?"

Brenna shrugged. "We'll see."

Brian appeared in the doorway, looking about as haggard as Brenna felt. There had been little time for sleep since the weekend. Jake stepped out into the hallway to talk with his deputy.

When they came back inside, Brian told everyone, "Siren's Call is locked up and has a deputy stationed outside."

"That makes me feel better," Brenna said with sarcasm. "I'm sure the Woman in White will quake in her ghostly shoes."

Brian's tired green eyes flashed in anger. "Hey, it's all we can do at this point. Your magical solutions haven't been working too well."

Instantly contrite, Brenna said, "I'm sorry, Brian."

"Whatever." He crossed the room to his mother. Diane broke away from the others to wrap Brian in her arms. "How is Grandmother?" he asked.

"We're waiting to hear from the surgeon," Eva Grace told him.

Jake stepped up and squeezed Brenna's shoulder. "It's no big deal," he reassured her in a quiet voice. "Brian knows everyone is exhausted, and he's just really worried about his grandmother. He knows you didn't mean anything." His ability to sense her thoughts was both comforting and disconcerting for Brenna.

Brian was grim. "The deputies found the shard of glass that most likely injured grandmother. It looks like a knife, like it was made into weapon to do just what it did—stab her."

"There are just too many things we can't explain." Brenna turned to Fiona, willing her sister to bring up Celia's warning. They needed to fit all of the pieces of the puzzle together.

Jake made another announcement. "I also got a fax about Sandy Murphy late this afternoon. The coroner said she died of a massive coronary."

"She was only twenty years old!" Eva Grace protested. "Young and healthy. She ran marathons."

"I know," Jake said. "I called the coroner, and he said he wouldn't admit it in court, but if he had to guess, he'd say she was scared to death."

"Is that even possible?" Brenna asked.

"I'm just telling you what the report said. I'm frustrated and wish like hell that Garth were here. He was better at dealing with supernatural problems than I'll ever be."

Eva Grace sagged back in her chair. "I don't think he would have a clue what to do about this, Jake." She looked around the room. "The Woman in White has visited my shop twice. Killed one person and injured another. She's after me."

Aunt Estelle took her niece's hand. "Remember, we think what killed Sandy was a demon."

"But the Woman was in front of us tonight," Eva Grace insisted. "She tried to kill Doris."

Delia left Aiden's side and went to Eva Grace as well. "The Woman is breaking her pattern."

Brenna nodded in agreement with her mother. "This is the second time she has appeared to us without taking a tribute. Nowhere in any of the history that we've found is there record of her manifesting to Connellys like this. Surely that means something."

"Maybe she's taunting us," Lauren said from the doorway. Brenna's beautiful cousin stood arm in arm with Maggie. Only then did Brenna realize that these two members of the coven had been missing from the waiting room. She had not seen Maggie since the ambulance arrived at the shop for Doris.

Tears were streaming down Maggie's face. The tight bun of auburn hair she had sported earlier was loose and fell around her shoulders. She looked more like herself, but even more frightened than usual.

"What if the Woman comes after my Sophie?" She

referred to her four-year-old daughter. "I'm not sure I understand what happened tonight. My husband wants me to go away and take Sophie with me."

Sarah stood. "That's nonsense, Maggie."

"But Ian doesn't understand any of this."

"Hogwash," Frances told her with spirit. "Ian Mills' family has lived in Mourne County for at least a century. He knows very well what's going on. He understood what he was taking on when he married a Connelly witch. Good god, he has a touch of fae himself, from his great-grandfather's side."

"That's right," Aunt Diane said. "And I talked with Ian myself about everything when you two became engaged, Maggie. Since your mother doesn't have magic, I knew I needed to explain some of this to him."

"But this curse seemed so far away then," Maggie said, sobbing. "I didn't know until I had Sophie how awful this could be."

"None of us knew until now how we would feel about it." Lauren's face was pale against her auburn hair. "I never thought I could die until tonight."

"But you didn't," Sarah pointed out. "We fought off the Woman."

"You fought off something," Aiden put in. "Are we sure it was the Woman?"

"We saw her." Brenna frowned at her father. "Didn't we all see her?"

"Yes," Delia said. "But was it her or a clever disguise?"

Sarah insisted, "Whatever it was that confronted us tonight, what really matters is that we drove it away."

Delia cocked one slender eyebrow at her mother. "For now."

Brenna looked around for her sister. Fiona sat rigid in a chair, her face pale, her arms clasped around herself. "Don't you need to say something?"

Fiona shook her head. "Not now."

"Yes, now," Brenna urged her. "Tell everyone."

"What's wrong?" Sarah demanded. "What's happened to Fiona?" The coven leader went to her youngest granddaughter, grasped her chin, and studied the young woman's face. "Are you hurt?"

Fiona could never lie to Sarah. "Aunt Celia came to me."

The blood drained from Sarah's face. "Celia? You're sure?"

"Very sure." Fiona looked around the room in misery. "She said…" Her voice broke. "Aunt Celia gave me a warning."

"About what?" Sarah pressed.

Brenna sat down beside her sister, hoping to give her strength. "Go on. Tell it all."

"She said there's a traitor in the coven."

Immediate protests flew around the room. Frances took a step forward in anger. Maggie sobbed even harder. Brenna couldn't look at her relatives. This was too awful.

Sarah stumbled and would have fallen if Jake had not caught her. He sat her down in a chair. Marcus knelt at her side. Sarah turned her face into her husband's shoulder and wept.

Brenna was stunned. Losing control like this was not like Sarah. The events of the last few weeks appeared to be having an even worse impact on her than Brenna had feared.

"My Celia," Sarah said. "My dear, dear Celia."

The expressions of everyone there mirrored Brenna's shock. Several moments passed with only the sound of Sarah's quiet cries.

Sarah worked to regain control, pulling away from Marcus and looking around at all of them. "I always hoped Celia would speak to one of us. She died so young."

Delia spoke up. "We need to know exactly what Celia said about the coven, Fiona. Tell it just as it happened."

Fiona hesitated, swallowed hard and then closed her eyes. "It was after the circle was broken, while we were all watching what was happening with Doris. I was standing back a little. You know I don't like seeing blood."

"Nothing to be ashamed of," Frances said. "What happened to Doris was frightening."

Fiona gripped Brenna's hand. "I had blocked everything out but what we were doing so I could concentrate on the spell. It wasn't very hard. Not many spirits have spoken to me since Sandy was killed in the shop." She looked troubled. "I can't find several of the town's main ghosts. It's like they've gone into hiding."

"But you saw Celia," Brenna prompted. "When?"

"You and Eva Grace were helping Doris. I was freaked out by the blood. A voice whispered close to my ear and startled me. At first I didn't know what she said. Then Aunt Celia appeared in front of me."

Rubbing her face, Fiona sighed. "I was shocked to see it was her. I've never talked to Aunt Celia before." She looked at Eva Grace. "I would have told you."

"I know that." Eva Grace looked sad, as she always did when reminded of the mother who died when Eva

Grace was a baby. "Tell us exactly what my mother told you tonight."

"It's was pretty straightforward. She was in front of me, and she said, 'Beware of the traitor' Then she disappeared. By the time I came back to myself I was backed into the corner behind the counter, and Brenna and Jake were talking to me."

"Did she say who the traitor was?" Brenna asked.

"There is no traitor." Sarah's voice had regained her normal authority. "We're family, and we've never had anyone betray us." She gave Fiona a sympathetic smile. "Celia didn't specifically say the traitor as in the coven, did she?"

Fiona looked confused. "She warned me against a traitor. I assumed it was a traitor in the coven."

"But maybe that's not what she meant," Sarah said in triumph. "Maybe she was talking about someone outside our circle"

Her gaze landed on Jake. His eyes widened.

Brenna jumped to his defense. "Now wait a minute—"

"Jake was Garth's best friend," Eva Grace broke in. "He wouldn't do anything to hurt us."

"Maybe not intentionally," Sarah retorted, still staring hard at Jake. "Look at the happenings all over town. People who have never been violent have done things completely against their natures. Perhaps our friend here is infected."

Jake was speechless.

Brenna muttered a protest. "That's not possible. The night in the diner when the werewolf came out, Jake had to fight his own change. He fought and won. That's the kind of strength he has. He wouldn't give in to a demon and betray us without a tremendous battle."

She realized Jake's victory over the evil that night was when her feelings for him had begun to soften. He was good inside, she felt. Truly good. But he shocked her with his next words.

"None of us can be sure of what we're capable of." He looked at Sarah, a mixture of guilt and pain in his face. "I know from experience in my own life that control isn't always possible."

Smug now, Sarah looked to the rest of the group for support. Brenna was infuriated with her grandmother for planting this seed of doubt about Jake. Why was Sarah doing this?

Aid came from an unlikely source.

"This is insanity," Delia said.

"Utter nonsense," Aiden agreed. "There was no demon inside Jake tonight. He did nothing that showed the slightest hint of betrayal."

Brenna took Jake's hand, threading her fingers through his. "Of course, Jake did nothing to hurt us. But look at us, turning on each other, casting blame on someone who has been a friend. Maybe the demon is infecting us all."

Aiden appeared thoughtful. "Brenna could be right. As far as the spirit who spoke to Fiona, it's possible the demon took Celia's form to spread dissension in our ranks."

Fiona paled, and Eva Grace put an arm around her.

"How can we tell what's the work of a demon and what's not?" Brenna asked.

"There's no easy answer," her father replied.

Delia turned to Sarah. "You're grasping at straws to explain why this happened to Doris tonight. The simple fact is we should not have done that restorative spell at all. You made a mistake. We were wrong to go along with you."

Sarah protested, and Frances stepped forward. "Sarah was simply trying to something positive. Eva Grace has lost so much. Who can blame Sarah for wanting to put her shop back together?"

"But who knows what dark magic we set free?' Delia mused.

"That's not possible," Sarah insisted. "We're a family of witches who have stood together through good and bad times. We let no evil in. Why, in our history, any hint of black magic has met with banishment."

Brenna disagreed. "Maybe Willow was right. Maybe we're losing control of our powers and of the town.

As usual, Fiona defended her grandmother. "That's not true. If not for Connellys, who knows what would have happened to this town in the past."

"But what's happening now?" Brenna demanded. "We all saw the Woman in White at the store tonight, and she's never appeared anywhere but on Connelly land near the falls. Why has that changed?"

"Because we were all assembled there?" Eva Grace offered.

"We've assembled often in the past week." Brenna studied her family. "Why wouldn't she take us while we're at the home place?"

"Our protections are too strong there," Sarah insisted. "It was the Woman who came tonight to the shop. You all knew it was the Woman in White. We know it's time for her. It was inevitable."

This blind acceptance made Brenna crazy. “Yet we were able to repel her with magic. Has that ever happened before?”

Sarah exchanged a glance with Frances. “Well, no, but—”

Brenna opened her mouth to reply when a dark-haired man wearing surgical scrubs entered the room.

“Are you all the family of Doris Barton?”

“Yes.” Sarah got eagerly to her feet.

“I’m Dr. Hargrave. Ms. Barton made it through the surgery. I was able to repair her carotid artery. Fortunately it was just nicked. She’s very strong, but the next twenty-four hours will be key.”

“Thanks be to the goddess,” Sarah murmured. A chorus of voices echoed her relief.

The doctor surveyed the group. “Which one of you is the empath?”

Eva Grace nodded. For the first time, Brenna noticed how weak her cousin seemed.

Dr. Hargrave hurried over and placed his fingers on Eva Grace’s wrist. “Whatever you’re doing for Doris, you need to stop. She’s in a deep sleep and her vitals are stable. She’ll be all right for the next few hours.”

Relaxing and letting out a deep breath, Eva Grace reached for her purse and pulled out a tea ball. “Could someone get me some hot water?”

“Of course, dear.” Estelle hurried to the hot water and coffee provided in the room.

“Is it ginseng?” Dr. Miller asked.

Eva Grace nodded. “It should help me feel better until I can rest.”

“It’s very effective.”

When Eva Grace gave the doctor a questioning

look, he smiled at her.

"My grandfather is a Cherokee healer, and their methods are very similar to yours in that good health relies on harmony with man, animal, and plants."

Brenna was pleased to hear this coming from a surgeon. It wasn't often that men and women of science were so accepting of the ancient remedies her family practiced.

Frances handed Eva Grace a paper cup and the young woman dropped the tea ball into it. The scent of ginseng wafted up, and Eva Grace drew in it.

Brenna decided she liked the doctor. "Do you use any of your grandfather's methods?"

"I have an herb garden." His grin was wry. "Actually, my gardener maintains a beautiful patch of herbs for me. I don't use them much, but my grandfather is still sought out for healing and medicinal help. Like me, my father has a medical degree, and he uses some of the herbs for minor illnesses. I use them mostly because I enjoy cooking."

The doctor checked Eva Grace's pulse again.

"I'm feeling better already," she said.

He appeared pleased. "You saved Doris' life. She could have bled out if you hadn't intervened."

"You're sure she'll be okay?" Diane asked, teary-eyed. "She's my mother, and this is her grandson." She gestured to Brian.

Dr. Hargrave rose. "You can both come back with me to see her for a few minutes. Then you all should go home. No visitors tonight."

Diane and Brian followed him out of the room.

The rest of the coven looked at one another. Before Brenna could speak, Sarah held up a hand. "I'll hear no more talk of traitors tonight." She turned to Jake. "I'm sorry I accused you. I don't want to believe the traitor could be one of my family. Most likely Aiden is correct, and it was the demon who spoke to Fiona instead of Celia. After all, she's never come to us before. Why should she now?"

Brenna could think of many reasons why a family ghost might want to help them in their hour of need. Most of all, however, she was glad Sarah had set to rest any question of Jake being the traitor.

His expression somber, Jake took Sarah's outstretched hand. "I understand. It was natural that you think it might be me."

"But it wasn't." Brenna shot a resentful glance at Sarah. She turned to the others. "What do we do now? Are we just going to wait around for someone else to be hurt or killed?"

"Please keep it down," a nurse said from the doorway, her expression severe. "I believe the doctor said you could leave."

Aunt Estelle hung back to wait for Diane and Brian, but the rest of them headed out to the parking lot. It took great effort for Brenna to hold onto her temper.

Jake put a hand on her shoulder. "Let it go, Brenna. I'm not upset with Sarah's accusations. This was a terrible night, and everyone's feeling the strain. Come stay with me."

Grateful that she didn't have to go home and argue about all of this any longer, Brenna followed Jake to his cruiser. She saw Sarah look her way and turned her head. Maybe Maggie had the right idea. Maybe all of them should just run and hide.

Chapter 19

"Sarah and I fought off the Woman in White with magic tonight. I need to know if that has been done before," Brenna said as they entered Jake's living room. "There's so much I need to know. If no one's going to help me, then I'll just have to do what's needed on my own."

"And how do you think you'll do that?" Jake put his hat on a table near the door, removed his holster and put his gun in the safe on top of a bookcase. "The whole coven hasn't been able to defeat whatever this is, a lone witch may not fair too well."

"Do you think Aunt Celia's spirit was the demon?" Brenna followed him to the kitchen and grabbed bottle of water from the refrigerator. She set a bottle for him on the counter.

She was making herself at home Jake noted with discomfort. "I don't know. Do you think she was real?"

"I'm asking for your opinion."

"I may be a shifter, but I don't know much about demons and ghosts."

His answer seemed to upset her. "You're still angry about Sarah's accusations, aren't you?"

"I told you I wasn't." If anything Sarah's words reminded him of who he was and what he was capable of. He needed to keep that foremost in his mind to keep Brenna at arm's length.

She regarded him with her head cocked to the side. “You don’t have much faith in yourself, do you?”

“Why do you say that?”

“What you said tonight about control.”

“In the blink of an eye, I am a predator,” Jake reminded her. “I’d be foolish not to acknowledge that.”

“It’s more than that. What’s made you this way, Jake?”

He had a flash of memory, of blood and gore. Carnage wrought by him. He took a step back. She was in his space, meddling in matters that were none of her concern. What happened to keeping it casual?

He breathed in and released it slowly, working hard to resist anger. “How about we just chill out? “

She looked as if she might argue then raked a hand through her auburn curls. “You’re right. This was a terrible day. I’m angry at myself because I want to run away from my family again.”

Her vulnerability dissolved much of his unease. Her name was a sigh on his lips as he pulled her close. “What do you want to run from most? Your family or the Woman and her curse?”

She turned her face into his chest. “Both of them. I’m angry with Sarah because she’s not taking advantage of the strength of the family. She’s trying to make all the decisions alone.”

“And your parents?” he prompted.

She was silent. “I was surprised how they defended you tonight. How logical they were.”

“Makes it hard to hate them so much, right?”

She groaned and put her arms around him. “It’s very disconcerting that you understand me.”

He laughed. “I wouldn’t go that far. After all,

you're a witch."

She tipped her head back and looked up at him. "Does that bother you?"

"Why would it?"

"So you've known witches other than the Connellys?"

"One really well. I was eighteen, living in Boston. As you know, we shifters are often able to sense one another. I ended up with some other kids with special abilities who were on the streets. There was a witch who used to let us sleep at her house now and again."

"Another good witch like Eva Grace."

He shook his head. "Not entirely. She made a living working for a couple of mobsters, brewed up potions for them to use on their enemies."

Brenna frowned. "The craft says do no harm."

"She had lost her way. Her family shunned her."

She shivered. Even though she moved away, her family's power and strength reached across the miles to steady and comfort her. Their teachings and creed of honor were her foundation. "Do you know why her family put her out?"

"It had something to do with a wizard she fell in love with. He wasn't the best sort, I guess. Her family asked her to give him up, and she wouldn't. They made her choose. She took him, but in the end he left her alone. It confirmed my feelings about the uselessness of love and commitment."

"Confirmed?"

"Yeah, the worst thing my mother ever did was love my father." His admission slipped out, but before Brenna could pursue it, he released her and stepped back, picking up the bottle of water. He was done with true confessions for the night.

Taking a cue from him, Brenna changed the subject, "I'm worried about Eva Grace and Fiona. Maybe I should call them."

"It's late. They're probably asleep."

"Fiona was terrified that Aunt Celia's ghost was actually the demon in disguise. At the same time, she doesn't want to believe there's a traitor in our midst, either."

Jake shook his head and took another sip. "None of this feels right to me. Despite your differences, your family is strong when you're together. Tonight, your power was amazing."

"But someone broke the circle." Brenna bit her lip.

"Who do you think it is?"

She sighed, but she didn't hesitate to answer. "It could be my mother."

The response didn't shock Jake, but he didn't see the logic. "Why would your mother try to put more hurt on your family than what the Woman in White can inflict?"

"She left here to live a life separate and apart from our family. Maybe she didn't intend to break the circle tonight, but she's not really a part of us any longer."

"You could have fooled me. She jumped right in to save Doris."

"That could have been for show."

Jake still wasn't buying the theory. "I know that I'm an outsider, and I never met her before now, but she seems to really care what happens. She and your father warned Sarah against the spell."

Brenna didn't like his defense of her mother. "If not Delia, then who? Not Fiona or Eva Grace. And

Doris was the one attacked. What's your theory?"

"Oh, no, I'm not playing that game." Jake drained his water. "It's fine for you to criticize everyone in your family, but I'm not going to. And the truth is, I don't have any idea."

"Damn." Brenna dragged a hand through her hair. Her expression was fearful. "What if it's Sarah, Jake?" She began to pace, her body vibrating with anger and tension. She moved from the kitchen to the living room and back again. "What if something has happened to Sarah that we don't understand? She's been neglecting the coven. She ignored good advice about tonight. Willow says she's losing control. She didn't have enough strength to fight the Woman in White until I joined her. "

"But together you sent her running. Perhaps you can do the same when she comes back."

"But when will that be? When Aunt Celia was taken, she was with my mother. They were alone at the falls. There was no one there to help my mother fight for her sister's life. The Woman took her right there. Just like she took Garth."

Brenna's agitation stirred the air. The candles on the stone fireplace mantel lit and extinguished repeatedly. Kitchen cabinets opened and closed. The unopened mail on Jake's dining room table began to sort.

He took Brenna by the shoulders. "You need to calm down. " He knew better than suggest she try to rest, even though it was after one in the morning and neither of them had gotten any real rest during the day. "Why don't we see what we can find on the Internet?"

"We won't find any answers there. The answers are

in missing pieces of *The Connelly Book of Magic* and in the history of this town." Brenna walked away from him and tossed her empty bottle in the recycle bin beside the back door. "I think I need to go to talk to Willow. Would you go with me?"

"I don't think you need to do that either. Going to see Willow will make Sarah angry."

"But if she's the traitor, maybe that's what I'm supposed to do."

Jake went back to the kitchen and took a bottle of Jameson's and two heavy, old-fashioned glasses out of the cabinet. "I don't usually drink liquor when it's possible that I could be called in, but we've both had a long, hard day. In addition to all the stress you endured when your aunt was injured, I suspect you used some huge energy helping with the restoration spell."

He poured three fingers of whiskey in each glass. "You also put a lot of yourself into helping Sarah battle the Woman in White. It's late, Brenna. You don't need to go anywhere else tonight."

With a sound of reluctance, Brenna reached for the glass he held out to her. "I'm not much for drinking whiskey."

"Considering Garth gave me this for Christmas two years ago and it's still more than half full, I can say the same." Jake held up the glass and studied the amber liquid in the light. "According to Garth, there's no wrong way to drink Jameson's, but the best way is to take a sip, hold it on your tongue until the burn goes away, and then swallow. You get the full flavor of the whiskey without dulling your taste buds."

He lifted his drink. "Shall we?"

Brenna tipped her glass against his and said,

"*Sláinte.*"

Though her eyes watered a little, Brenna smiled when she swallowed the heady drink. "Garth was right. I've always had it with cranberry juice or ginger ale, but you really do get a better experience of the flavor this way. I think I'll finish mine during a hot bath."

"Good idea. Towels are in the hall closet, and I'll get you a T-shirt and the robe I never use," Garth said. "I'll throw your jeans and T-shirt in the wash, although it's doubtful the blood will come out entirely." He gave a rueful glance at his own blood-spattered khaki uniform. "I think our clothes are toast."

Brenna set her glass down and walked into his arms. "Thank you for letting me stay. " She stepped away from him and grinned. "Just remember, you have to tell me if you really don't want me here."

Jake watched her walk away. Despite their interaction, things were back to the way he wanted it between them. This was the way he liked relationships. Casual, friendly sex. Commitments were forbidden territory for those of his nature.

After imagining Brenna's naked body reclined in his tub, he opted to get the T-shirt and robe for her and close the bathroom door. He went to the cluttered desk that served as his home office, revived his sleeping laptop and checked the few people who were available to him through instant messaging.

Dr. Rodric McGuire was online as usual. It was morning in Edinburgh, Scotland, and Jake knew his studious friend would be retiring soon after a night of work. As a paranormal researcher, Rodric spent most of his nights in a castle or another building older than America waiting for ghosts, demons, and other beings that enjoyed darkness. Rodric was a researcher who had done a study of shifters in Special Ops in the military. He, Garth, and Jake became fast friends and usually met once a year in Scotland for hunting, drinking, and vicious games of chess.

Rodric had been distressed when Jake sent him a message about Garth's death, but with the events in New Mourne, there had been little time for Garth to speak with him since.

Five minutes after Jake sent his message, his phone rang. He grabbed it before it disturbed Brenna and greeted his old friend.

"I'm so glad to speak to you at last." The lyrical tones of his Scottish heritage sang in the doctor's words. "I can't believe Garth is gone."

"None of us can." Fresh grief roughened Jake's voice.

Rodric asked about Eva Grace and Garth's aunt, then got straight to the matter. "You said in your IM that you need my help."

Jake related the situation in New Mourne, including the attack by the vine on Brenna, the death of Sandy Murphy and tonight's spell gone wrong that left an elder aunt in the ICU.

Rodric cursed Celtic gods, goddesses, and various other deities. "There's more going on than the family curse. That's obvious to me."

"To Brenna, too. The rest of the family seems reluctant to accept that, although the elders have admitted to tangling with a demon in the past."

"Then it could well be the same now," Rodric said.

"One more thing you might be interested in." Jake paused for effect. "Aiden and Delia Burns are here."

"I'll be there as soon as I can," Rodric said and hung up.

Smiling, Jake closed his cell. He wasn't surprised that Rodric knew of the famed mystical researchers. The good doctor would want to be in on the resolution of the Connelly's family drama. What Jake hoped was that Rodric would be able to help them figure some of this out. The sooner he arrived, the better.

He turned as Brenna appeared in the doorway from the hall. She looked like a creamy cupcake, her skin soft and damp, her auburn curls drying in disarray around her face. Her robe opened to reveal smooth, silky legs beneath his baggy white T-shirt.

"Want to go to bed with me?" she asked.

He moved toward her, grinning. "There's nothing I'd like better, but you're exhausted. I'm not a desperate teenager." Jake realized his loins didn't agree with that statement, but he fought down his desire.

He kissed her softly, threading his hands through her hair. Then he took her hand and led her down the hall. "Come on. Let me tuck you in, and you'll have sweet dreams for sure."

She gave him token resistance, but he insisted she climb into his big oak bed and try to settle down. He sat by the bed as she mumbled about what she needed to do tomorrow and finally gave in to sleep. When her breath steadied, he slipped out and gazed longingly at the dark woods behind his house. He needed a run, but he wasn't comfortable leaving Brenna alone.

A loud hissing sound pulled him to the back door. A barn owl perched on the lower limb of the red oak just beyond the house. The owl blinked at him and hissed again.

"You're Brenna's bird," he said aloud, admiring the pale brown wings and stark white face in the moonlight.

The owl watched him, eyes steady and true.

"You'll keep her safe?" Jake asked.

The owl hissed again. Feeling he had protection in place, Jake let go of the restraints of his human form. The tiger took control and in moments he was racing through the undergrowth chasing a rabbit that would serve as a nice appetizer.

An hour later, refreshed and sated, Jake stood under a hot shower feeling better than he had in days. His mind was clear and his body loose. He knew he was ready to help Brenna intensify her search for answers.

Brenna stirred as he slipped in beside her, and she snuggled against him. This time Jake didn't argue with his libido. Surrounded by the scent of honeysuckle and Brenna's supple skin, he buried his face against her warm throat. When he licked the delicate skin, Brenna came awake on a moan.

He slipped his hands under the T-shirt and slid it over her head. His hands glided over her body, appreciating the curves and muscles. When his fingers grazed her hip, she pressed herself against him.

Jake took her lips and nibbled. She ran a palm across his chest, and he deepened the kiss, drinking from her like a dying man. He pulled her close and pressed his erection against her. Brenna parted her legs and made little movements that made him glad he as a man.

He moved his hand down her body, slipping his fingers inside her. She responded with abandon. As she pumped against his hand, he took her nipple into his mouth. She rode the crest and slumped against him when she came. Before he could move to take her, she pushed him down and crawled on top, taking him in as she settled.

She set a slow, mesmerizing pace that left Jake helpless to do more than hold on to her. Watching her beautiful body move above him, Jake felt more than physical response. He tried to push the feelings away, as he had in the past, but Brenna touched his core in an unfamiliar way. She brought him to completion, and then draped herself over his body, sated and sweet smelling.

Before his breathing slowed, Brenna gave him a wicked grin. He thought she was going to suggest they make love again. Even though he was supernatural, he didn't know if that was possible.

She laughed as if reading his thoughts. "I'm starving, shifter. Got anything to eat?"

Chapter 20

Since the phone didn't wake them during the night, Brenna assumed the town was still peaceful. Eva Grace called to tell her Doris had made it through the night and was doing better than expected. Brenna and Jake slept in, made love again and enjoyed the breakfast he prepared.

Although she knew why she wanted to stay with Jake last night, she was surprised at her reluctance to go home.

"I like this," she admitted to herself as she drove away.

In the rearview mirror, she saw him watching her leave. She felt a strong temptation to turn around, to wrap herself around his long, lean body, and have her way with him once again. She was well acquainted with passion, but Jake took her to new heights. At the same time, he made her feel comfortable. There was no pretense. She could be herself with him.

An ill-advised development, she reminded herself. She would not get involved while in line to die. Jake was a distraction. Her sole concern should be breaking the curse. Connellys before her focused on their normal lives—Sarah wrapped up in raising her daughters' children and Delia wrapped up in Aiden. They might have made progress if they had stayed the course.

Brenna hoped she could get to her room without

talking to anyone. Sarah and Marcus were usually in their studios by this time each day, and as she pulled into the driveway, she noted her parents' rental car was gone. Though she knew she could spend the night wherever she chose, she didn't want to explain herself to anyone in the family right now.

"But I have no such luck," she muttered as Fiona's van came up behind her.

Taking a deep breath, Brenna got out. She prepared herself for Fiona's anger for making her tell the family about Aunt Celia.

Fiona cranked down the window on her old van. "I was out this way to check out a story for my webcast, and I thought I'd stop by. Are you just getting in?"

Relieved there was no hostility in her sister's tone, Brenna replied, "Yeah, I stayed at Jake's."

"He's a good guy. You could do worse."

Not ready to discuss exactly what she was doing with Jake, Brenna changed the subject. "Have you found a new haunting?"

"We're going to tape a webcast at the old Beech Chapel cemetery up the road. I've been getting some new voices from there, so I went up to plan the shoot. "

"Anything that could help us figure out who the Woman in White is? There are some really old graves there."

Fiona shrugged. "We'll see. Just like last night, I'm not connecting with anyone today."

Brenna frowned. Her sister's lack of spiritual communication was strange. "What do you think is happening?"

"I'm trying not to worry." Fiona drummed her fingers on the steering wheel. "I talked to Brian earlier.

He said there wasn't a single call into the sheriff's department last night. That's the first time since Garth died we've had a quiet night in town."

"That explains why Jake got to sleep in this morning." Brenna knew she should be relieved no one was painting graffiti, shooting a spouse or beheading chickens. Instead, she was uneasy.

"I'm headed to the hospital to see Doris. Want to come along?"

Recognizing the olive branch, Brenna nodded. "Can I change into something a little less bloodstained and rumpled?" She indicated her ruined jeans and Jake's T-shirt.

Fiona cut off the ignition and went inside while Brenna went upstairs. She chose khaki shorts, a faded Atlanta Braves T-shirt and sandals. She even took the time to brush her hair, slide on a pair of dangly earrings, and add a little mascara and lipstick. After all, she might see Jake while in town.

A meow of disapproval made her turn. Tasmin leapt onto the bed, looking disgruntled.

"I'm sorry." Brenna stroked the cat's gray fur. "I promise I'll see you later."

Tail straight in the air in a feline Bronx salute, Tasmin turned her back.

"Have a great day yourself," Brenna said, laughing as she went to join her sister.

Equipment rattled in the back of the old van as Fiona guided it over the familiar road to town.

"Anything new on Aunt Doris?" Brenna asked.

"She may get out of ICU today."

"That's amazing."

Fiona swallowed hard. "I was sure she was going

to die before we could get help. There was so much blood."

Brenna did her best to hide her smile. Fiona could face the nastiest ghost with superb calm, but a paper cut made her go pale. "What's the report from everyone else this morning?"

"Everything at the store is back to normal except for the mess from last night. Eva Grace and Lauren are planning to do a cleansing spell this afternoon."

"Do they need us?"

A line appeared between Fiona's eyebrows. "You think Eva Grace and Lauren need help with a simple cleansing spell?"

"I didn't say that."

"You implied it."

Brenna released a frustrated breath. "That's not what I meant."

"Eva Grace is trying to smooth over the discord in the coven right now."

"And I suppose you both think the *discord* is my fault."

"You believe there's a traitor in our family. How can you even imagine one of *us* would betray the coven?"

"That's what Celia said." Brenna spoke through gritted teeth.

"I believe Dad is right about Aunt Celia's ghost being a demon's trick."

Brenna was torn on her own opinion. "But don't you think it might have been her?"

"She said to beware the traitor. I assumed she meant a traitor in the coven, but as pointed out last night, I could be wrong. Besides, even if it was Aunt

Celia, she's a ghost, an unpredictable spirit. I learned a long time ago not to trust everything spirits tell me. That's why I didn't want to tell anyone last night."

"How do you know she's unpredictable when you've only seen her once?" Brenna's eyes narrowed as she studied her sister. "Why are you so eager to side with Sarah?"

"Sarah is the coven leader, the one we turn to when we need advice and counsel. It's not wise to have conflict with the strongest witch we know. Plus, she's our grandmother, and she raised us. That should count for something."

"It's also not wise to ignore warnings from ancestors."

Fiona pursed her lips and glared at the road.

Brenna stifled a sharp retort. She had no desire to fight with her sister.

The rest of the drive passed in silence. At the hospital, anger still stewed between them as they learned that Doris was in a private room.

Though their great aunt looked weak and pale and had a bulky bandage on her neck, she was awake. Eva Grace was arranging crystals on the table. Lauren was with her, chanting softly. When she finished, Brenna and Fiona stepped into the room.

"Hello." Fiona leaned down to kiss the elderly woman. "You gave us an awful scare."

Doris nodded weakly. The wound in her throat prevented her from talking.

Eva Grace patted the elder aunt's hand. "According to the doctor, her progress is remarkable."

"You're going to be fine, Aunt Doris." Brenna smoothed the covers. "We all know you can't keep a good witch down."

Doris drifted off to sleep while her nieces fussed over her. Lauren and Eva Grace discussed what they needed to do at the store that afternoon. Neither of them mentioned the family disagreement from last night, for which Brenna was grateful. Fiona sat at the bedside, still holding Doris's hand while Brenna moved restlessly around the small room.

Hospitals were too clinical. The walls should be a soothing color. Herbs should grow in little pots on the windowsill for healing and comfort. The light was all wrong as well. They needed pink bulbs to soften the edges. She looked at Eva Grace and wondered if her cousin would consider suggesting changes to the handsome doctor they met last night.

Although it was too early for Eva Grace to be thinking of anyone other than Garth, Brenna thought Dr. Hargrave was a perfect candidate to remind Eva Grace she was very much alive.

Maggie arrived next with a massive bouquet of day lilies. Brenna recognized them from Frances's garden and shivered a little. Doris woke up and smiled at the blooms, obviously pleased to have them.

Looking refreshed, Maggie spoke gently to the elder aunt. Maggie's hair was back in its usual smooth style, her attire a pair of white cropped pants and a deep blue top. She was much more like herself today, and like the others, she made no mention of demons, traitors or the Woman in White. Obviously, none of them wanted to disturb Doris's rest.

Brenna studied the familiar faces. Really, the five of them could be sisters. They all had green eyes and varying shades of red in their hair. Eva Grace's was dark cinnamon. Fiona's brunette tresses were streaked with fire. Brenna, Lauren and Maggie were all auburn-haired, and all three were tall and statuesque. If you looked past the fact that Lauren dressed for maximum sex appeal and Maggie preferred sweater sets, those two cousins could be twins. All five of them were so much alike.

All of them possible victims for the Woman in White.

And one of them perhaps a traitor?

Brenna's heart pounded in fear.

By the goddess, she hated suspecting the women she loved most. She just wanted this nightmare to be over.

Too many questions, and she needed to find some answers.

It wasn't long before Doris fell asleep again. Eva Grace and Maggie said they would stay until Aunt Diane arrived to sit with Doris this afternoon.

Lauren was planning to take the night shift. "After all," she purred, "I'm accustomed to being up all hours of the night."

Fiona gave Brenna the gagging sign behind Lauren's back. Lauren chattered on about her social life, and Fiona made similar faces behind her all the way to the parking lot. Brenna coughed to cover her laughter. Lauren never suspected Fiona was busy behind her.

Parting from their cousin, the sisters approached the van. Brenna was relieved to feel Fiona wasn't so angry with her now. "Got any plans for the next couple of hours?" she asked.

"Just some research for a client. Her husband

claims her dear departed great-grandmother is driving the family crazy trying to find her favorite pearls." Fiona laughed as she started her car.

"Do you think you can find them?"

"That's the funny part," Fiona said. "This particular ghost told me years ago her great-grandmother sold the pearls to buy the family home."

"So why not tell your client that?"

"The client is the wife and every time she gets angry with him, she invites me in to look for the pearls again. He's always looking for easy money and the thought that those pearls are hidden somewhere just drives him crazy. It gives his wife a good laugh."

"That's kind of mean," Brenna observed and laughed as her sister started the van. Fiona was such a softie most of the time that Brenna appreciated that she had a streak of mischief.

"How about going with me to see our cousin Inez?" she invited Fiona.

"The cousin who has all the history?"

"She may know something important about the Woman in White. As you heard last night, neither Sarah nor any of the elder aunts have bothered to explore her records."

Fiona drove them to The Meadows, "a caring facility where the residents' needs are the priority," according to the sign at the entrance. It was a pleasant looking building with a wide front porch lined with rocking chairs. Four women and two men watched as Fiona and Brenna walked up to the door.

"I hope you're here to see me," one of the men said to Brenna.

"Nah, Charlie, it's me. I'm younger than you," the

other man put in, eyeing Fiona.

"You're ninety-two."

"Yeah, but you're ninety-seven, and I can tell they'd like a younger man."

Brenna and Fiona were still smiling when they arrived at Inez's room, an overly cheerful place that only had one thing missing—the lady herself. Set up like a comfortable studio apartment, the room had a purple velvet loveseat decorated with crystal buttons that battled with the primary hues of the bed's patchwork quilt. Beside the loveseat was a blue recliner lift chair. Lacy lavender curtains were on the two small windows.

Several bookcases were filled with leather-bound journals. Brenna noticed that years were embossed in gold on the spines. Curious, she pulled a journal out and opened it. Neat, precise handwriting filled page after page, telling the story of her marriage and family in an easy manner that related events with the humor or tears they deserved.

"Inez recorded almost every day of their lives and it's actually interesting." Brenna flipped through the pages, catching familiar names. "I'd love to read all of these."

They turned as someone entered the doorway. Though the woman was ancient, her voice was strong. "Oh, look, I've got company."

A teenager who wore the mint-green smock of a high school volunteer helped Inez into the recliner. With the regal gesture of royalty, Inez dismissed the volunteer with her thanks.

When Brenna started to speak, Inez held up a hand. "No, let me see if I can recognize you. It's a little game

I like to play to exercise my brain."

She studied both of them, moving from Brenna's face to Fiona's and back. After a moment her eyes lit with delight. "You're Sarah's granddaughters, aren't you?"

"Yes, ma'am," Fiona said. "We're Delia's girls. We'd like to visit with you a while if you have time."

The older woman cackled. "It's not like I'm going anywhere else."

Brenna and Fiona sat gingerly on the purple loveseat.

"I hope you don't mind that I looked at one of your books," Brenna said, holding up the volume she'd been scanning. "It's amazing that you kept these journals."

"I love to share my memories, especially with family."

"We'd like to talk to you about the Connelly family history," Brenna said. "To get right to the point, we're hoping to find some information about the Woman in White."

Inez's bright smile dimmed. "Even though the Woman did not threaten me, my only daughter lost a friend to her, one who was like another of my children. My sweet Maeve still misses your Great Aunt Rose every day."

Tears glistened in Inez's eyes. "Your grandmother and her sisters nearly grieved themselves to death when Rose was taken. I've always thought that was why Sarah went wild and took up with that gypsy."

Brenna and Fiona exchanged a glance. Sarah had nothing to say on the subject of their biological grandfather.

"Did you know him?" Brenna asked.

Inez sniffed. “Good heavens, Sarah barely knew him. All he did was put two babies in her belly and take off.”

“She won’t talk about him,” Fiona said.

Inez peered into Fiona’s face. “Well, you look a little like him with your dark hair and maybe the cut of your cheekbones.” She sighed. “I’m just glad Sarah found a good man at last.”

“We all love Marcus,” Brenna agreed. She nodded to the room’s bookcases. “Are all of these books your journals?”

“All but that case.” Inez pointed behind her. “Those are the records I’ve been able to obtain about our community and the Connelly family.”

Brenna itched to dive into those volumes.

Inez added, “I began writing in a diary when I was ten years old. I wanted to be sure there was a history of me, that future generations would know I existed.”

“Why would a ten-year-old girl worry about that?” Fiona asked.

Inez used the chair to lift herself to standing and tottered over to the tiny kitchen area. “Would you like some tea, ladies? I haven’t had visitors other than my children and grandchildren for a while, and I love to entertain.”

“Of course,” Fiona said. “Can I help?”

Inez didn’t hesitate. “Yes. The cups and saucers are there, and I have a stash of cookies under the sink. If I don’t hide them, my great-great-grandson helps himself.”

When they had everything prepared, Fiona brought the tea tray to the coffee table. Inez returned to her recliner, adjusting it so she sat comfortably.

"This china is beautiful," Brenna said admiring the flowers on the delicate cup.

"It belonged to my husband's great-grandmother. I was thrilled when his mother gave it to me." The old woman's voice strengthened with pride. "It was imported from Ireland. The Connellys never forgot their roots."

"You were going to tell us why you started keeping journals," Fiona prompted.

"I was left on the back steps of a church in Dahlonega. The minister and his wife, who were childless, became my parents. They were very strict. I was determined to gain my freedom as soon as I could, so I ran off with Craig Connelly six months after his first wife died in childbirth. He had three small boys, but I knew I'd be freer with him than I ever would with my parents." Inez stopped to drink some tea.

"And were you happy with him?" Brenna asked.

"Absolutely," Inez said with a laugh. "We had a home crowded with love and children—his three and our four—and the Connellys accepted me without hesitation. My daughter Maeve has some magical abilities, being a female Connelly, though she chose not to develop them. She was too heartbroken when Rose died. She distanced herself from the family. But for the first time in *my* life, with the Connellys, I knew what family was. Surrounded by all that magic, I wanted to be a Connelly witch, too."

Brenna nodded. "Is that why you began collecting family history?"

"History can become very important to someone who has none of their own. Let me show you something that Craig and I found on Connelly land."

She started to get up again, but Brenna put a hand on her knee to stop her. “Let me get what you need.”

“It’s the wooden box on the bottom shelf over there,” Inez said. “Like my great-great grandson, I like to keep my treasures.”

Brenna retrieved the box. Inez took hold of it eagerly, but her hands trembled.

“Are you okay?” Brenna asked Inez.

The woman was focused on the box. “Why, I’m just fine, Brenna dear.” She opened the lid with great care. Small artifacts rested on velvet—several arrowheads in various sizes, some broken pottery, and a long, sharp, shiny rock that looked lethal. Inez picked it up.

“This is a skinning knife,” she said. “The Cherokee were great hunters.”

Fiona leaned forward and took one of the arrowheads. Brenna started as Fiona jerked and began to shiver.

“What is it?” Brenna grabbed her sister’s other hand.

Fiona flinched, as if in pain.

Brenna had to pry the arrowhead from her sister’s grasp. Though she felt nothing from it, she was quick to return it to Inez’s box. Fiona took a deep breath and leaned back, visibly shaken.

Alarmed by her sudden pallor, Brenna refilled her cup with tea and added a liberal amount of sugar. “Drink this.”

Fiona complied, some color returning to her cheeks as she gulped down the hot liquid. “That was strange,” she said. “I was in a dark, cold place. Someone was screaming in pain.”

"Who did you see?" Inez asked, her tone sharp. "Who was it?"

Fiona frowned. "I couldn't tell."

"You're sure?"

The elderly woman's intensity struck Brenna as odd. "Why do you consider what's in this box so important? The Cherokee once populated these mountains, so finding traces of them is not so rare. Many families have collections like these."

Inez blinked and appeared disoriented. She held the box out to Fiona again.

Fiona eyed the artifacts with reluctance, but with her gaze locked on Inez's, she reached for the long skinning knife.

The sunlight beaming into the room dimmed. A sense of foreboding rose like a tide in Brenna. "Don't touch it!" she cried in alarm.

"Take it and tell me what you see," Inez coaxed.

"No." Brenna put herself between Inez and Fiona. She called to the goddess and bathed the older woman with pink, translucent light.

Inez shuddered, and then sagged back in her chair, the open box in her lap. She looked alarmed at Fiona and Brenna, and pressed a hand to her mouth. "The devil. I felt him."

"The demon," Fiona murmured, staring at the box. "Is he in this collection?"

"No," Inez exclaimed and clutched the box.

Brenna steeled herself for a change in the woman, but it didn't happen.

"Craig told me to keep these," Inez explained. "He would never tell me to keep something evil."

"But what happened?" Brenna patted her on the

arm, fearing the frail woman would harm herself by being so upset. "What did you feel?"

"Like I was watching everything on TV or maybe in a mirror."

The dark side of the mirror. Brenna recalled Willow's warning with a shiver.

"Was someone telling you to hurt us?" Fiona pressed.

Inez shivered again, visibly shaken. "I've never hurt anyone in my entire life, but I was thinking about that knife at your throat. It was the devil, the very devil himself had hold of me." She began to cry.

Brenna took the box and put it back on the shelf. She paced the room and put a protective spell in place while Fiona soothed Inez and freshened her tea. The room was warmer than just moments before. Too hot, she decided. The demon had briefly taken over Inez, but the black magic was weak, possibly from the blow she and Sarah had dealt him last night.

She turned back to Inez and Fiona. "I wonder what Inez has that the demon doesn't want us to discover."

The older woman straightened in her recliner, tears drying. "I've kept all of these things for so many years. So many times my children begged me to let them take it all away, but I wouldn't let them. Maybe I've been waiting for you. Maybe there is something here to help you end that wicked curse."

"But where do we start?" Brenna gazed at the shelves full of books. If there was a secret buried here, it would take time to find it. And the Connellys were running out of time.

"We'll start with the Cherokees," Inez proclaimed, gathering her faculties about her once again. "The demon came at me when Fiona touched the arrowhead. Surely that's a clue." She twisted around to survey the books on the shelf behind her.

A few minutes later, they had over a dozen volumes open—history books and journals—and were searching for a scrap of local Native American history that would tell them something.

Fiona looked up from one of the history volumes. "They got along really well—the Cherokees and the Connellys—because they both had such strong beliefs in the magic and power of the elements."

"I love the Cherokee legends and stories. They're wonderful storytellers," Inez said, "just like many of the Connellys, but your family wasn't as willing to talk. We all understood the need for secrecy about the magic and the witchcraft, but sometimes that made it difficult to get family stories straight."

"What did they say about the Woman in White or the curse?" Fiona asked.

"Craig told me to leave that alone," Inez replied. "Even when Rose was taken, no one wanted to open up about the history. I tried to talk to Sarah after her daughter was taken, but she couldn't speak of it. She was so heartbroken."

And foolish, Brenna thought. Sarah should have let Inez help.

"We're running into the same walls," Brenna told her. "We've been trying to find out why the original Sarah Connelly made such a terrible deal."

Inez was distracted. She was flipping through the pages of one of her journals. "I thought I had written down a story someone told me about the Cherokee." She frowned. "It's not in this one."

Brenna flipped through the pages of another journal Inez had directed her to pull out. “I have to ask—how did you find time to write all of this with seven children?”

Inez laughed. “I was determined. You won’t notice unless you read all of them, but there were days when I only recorded a few lines. I couldn’t write every day, but I tried to get something down most days. As the children grew older, it became easier. My granddaughter works for a publisher in Atlanta and she had them bound for me.”

“I imagine you could tell me about some of the ghosts I encounter.” Fiona said. “There are a lot of restless spirits in our town. Many can’t let go and move on to the other side.”

Inez studied Fiona’s face. “It must be difficult for you to deal with all those ghosts.”

“It can be stressful,” Fiona admitted. “But it’s also rewarding when I can help someone move on or pass along a message to a relative or friend.”

Inez turned to study the shelf behind her again. Brenna sensed the elderly woman was growing fatigued, and she was jumping from one subject to another.

“Maybe the legend I’m thinking about isn’t in the journals.” Inez pointed to the bottom shelf. “Bring me that book on the end of the row. I think the title is *The Ghosts of Northeast Georgia*.”

Brenna found the book, and Inez turned the pages with impatience until she found what she was looking for. “This is it,” she said. “Let me tell you the story.”

She leaned forward, her eyes bright and voice growing husky. “The first white men in this area were missionaries who came to save the heathens." She chuckled. "I shouldn't laugh, but it's funny because the Cherokee were a very civilized people. They were hunters and lived in clans, much like the Irish. They respected all living things and were in awe of the Great Spirit."

She was quieter as her eyes focused on a distant point. "One of my good friends was a direct descendant of the original Cherokee families. He told me an old story passed down by the families for centuries. It was about a missionary who discovered his daughter had fallen in love with a young Cherokee brave. The missionary was so angry he kept her tied up for weeks. Eventually her young brave and his friends rescued her."

Fiona said, "Sounds a little like a Cherokee version of *Romeo and Juliet*."

Inez agreed. "That story still rings true today with racial hatred so prominent. Supposedly, the missionary searched for days in a mad rage. He even kidnapped the young brave's friend and tortured him to death without learning anything."

Fiona shivered.

"What is it?" Brenna took her sister's hand.

"I don't know. I just remember the screaming when I touched the arrowhead." She patted Brenna's hand. "I'm okay. Go on, Inez."

"Yes, what happened to the daughter?" Brenna asked.

"I was able to dig up several theories," Inez said. "Some stories say she crept back to her father's house in shame with her baby by her Cherokee mate. Those versions say she was insane, so crazy that she killed her baby. But other tales have her father finding her, dragging her home and killing the baby himself because it was a half-breed. So she killed him and then took her own life. Threw herself right over Mulligan Falls."

Brenna drew in a sharp breath, trading a startled glance with Fiona.

Inez turned the book she held around and pointed to a crude sketch of a woman. "Her death at the falls is just about the only part of the story that's an irrefutable fact. One of the other missionaries drew this picture and put in the date of her death, leaving off her name, but noting she was damned for eternity for taking her own life. The picture survived, and it's in the town library somewhere. I believe the date was around the mid-1700s."

"Not too long before our ancestors settled Mourne County," Brenna said, studying the sketch again.

"How awful," Fiona murmured. "What happened to her brave?"

"Some stories say her father killed him. Some say he was sold into slavery. Others tell that he abandoned his pretty blond wife when she went stark raving mad."

Brenna traced a finger over the features of the woman's picture in the book. Though the drawing lacked definition and detail, this could be the entity encountered by the falls and seen last night in the shop.

"Do you think this is the Woman in White?" Fiona said, giving voice to Brenna's thoughts. "Only a tortured soul could stay around this long."

"The woman we saw with Garth was pretty, like the young woman in this drawing." Brenna stared down at the face on the page. How could someone who looked so innocent be so evil? Who was this woman and what had really happened to her?

"Do you have all the versions of her stories written down?" Fiona asked.

"Of course, in one of my books," Inez said and pointed to the shelves filled with dozens of leather-bound volumes. "I'm sure it's in one of those."

Chapter 21

On Friday, the sheriff's office had an abnormally quiet morning. Gladys was doing her weekly dispatcher's report, Brian was typing up an incident report, and a resident was snoring in the back, sleeping off a bad binge brought on by yet another fruitless search for an ancestor's priceless pearls.

Jake still didn't feel comfortable in the office he inherited from Garth, but he was easing into it. Garth's things were gone, given to his aunt, so the room was a little bare. Maybe that was for the best, Jake thought as he sipped coffee. He was only the acting sheriff. He might not want to stay in the role.

He felt blue, thinking of Garth this morning. Maybe that was why he wasn't enjoying a respite from crime. The calm felt ominous. It reminded him of being on active duty, of the breathless pause he always felt just before his unit started a new mission. Anything could happen.

Brenna thought it was a false break in the action, too, especially since the demon had tried to take over their elderly cousin. She was in sharp disagreement with her family. Sarah was sure they had driven away the Woman in White at the shop on Tuesday night. Few of the other witches disagreed with her.

Jake suspected Delia wasn't convinced the trouble was over, although she seemed reluctant to fight with

Sarah. Fiona still had trouble connecting to spirits, so she was distracted by that. He wasn't sure about Eva Grace. She remained shell-shocked by the deaths of Garth and Sandy, so it was difficult to know what she was thinking.

The bottom line was Brenna's mother, sister and closest cousin weren't giving her any support in her quest to thwart the family curse. Like the others, they wanted to believe Sarah was right and the curse was finished.

Brenna couldn't. Last night, she cried while telling him about the fight with Sarah. He didn't think Brenna cried easily. She and Sarah had quarreled so long and so loud that Marcus stepped in. Brenna worshipped her grandmother's husband, and his anger had hurt. She said she no longer felt welcome in the house where she had grown up. She'd spent the night with him again.

Sipping his coffee, Jake frowned. Of course Brenna ended up at his house for the night. That was becoming a habit.

The phone intercom buzzed. "Fred Williams is on line one."

"Thanks, Gladys."

He sighed before punching the button. "Morning, Fred, how's it going today?"

"That's what the Board of Commissioners wants to know. We've called a meeting for eleven o'clock. We want a full run-down on everything that went on in town after Garth died."

"You've got my latest report," Jake replied, trying not to be irritated. "And everything is very calm today. We haven't even had one call."

"We can't expect that to last."

So the commissioner was of the same opinion as Jake and Brenna. That was interesting. “What makes you think the trouble will start again, Fred?”

“I just know. See you at eleven.”

The dial tone rang in his ear as Jake said, “Sure, Fred, I’ll check my calendar to see if I can make it.”

He put the phone in its cradle and took another sip of coffee. It tasted bitter now. For a preacher, Fred Williams sure gave him a lot of hell. Letting out a long breath of frustration, he punched the intercom button.

“Brian, I need the most recent incident reports and the graphs you made comparing this year with the last two, please. I’ve got a BOC meeting in an hour, and I need three copies of everything and the master for me.”

“No problem.”

Jake went to the small break room, dumped his now cold coffee and poured a fresh cup, adding a spoonful of sugar to ease the bitterness. He wished a spoonful of sugar would make the BOC easier to take.

Garth had faced their wrath often. So far they had gone pretty easy on Jake, even during the recent troubles. He suspected that would change today.

He headed to the meeting with his report about an hour later. It was short walk since the commission room was in the courthouse just like the sheriff’s department. The politicos sat behind a half-moon desk at the front of the room. Walking down the center aisle, Jake felt three pairs of eyes boring into him. Harry Chambers, Riley O’Neal and Fred Williams didn’t speak until Jake passed out his reports and took a seat on the front row of folding chairs.

They flipped through the reports and muttered to one another in low voices. Jake watched them and wondered what they would do if confronted by a tiger.

Riley O'Neal sat on the left. Jake thought he'd heard somewhere that Riley's ancestors were druids. There'd been rumors for years that Riley used an ancient spell to become invisible. Jake didn't know what Riley did. He didn't think it was anything illegal, but he also wasn't sure how Riley had built his family's compound of houses, pools and horse barns.

Harry Chambers lived in The Enclave and was the retired CEO of a textile company. He'd orchestrated the sale of the company just before the economic downturn, his millions safely invested in healthy stocks and gold. He was the leader of Neighborhood Watch and embroiled in county politics.

Fred spoke first. "We're here today because people in our town are frightened and upset. What are we going to do when the crime wave starts again?"

"We're not exactly looking at a gang war in Newark," Jake said. "We'll respond, just as we've done for the past week."

"We've had two murders," Harry said. "You've got good, honest citizens worried about leaving their houses. Some of our residents are getting guns, with legal permits, of course."

"That's not always a good idea, Harry," Jake said.

"These people need to feel safe. They moved here from Atlanta to get away from crimes and fear. We've built a wonderful community and made it secure, but we know what's happening in New Mourne will eventually make its way to The Enclave."

"That's not necessarily true, Harry," Fred said. "My family has been here for a long time, and there have been other times of unrest and everything worked out. We just need a little cooperation."

"What happened during those other times of unrest, Fred?" Jake asked.

"Bad times, crimes and misdemeanors," Fred said, "and the church people did lots of praying. It's how we've always responded to evil."

Jake rolled his report into a tube. "I know about some of that, Fred, I've been doing some research. It seems there was always trouble in New Mourne at certain periods in the town's history." He shared a long look with the pastor. He would bet his cabin the man knew everything about the Connelly family curse and the troubles that came to town with it.

Fred looked at the other two men. Harry nodded. Riley clasped his hands on the table. Jake felt his stomach tighten. Something bad was coming.

"We think it's time to look again at allowing the security guards for The Enclave to be a local police force," Fred said amiably. "We all believe it's important for our citizens to feel safe."

"Even if you add a police force out there, you know Georgia law states the sheriff is still in charge," Jake said.

"Looks to me like you could use the help," Harry said. "And it would give our men more authority."

"Where will these men get their training?" Jake asked. "Will they be former police officers? Many of them are retired and unable to meet the physical standards for a sheriff's deputy."

"Are all of your deputies fully up to snuff?" Harry asked.

Thinking of his oldest two men, who were nearing retirement, Jake shifted in his chair. He looked to Riley, hoping for support. The man's dark eyes glimmered, but he said nothing.

Jake straightened his shoulders, knowing he had to face this on his own. "Let's not be too hasty with this."

"We know there are things that need to be worked out—" Fred stopped, his face paling visibly as he stared at a point over Jake's shoulder.

Jake turned to the door, surprised to see Brenna's parents coming toward him.

"Celia," Fred said in an awed whisper.

Riley touched the minister's arm and said, "It's Delia Burns, Fred."

Jake watched Fred's inner struggle for a moment, seeing that control didn't come easily.

"Of course," Fred said. He nodded to Delia and Dr. Burns, then abruptly picked up his copy of the report and stood. "I think that's all for today," he told the other commissioners as he left the room through the side door.

Harry and Riley watched him leave, and then turned back to Jake. Harry said, "We'll discuss this at length during the next meeting."

As the two men left, Jake stood to greet Brenna's parents. He hoped they weren't here to report more trouble.

"Was that Fred Williams?" Delia asked.

"You know him?"

"We grew up together." Delia laughed. "Fred was always stuck on himself. Very handsome, of course, but vain and selfish. He was president of his senior class and thought he ran the world. I didn't like him."

Jake had to laugh. "He hasn't changed much."

"I'm not surprised." Delia gave Jake a concerned

look. "I bet dealing with him is a pain."

"A big one," Jake admitted. "What brings the two of you to the courthouse?"

"We were looking for you," Dr. Burns said. He hesitated. "We wanted to talk about Brenna."

Jake frowned. This wasn't a conversation to have in a public meeting room. "Let's go back to my office."

County employees in nearby offices directed curious stares their way as Jake led the Burns up the stairs. He supposed they were used to stares. She was uncommonly beautiful with her bright red hair, delicate skin and petite figure. Aiden had a distinguished presence. Together, they exuded a European air.

As they went through his outer office, the couple greeted Brian and called Gladys by name.

Jake offered them tea and coffee, but they declined as they went into his office and sat. He closed the door, afraid if he didn't Gladys might strain her neck trying to listen to the conversation.

"What's going on with Brenna?" he asked as he took the chair behind his desk.

"We're worried about her," Delia said. "She's convinced Celia's warning about betrayal in the coven is serious. To say Sarah doesn't agree is an understatement."

Her husband added, "In the journals she got from Inez, Brenna found evidence that there's been discord in the coven before."

"We can't dispute that we Connellys haven't always been devoted to one another." Delia sighed. "But Sarah will not have it. Brenna is threatening to leave."

"She and Brenna have been at it again all

morning," Dr. Burns said.

Delia rubbed her forehead. "Those two have matching tempers, and neither of them gives an inch."

"Sarah's worse than Brenna," her husband said.

"Aiden." Delia's voice had a warning.

"Sorry, sweetie, but it's true."

Delia sat forward in her chair. "Jake, we know you and Brenna have been spending a lot of time together."

Jake shifted in his seat, not quite able to meet Brenna's father's eyes as he thought about how he spent his time with Brenna.

"Eva Grace thinks the world of you," Delia continued. "She says Garth loved you like a brother. We'd like you to talk to Brenna. Maybe you can help her see how unwise it is to leave her grandmother's home."

Jake laughed. "You think Brenna will listen to me?"

"It's more likely she'll listen to you than either of us," Dr. Burns said. "She doesn't exactly trust us."

"Oh, Aiden, she despises us," Delia said quietly. "We're concerned, Jake, and we thought you'd be the best person to talk to about it."

"What about Fiona and Eva Grace?"

"They agree with Sarah, so for maybe the first time in her life, Brenna's on her own," Delia said.

Jake rubbed his chin and wished he had a cup of coffee and a donut with sprinkles. A cake donut, in fact. Yeah, that's what he needed…and to be anywhere but here.

As a loner, like most of his nature, he wasn't used to family dramas like this. He had never been approached by the parents of a…lady friend?

Girlfriend? He knew he was already embroiled in it, but did he want to get deeper? Weren't he and Brenna just pals, just enjoying each other? Wasn't it stupid of him to get in the middle of a family feud?

He knew all of that, yet he couldn't look into her mother's green eyes full of concern and turn her down. "I'll think about talking to Brenna," he said at last. "I can't guarantee she won't turn me into a toad, but I'll try."

"Delia made me a turtle once." Dr. Burns' tone was matter-of-fact.

"A tortoise, my love," Delia corrected him. "I made you a big, beautiful tortoise once when you were trying to rush me as I was getting ready for a party. I needed you to slow down."

He took her hand and kissed it. "I guess I did deserve that spell."

"And I turned you back." His lovely red-haired spouse smiled at him. "For that you can be grateful."

Jake gulped. "So Brenna really could turn me into a toad?"

Delia considered him a moment. "Well, it might be difficult, given that you're already a tiger, but Brenna's very talented."

"She summoned the wind when she was two," Dr. Burns said with pride. "Sarah called us. I think we were in Turkey."

Delia beamed. "Brenna is an exceptional witch." Her eyes narrowed as she studied Jake. "I do hope you realize what you're getting into with her."

He wasn't sure he liked that terminology. He hadn't intended to get into anything but justice for his murdered friend.

The couple stood. Dr. Burns shook Jake's hand and Delia thanked him. "I hope you will talk to Brenna."

"I'll try."

Delia spoke to Gladys on the way out as Aiden waited patiently by the door. The older woman hugged Delia, and they parted with plans to meet for lunch.

Jake walked over to the coffee pot and poured a cup, thankful it was freshly brewed.

"How do you know Delia?" he asked Gladys as he studied the donut remains in the box from the morning. None of the broken, hardened pieces looked appetizing.

"She was a friend of my daughter."

Jake knew Gladys' daughter had succumbed to leukemia before her fifteenth birthday.

"The Connelly twins were so good to my girl," Gladys added, looking toward the door where the Burnses had exited. "When all the other kids stopped coming by the house, the twins still visited. Celia even tried to heal her, but the cancer was determined to take her. Even magic couldn't help."

"So Eva Grace's mother was a healer, too?"

The older woman nodded. "She had the sweetest, kindest soul." Gladys sighed. "We all nearly grieved ourselves into the grave when she was killed. I knew how Delia felt, but I was too wrapped in my own grief to help her. I just don't know how Sarah carried on."

"I guess she had to think about raising Eva Grace."

Gladys clucked. "Oh, my, now that was a shock when Celia came home pregnant. She had been out west at some fancy school. She never even told Sarah she was expecting. Just came home, big as a barn, and delivered Eva Grace at the same time Brenna was born."

"Kind of amazing. Twins having almost twins."

"But Celia was never the same after that," Gladys continued. "And then she died, like a young Connelly witch always does."

The words hung in the air.

Gladys's eyes filled with tears. "I hope that doesn't happen this time, Jake. But I'm afraid." She blinked. "You know it's not over."

"No, it's not," Jake said as he patted the older woman's arm. Fear twisted his gut.

There must be something he could do to protect his witch and her family.

His witch.

Oh my God, he thought. What in the hell was he doing?

Chapter 22

At Jake's cabin, Brenna pulled her SUV to a stop. His cruiser wasn't around, so she pulled over to the side. Hot summer air closed in as soon as she shut off the engine. Even here in the tall trees, the heat was oppressive on this Friday evening. Since Tuesday, the days had been steaming and the nights unnaturally warm. The weather seemed ripe for a thunderstorm, but no clouds appeared and no moisture fell.

"I'll fix that," Brenna murmured.

She got out and raised her arms to summon the wind. A breeze responded, but it was like heat radiating from a fire, a wave of heavy, smothering air. She cursed in frustration, then closed her eyes and cleared her mind. Still no cooling rain came.

Brenna kicked at the dry grass beside Jake's driveway. Just as the town's ghosts weren't responding to Fiona, the elements were not cooperating with Brenna. Last night, after arguing with Sarah, she tried to call up a storm to rattle the windows of the home place. All she got for her efforts was some distant heat lightning.

She left Sarah's house this afternoon. She just couldn't stay there and wait for the next terrible thing to happen. The coven needed to be doing anything they could to find a way around the curse. If there was a traitor in their midst, Sarah should ferret her out. They should be making sure no demon remained to make mischief in town. Instead, they did nothing.

Brenna wanted answers. Her grandmother wouldn't act. The rest of the coven wouldn't move against Sarah. So how could Brenna stay at the home place another minute?

She thought about going to Eva Grace or Fiona and asking to stay, but she didn't want to put her sister or cousin between her and Sarah. Brenna also knew she needed to stay close to Connelly land, that her strength was needed more than ever in the coven. Coming to Jake's was a natural solution.

Feeling it was natural to turn to a man for help was alien to Brenna. At least to the person she used to be, but every time she tried to distance herself from Jake, something made her come back. He felt like her only ally.

A sexy ally who preferred to be alone.

What was he going to say when she asked to stay?

Trying not to worry too much about that, Brenna looked around. She liked that Jake had cleared as few trees as possible. His lawn was a small patch of grass with bushes and shrubs of various sizes and heights growing near the house and the edge of the woods. She recognized strawberry bushes and oakleaf hydrangea, plants she had seen in Aunt Frances's garden. Perhaps she could get some work done on the illustrations for the children's book while she was here. The events of the past week had preoccupied her when she should have been working.

She got out her sketchpad, and then walked around to the small back porch where the shadows were deepening. It was hot, but peaceful. No wonder Jake loved it out here. She let the quiet soothe her frazzled brain as her pencil flew over the page. She drew the pointy-tipped leaves of a strawberry bush with a yellow-green flower drooping in the heat. Beneath the plant, the book's small caterpillar hero slept in the shade.

Brenna was absorbed in her drawing until she heard a noise overhead. She looked up as her now-familiar owl came to rest on the branch of a tree nearby. "My, but you're out early again today," she said.

The bird rotated his pale face, as if looking over his shoulder.

Brenna chuckled. "Are you expecting someone?"

The owl turned his head back to her and hissed.

"I know. It doesn't seem very smart to leave home now that I've done it," Brenna said as she stood and walked toward the tree. "But I felt like I had to do something. Sarah and I were arguing several times a day. I was miserable. She was miserable. Leaving seemed like the best choice."

The owl screeched.

"Well, you don't have to get nasty." Brenna turned at the crunch of tires on gravel. Jake was home.

She looked back up. The owl blinked his knowing eyes. "Could you at least tell me where I can go if Jake won't let me stay here?"

Once again the owl screeched.

"Brenna?" Jake called from the side yard. She stepped around the corner.

They both looked up as the owl flew away.

"I'm here for dinner," Brenna lied. "I thought you might have something wonderful in that freezer of yours."

He held up a brown sack Brenna knew was from the diner. Her stomach growled at the delicious aroma. "Is that meatloaf?"

"Lucky for you I got a double order," Jake said as he unlocked the back door. He waited for her to go inside and followed her. In the kitchen, he got out two plates and put them on the table with silverware while she unpacked the food. He grabbed two soft drinks out of the refrigerator, and they sat down.

Brenna ate mashed potatoes, gravy and savory meat, smiling in pleasure. "That's good. I was starving."

Jake regarded her with a frown. "There's something really wrong, isn't there?"

Brenna ate some meatloaf before responding. "I need a place to stay."

"What's wrong with your place at Sarah's?"

Brenna ate the last of her potatoes and licked the fork. "I sort of ran away from home."

"Teenagers run away, Brenna. Grownups leave. I know. I've dealt with a few of both situations. What's up?"

"I just needed some space, and I thought I'd see if I could stay here a few days until I find an apartment."

He was silent and looked reluctant.

Brenna never really thought he would turn her down. "I'll be working on my sketches for the book and studying Inez's journals for more on the Woman in White. It's just a temporary plan, Jake. I'm not moving in for good."

That suggestion seemed to jar him. He got up and opened the refrigerator to get out a beer. "I'm not sure about this, Brenna. You've got family all over town."

"My family is not happy with me right now."

He shifted from foot to foot and took a long sip of the beer.

Brenna felt her face flame. "Okay, so I won't stay." Feeling rejected and humiliated, she got up from the table and took her plate to the sink. She couldn't look at Jake.

She rinsed her plate and silverware. "Thanks for dinner. I'll call you—"

"Brenna." She looked up and into his troubled gray-blue eyes. He stepped close and lifted a hand to her cheek. "You can stay."

"No, you're not comfortable with me here—"

"Stop it," he said, cutting her off by pressing a gentle kiss on her lips. He stepped back, his fingers threading through her hair. "You're upset. You don't need to be alone. Stay here."

She relaxed against him, enjoying the feel of his hard muscles as her arms closed around him. "There could be some benefits to this." She lifted her lips to his again. "You might enjoy them."

He put his hand up to stop her. "I think we should sleep in separate rooms, keep this on a roommate basis."

She blinked in surprise. "Roommate?"

"Neither of us wants to get confused here, do we? This isn't serious. You're not moving in with me."

She thought he made that a little too clear. His reluctance was enough to crush a girl's ego, but he was right. She had established the boundaries of this relationship, the same as she always did with males. Just for fun. Just temporary. No doubt it was the situation she was facing with her family curse and the intensity of the last two weeks that made her feel so connected to Jake, so different than she had felt about other males.

So she smiled into his eyes and pushed aside her disappointment in his response to her. "I understand what you're saying, Jake. I'm just staying with you for a day or two. I'm going to look in town tomorrow for a rental."

Was it her imagination, or did he start to protest?

When he said nothing, however, Brenna said, "I guess I should go get some of my things out of the car."

"I'll help."

"I'll get it…roomie," she responded, keeping her tone light as she headed for the front door. "I'll let you finish cleaning up the kitchen."

Outside, she retrieved a few essentials from her SUV. She was stacking her small bag on the handle of her rolling suitcase when she heard an angry yowl in the woods. Frowning, she peered into the twilight. A plaintive meow sounded from nearby, and a gray cat materialized from the shadows.

"Tasmin?"

The cat yowled again.

"How did you get here?" Brenna crouched to stroke her. "You came all the way from Sarah's? Was it a scary walk all the way through the woods?"

Tasmin sat down and gave Brenna a look of feline superiority. She wasn't one to be frightened by a simple walk through the forest.

"All right, so you're very brave," Brenna murmured, "but you got yourself dirty." She picked small sticks and burrs out of the cat's thick gray and white fur. "All because you couldn't keep away from me. Interesting that you knew exactly where I was headed."

The cat meowed and bumped her head against Brenna's leg.

"I guess this makes it official. I've got a familiar." She picked Tasmin up and hugged her until she purred loudly. "Now all we have to do is convince the tiger you should stay here, too."

She turned back to the car to pull out a shopping bag full of shoes, piled her bags together and dragged them across the yard. When she walked in the front door, the cat squeezed around her and jumped on the couch.

"What the hell is that?" Jake asked as he came out of the kitchen.

Brenna laughed. "I'd think a tiger would recognize one of his own."

"In no universe is that animal one of my own. Tigers are majestic and heroic. Domestic cats are…small."

Tasmin jumped down to sniff Jake. After she finished getting his scent, she sat down and began licking a paw.

"Obviously she appreciates your grandeur," Brenna said as she pulled her bags over the threshold.

Jake frowned at her but walked over and took the bags down the hall. Tasmin followed him. With a laugh, Brenna fell in behind them.

The guest bedroom, painted off white, had nothing on the walls. There was a small chest of drawers, a cedar chest and a bed with a brown bedspread that made Brenna think of piles of dead autumn leaves.

"Your decor is flawless," she said. "Thanks again,

Jake."

"You're welcome. And beggars can't be choosers."

He set her suitcase on a cedar chest at the end of the bed and watched as she emptied the shopping bag of shoes into the closet floor. She sensed his disapproval of her disorganization. From what she had seen of his house, Jake was very tidy.

"Have you thought about how your parents feel in all of this?"

Brenna was surprised.

Tasmin looked up at Jake as though the man had lost his mind.

"My parents? What the hell do my parents have to do with anything?"

He looked uncomfortable. "They came to see me today." He told her what her parents asked him to do.

Brenna felt a spike of anger. "They had no right to ask you to talk to me about anything. They're not a part of my life."

"That's not true."

"So now you're best buddies with Delia and Aiden?" Brenna snapped. "That's just wonderful."

"Don't get angry with me," he shot back. "They came to me, but their argument made a lot of sense. Is it helpful for you to be arguing with Sarah like you are? Does it protect anyone for you to leave home?"

He was verbalizing the questions Brenna had been asking herself since she packed her car. Tasmin studied him as if she agreed, then looked at Brenna and flipped her tail.

"Oh, shut up," Brenna told the cat. She glared at Jake. "You expect me to believe my parents give a rat's ass about what happens to me? *My* mother?" Brenna snorted.

"You've got a legitimate gripe about Aiden and Delia not being picture-perfect parents," Jake continued. "But right now, when their daughters need them most, they're here. That's not the worst thing, Brenna. Not by a long shot."

"Maybe this wouldn't be happening if they came home before now."

"They're not the only ones who left town. You were gone for three years."

Her anger heated, the air stirred, and the window shot up with a bang. Jake flinched. Tasman looked at her in disapproval. Brenna knew she still needed to work on not letting her emotions spill over in magic. Once upon a time, she had better control.

She took a deep breath. "Comparing my leaving to my parents going away is low, shifter. You didn't grow up here. You found your haven after traveling around the world. What was here for me?"

"Your life, your family."

"My parents were halfway around the world in a cave in Ireland or Scotland or England. But I'm supposed to stay here?"

"Other than your parents, all of the people who care about you were right here," he insisted, not backing down. "You and your mother are more alike than you think. You just have different priorities and ideas about what is important."

"What's more important than raising your children? What's more important than nursing a child through chicken pox or a bout of stomach flu? What's more important than helping a young girl become a responsible adult?"

"People often do things to their children they think they will never do."

They said nothing to each other as Tasmin gave them both a dismissive look and left the room.

Jake shrugged and looked past her. "That really is an ugly bedspread. I got it at a thrift shop."

Brenna went to him, blocking his view. He had hinted at this before, and now she wanted to know. "What do you mean? What happened with your family?"

He left the room, and she followed him to the kitchen. Pulling another beer out of the refrigerator, he offered it to her, but she shook her head. He twisted the cap off and drank half of it in one gulp.

"Do you know anything about the mating habits of tigers?" he asked.

"Not really."

He finished his beer and tossed the bottle in the recycle bin with such force it broke. Brenna jumped, but she didn't move. "When tigers mate, the male has almost nothing to do with raising the cubs. They are completely dependent on their mother for sustenance, protection and education. She sometimes even eats their feces so predators can't scent them. Tiger mothers are amazing."

"I thought you said your mother wasn't a shifter?"

"No, she was human, but she was fiercely protective. She had to be, because my father didn't care. He liked to pretend I didn't exist."

When he reached to open the refrigerator again, Brenna stopped him. She had never seen Jake drink more than two beers. He was upset and needed to talk, not get drunk. She gestured toward the dining table.

"Sit down and tell me about your parents. Please."

They sat across from each other, and he continued without looking at her. "When my mother got pregnant, she got a job as a secretary. My dad kept working shows when he could. He came in and out of our lives."

Jake looked so bleak that Brenna wanted to hug him. "What about the times when he was gone?"

His smile was immediate. "My mom was great. She may have had to work every day, but she made sure I was cared for. As soon as she got home from work, she gave me her complete attention. I helped her clean and take care of the house. She's the one who taught me to cook. She had infinite patience. Life was great except when Dad came home. For some reason Mother always let him come back."

"She loved him?"

"Pitied him, I think," Jake said, frowning. "He hated what he was and what he did. She tried to get him out of show business, to work at something else. He was born in a circus. Performing was all he knew."

"So he didn't help you learn about shifting?"

"He told me it was a curse," Jake retorted. "Mother helped me accept who I was. For someone who didn't shift, she had an amazing understanding of what it feels like to have wildness inside. I think that's why my father hooked up with her in the first place, because her gentleness was a complement to his wild side. That's the crazy thing. I think he really needed her."

"She sounds like a wonderful person." Brenna couldn't imagine being that close to her mother. Her relationship with Delia had always been conflicted. It broke her heart to think of Jake losing someone he loved so much.

"My dad ended up in a show with an abusive trainer. The man sometimes forgot that Dad was a human part of the time. He used the whip once too often. One night after a show, Dad went berserk and killed him."

"Oh, Jake, that's horrible," Brenna murmured, reaching for his hand. "What happened? Did the police get him?"

"Dad came straight to the house. He asked Mother to help him. For the first time ever, she said he had to leave. They argued. Mother sent me to my room, and they were out on the patio, but I heard them. I heard what he said. Dad left, and Mother was outside, crying. I didn't know what to do." He stopped, emotion clogging his throat and affecting his voice.

Brenna squeezed his hand. "What could you have done?"

Jake shook his head. "But I should have done something. I should have known…"

"Known what?"

"What he would do." Jake's hands closed into fist. "I've never told anyone about this."

Brenna waited, sitting very still, saying nothing.

"I looked up just as Dad came over the fence. He was on her, ripping her to pieces before I could do anything."

Horror clenched Brenna's gut. Jake had watched his father kill his mother.

He stood and slammed his fist on the counter. "I should have helped her."

She got up and put her arms around his waist, laying her cheek against his back. "He would have killed you, too."

"That might have been for the best," he said.

"No, that's not true. What happened to your father?"

Jake turned to face Brenna again and held up a hand when she reached out to him. "Dad ran away, and I never saw him again. The attack was tagged a freak accident. As if a tiger could escape from a club on the strip, make it all the way to our house to kill my mom, then disappear into the desert." His laughter was bitter. "I lied to the police. I told them what they wanted to hear."

"So you don't really know that your father is dead?"

"He's dead to me," Jake retorted. "And he taught me a lesson about how quickly love can turn into hate and death. It's not something I'm going to forget." Defiance rang in his tone, as if he was challenging Brenna to argue with him.

She kept herself calm. "Jake, you should think of the other shifters you've known. People like Garth's family. They live peaceful, good lives and never hurt anyone. Your father had a problem, obviously—"

"Yes, and I am his son. I have the same problem."

Brenna struggled to find words of comfort and understanding. Before she could say anything, Jake distanced himself from her, looking wary.

"You should know this. I'm a murderer, too. Just like my father."

She thought she knew where he was going. "You were in the army. You had a duty—"

"I wasn't following orders." He grasped her shoulders and shook her. "I killed a man for no reason other than I wanted him dead."

Chapter 23

When Brenna didn't move, Jake tried to turn around.

She grabbed his hand. "Don't pull away from me."

"I just assumed you wouldn't want to be so close to a killer."

"Don't assume things about me, Jake. You'll end up having to live with disappointment."

"You're not shocked?"

Her gaze was steady. "Look at my family. Every generation someone dies, and yet we've gone on for over two hundred years, just supplying victims. We're murderers as well."

"It's not the same."

"How? Tell me what happened, and I'll judge for myself."

He had already told her enough secrets. These were stories he never planned to share with anyone. Why did he feel this responsibility to tell Brenna? He didn't owe her anything. What startled him, however, was the yearning he felt to tell her. Was this a spell? What was this witch doing to him?

She rubbed her thumb across the top of his hand. "I know things about you, things you probably won't let yourself know. So tell me about this murder."

He moved away. "What kind of things would you know about me? I'm a shifter, an animal. Tigers aren't exactly tabby cats."

"But most tigers don't have a human half either," she said.

"I didn't kill him as a tiger." He didn't look at her. The guilt was too much.

If she was surprised, she hid it well. Her deep green eyes remained calm. "Here's what I know. There's nothing evil in you. You wouldn't kill just for the thrill. Your sense of justice is too strong. There has to be a reason—personal safety, protection of others, no other choice."

Jake drew in a deep breath. She needed to know the truth about him. So he began. "It was my last tour in Afghanistan. I was exhausted. My men and I went out night after night, looking for insurgents and for leads on hidden Taliban members. It was grueling and frustrating work. We never knew what we would find. We relied on local citizens for our information."

Jake put his hands in his pockets. "It's a familiar story. We got a tip from a regular informant and went out to do a house-to-house search."

"How did you do it, day after day? I can't imagine."

"You do what you have to do. You know that. You would do almost anything to end this curse."

Brenna agreed and waited for him to continue.

"We posted men outside and were getting ready to search another house. It was a husband and wife, and one of the men was holding them in the front room while the others moved to the back. I won't give you the details except to say two of my men started into a bedroom and were both killed. By the time we'd taken out the insurgents, two more of my men were wounded.

One will never walk again."

Brenna took his hand.

The memories crowded into Jake's head, a horror he could never forget. "I had to write letters to the families of my men. I don't know why, but those two deaths were the hardest I've ever faced. I felt useless and incompetent. Even though we'd dealt with this informant several times in the past, I felt I should have seen something, known something was different."

"You weren't a telepath," Brenna pointed out. "How could you expect to know what another man was thinking? You said yourself you'd done this many, many times. He had been a reliable source, correct? Why would you expect this time to be different?"

"All I know is I couldn't get over it. Every time I closed my eyes, I saw those two guys opening the door and the lower half of their bodies being blown away." He squeezed her hand and looked straight ahead as he continued, "One night, I left the camp and went to where I knew the informant lived. I thought about confronting him as a tiger, mainly just to scare the shit out of him, but then I decided I wanted to talk to him."

The scene played out in Jake's mind. The black night. The hot, dry air. The smell of rotting garbage. A baby crying in the distance. Though humanity pressed in on every side, Jake had melted through the shadows, silent and deadly. Part of that skill was training. Part was his nature.

He told Brenna, "I snuck in the back and found the informant passed out drunk on his bed. I tied him down and threw a glass of water in his face. He started blubbering as soon as he came to, telling me he was forced to send my men into an ambush, claiming the

Taliban were holding his wife and son, and he had no choice."

He turned to look at her, his gaze level and direct.

"But I knew he didn't have a wife or a kid. He'd turned in his own brother and killed a female cousin for falling in love with an English soldier. I finally knew what had been bothering me for months—this guy was a rat bastard. I always suspected he would betray us someday. Even after what had happened, he would do it again. If not to us, to some other unit or someone else. He was filth."

When he paused, Brenna didn't look away. She took his other hand.

His voice flat and emotionless, Jake said, "So I slit his throat and left him where he was."

This time Brenna couldn't hide her shock. She sucked in a breath and closed her eyes. The muscles in her throat worked as she swallowed.

Jake looked at her, a dull ache in his gut. He cared about her reaction. He cared much more than he should.

Brenna steadied herself and looked at him again. "What happened next?"

"There was a cursory investigation, but they assumed he was murdered by the insurgents he betrayed by giving us information. I finished my tour two months later and left the army. Garth begged me to come to work for him in New Mourne."

Jake shook his head. "I almost didn't come. I had murdered a man in cold blood. After all those years in the military, I thought I learned to control the wild impulses inside me. I thought I wasn't like my father, but maybe I'm worse. It wasn't my tiger who killed that man. It was me."

Brenna's reaction was instant. "You're a good man, Jake, and what you've just told me doesn't change my view of that."

"I'm a dangerous man with a beast inside me."

"And you deal with that," she said firmly. She moved and put her arms around him. "I saw you fight off the demon that night in the diner. A bad man with a beast inside who craves killing would have welcomed the excuse to break free. You fought it."

"You don't understand."

"I understand that you can't wall yourself off from the world. All of us with special abilities live with challenges. We have impulses. Do you know how many times I've thought about infesting The Enclave with rats and snakes? In my opinion, that would get rid of a big problem in this town."

Thinking back to his meeting with the BOC, Jake had to agree. Yet he thought her argument proved his point about himself. "I didn't resist the impulse, Brenna. I killed that man. I didn't even have to shift to do it."

"And you live with the awful regret. You wouldn't do it again."

"I'm glad you're so sure." Jake shook his head. "I cared so much about those men I served with that I gave into my impulse." Which was why he should avoid deep entanglements.

"Yes," Brenna said her voice firm. "You gave in and you killed him as a man. As an angry, frustrated, heartbroken man. The story proves that you're not only shifter, but you're human." She studied him for a moment. "Which side of yourself are you more afraid of?"

The question shocked Jake. Damn this female. She forced him to examine himself much too closely.

Brenna pressed, “If you had to choose, which one would it be? Would you be a man with all those tendencies that men have to do right and wrong? Or would you run free as a tiger, a hunter and killer?”

The answer, Jake realized was simple. As a tiger, he couldn’t be with Brenna. And that’s what he wanted. More than anything, he wanted to be with this difficult, complicated and demanding woman. He held back the confession of love that started to tumble from him. Though his feelings had deepened, Brenna made it clear from the start that she wasn’t looking for a commitment.

“The good thing,” she continued, lifting a hand to his cheek. “Is that you don’t have to choose. You just have to try to be the person and the shifter you want to be. Someone that chooses right more often than not. Luckily, you’re in New Mourne. Because of that deal my family made, it’s easier here for supers to live at peace.”

“Most of the time.”

“That’s what we have to fix.”

Jake stood still, enjoying the warmth of her body against his. He needed to pull away, to return to the person who didn’t want a future with any woman.

She held him closer. “You’re a good man, Jake, and you did what you did to save lives.”

He turned and tightened his embrace. “God, Brenna, you almost make me believe I could live a normal life.”

He started the kiss with a delicate touch, but quickly took it deeper.

Jake found himself wanting to purr like Tasmin because of the warmth of her touch. He remembered her caressing his tiger in the forest. She'd been gentle and trusting, believing he'd never hurt her, just like she did now.

Even though he'd told her he'd killed another human being. Not in the throes of his beast, but as a *man*.

He did move away from her this time, pulling his hand out of hers. He couldn't do it. He couldn't trust and let go. He had to remember what happened before, what happened to his mother. He knew the tiger couldn't be trusted, and he couldn't give it a chance to prove him wrong. He had to keep Brenna at a distance.

"Want me to make us some coffee?" she asked.

"Sure." Anything to give him a chance to think, to regain his balance.

She began opening cabinet doors, and he realized she didn't know her way around his kitchen.

"Sorry, I'll make it."

The simple task helped him regain his calm. He got out a tin of coffee, a filter and filled the coffeemaker.

She set two mugs on the counter. "You take cream, right?"

"Or milk."

When he said milk, Tasmin came in from the living room and meowed.

"Oops, somebody else is hungry. Got anything a cat likes to eat?" Brenna asked.

"Are you kidding?"

"My bad." She laughed at his expression.

It was a husky, throaty laugh that made him want to kiss her until her toes curled.

He took a can of tuna out of the pantry, peeled off the top and dumped it into a bowl, leaving the oil on it. Tasmin dived into it like she hadn't eaten in days.

"Guess you do know what cats like," Brenna said.

How was it she made things feel so right in *his* home? That wasn't possible. They should be arguing about something or fighting over the issues with her family. How was it she looked so sexy and had that understanding smile?

His mouth came down on hers. Like sipping an elixir of the gods, he couldn't get enough. He wanted to drink from her until he was sated. Jake gave a brief thought to ripping her clothes off and pushing her down on the small kitchen table, but then he wondered why he'd want to deprive himself of enjoying the scent and texture of her skin.

He buried his face in her neck and drew in deeply. She smelled of the earth, a natural sweetness different from any other woman he had known. He wanted to lie against her like this for hours. He kissed the tender base of her neck and her body melted against his. Surrender from a strong woman was incredibly sexy.

She was warm and soft, extremely soft. The texture of her skin was like silk. He ran a finger down her cleavage, then over her breasts, barely touching her nipples. Her breath became shaky, and he marveled at the sensitivity of her response.

With an easy movement, he slipped his arm under her legs and lifted her. He carried her through the house to his big bed and set her gently onto the thick, soft comforter.

She began unbuttoning his shirt, and he stopped her so he could slip her thin tank top over her head. Her bra was a tiny piece of lace that easily popped open when he touched the hook. He cupped both of her breasts and dipped his head to kiss first one nipple and then the other. Brenna clenched her fingers in his hair and moaned.

"Take me now," she whispered. Her body moved against his with urgency.

"No." His strong arms stilled her. Slowly, his gaze steady on hers, he removed her jeans and his own clothes.

When she would have moved above him, he eased her back on the bed. His touch between her legs was light at first, then more insistent, and she climaxed quickly. Her body was still trembling as he took her up again. Only then did he slip inside her. Brenna shuddered as he pumped into her with slow and steady movements.

His tiger surged to life inside him. Even as he embraced the wild instinct to mate, he felt his human side. This was lovemaking, he realized, not sex. With Brenna, his dual natures were balanced. He felt whole.

Maybe it was because she wasn't quite human either. As they moved closer to the edge, her skin began to glow and her magic shimmered around them. He knew he wouldn't tell her, but he loved her.

He was lost. Utterly lost to a witch who was cursed.

After their passion was spent and Brenna slept beside Jake, he lay for a long time. Did his new feelings for Brenna make a difference in who and what he was?

She believed he wasn't a killer, but she was wrong. He knew would kill again.

To save her.

Chapter 24

While Brenna showered the next morning, Jake prepared a hearty breakfast.

She sighed as she surveyed the spread of scrambled eggs with cheese, thick slices of ham and Texas toast on the dining room table. "I can't keep eating like this. I'm going to be big as a barrel."

"A nicely curved barrel." Jake squeezed her bottom before he handed her a mug of steaming coffee.

Brenna laughed at his teasing tone. Last night had been very intense. She had worried how things would be between them this morning. She was used to ducking out of relationships at the first hint of emotional attachment. With Jake, she wanted to stay right here. The feeling was unfamiliar, and she would just as soon not confront it right now.

They ate breakfast together with companionable conversation.

Jake pushed back from the table as Brenna started on her second cup of coffee. "I need to go into the office and check on a few things."

"I'm going to do some sketching," Brenna said, "but I'll clean up while you take your shower."

She was sitting on the back steps with her sketchpad when Jake came out. She grinned. "There is definitely something about a man in a uniform."

They both ducked as the huge barn owl came out

of the sky and dipped toward the stoop.

“What the hell?” Jake muttered. “What’s he doing here?” When the bird swooped again, Jake took a protective stance and told Brenna to get back in the house.

“I think he’s trying to tell us something.” She pushed Jake out of the way and went out in the yard under the circling bird. “Come here, fella. What’s wrong?”

The bird stopped and perched on the tree limb where he’d been yesterday. Brenna almost expected the owl to speak. Instead, it took off again.

Jake and Brenna followed. The bird landed on top of Brenna’s car.

“He wants us to go somewhere,” Brenna said, starting forward.

Jake held her back. “Should we follow him? What if it’s the demon leading you into a trick?”

The owl hissed and unfurled his mighty wings. Brenna stepped in front of Jake in anticipation of an attack. The bird lifted again and flew around the yard, his strident call filling the air.

“We need to follow him,” Brenna said. “Let me go get my keys.”

“We’ll take my cruiser,” Jake insisted.

Because that was quicker, Brenna agreed.

They got in the cruiser and took off, following the bird. The owl flew a true course.

“He’s headed to Sarah’s,” Jake said.

Soon after, they turned into the driveway at the home place, but the bird didn’t stop at the house. It continued down the dirt road toward the barn just beyond Marcus and Sarah’s workshop. While Jake parked, the owl slipped into a ragged hole high on the wooden structure.

Jake headed for the barn door. Emotions and memories swamped Brenna, and she hesitated.

"What's wrong?" Jake swung the door open and looked at her.

"We played here sometimes as kids, but mostly we stayed away. Aunt Celia's things are stored in the loft, and Sarah didn't like us messing with them. Because we knew that, we were drawn to this place, of course, but it felt creepy to me. Kind of sad, too."

"You want me to go look for the bird without you?" Jake started into the shadowy interior.

Brenna shook off her trepidation and followed him inside. A rush of cold air enveloped them. The wind was as cold as January despite it being a hot June morning. The breeze carried the scent of clover, a smell Brenna remembered from those times when she, Fiona and Eva Grace had defied Sarah's instructions and looked through Aunt Celia's things.

She didn't need Fiona's sight to know this place was haunted.

"Aunt Celia?" she murmured as her eyes adjusted to the dim light. "Are you here?"

Jake paused at her side. "You feel something, too?"

Nodding, Brenna led the way to the ladder and up to the loft. The platform was crowded with boxes, old furniture and other items stored there through the years.

"Bless you," Jake said after Brenna sneezed.

She turned to the right, studying Celia's French provincial bed and dresser, once white trimmed in gold, but now gray from a heavy coating of dust. Boxes were stacked nearby, also covered in grime. She remembered rummaging through those, looking at Celia's clothes, turning the pages of college textbooks, sifting through photographs of her mother and her aunt with their high school friends. Fred Williams had been in some of those pictures, Brenna remembered. Odd how Fred had been part of their circle, but by all accounts Aunt Celia had been as accepting of others as her daughter was now.

Eva Grace had never been able to stay in the loft more than a few minutes when they went through her mother's things. Fiona had tried from a young age to get Aunt Celia to speak to her or to appear. Brenna wondered what her sister would see if she were with them now. Was their aunt standing here, watching Brenna? Had she sent the owl to lead her here? At that thought, the air warmed, and Brenna felt the emptiness of the barn. Celia was gone.

A scratching noise drew her attention to the left. From a dark corner, the luminous eyes of the bird stared at her.

Putting out his hand to stop Brenna, Jake moved carefully toward the owl. "Hey, buddy, got something you want to show us?"

The owl hissed but didn't move as Jake advanced on him.

Sticks, hay and other debris made a nest. Beside it was a cardboard box, top mangled and sides breaking with rot.

Placing his body between Brenna and the bird, Jake motioned her over. Brenna moved gingerly through rotting boxes past an old chair whose stuffing poked out of gaping holes. She looked down at the box closest to the nest and gasped.

"Shadows of Biddy Early," Brenna said.

"Who's Biddy Early?"

"The first Irish witch." Brenna dropped to her knees beside the box and reached for the yellowing pages on top. She looked up at Jake. "It's pages from *The Connelly Book of Magic*. I recognize the parchment and the handwriting. What the hell are they doing up here?"

The owl hissed one more time and then moved deftly out the hole in the barn to take flight.

Jake cleared debris away from the shuttered loft door and threw it open to the light, and then helped Brenna pull the box out where they could better see its contents.

"The wood of this box is rotten," he said as it disintegrated under his touch. "How is it that those pages are still whole?"

Brenna gave him a sidelong glance. "Magic, of course. Even bugs are smart enough to leave it alone." She began reading. "Looks like these are from the 1800s just before the Civil War."

He sifted through the box, separating pages of the book from other debris and handing them to her to read. She became excited as the words began to make sense. "It was another dark time here in the county. Lots of unexplained events, even murders and a rash of arson."

"The same pattern we're going through."

"This continued for several months as the Yankee Army marched through the state." She read on as Jake retrieved more pages. "The witches gathered at the Connelly house for several days, working on spells and potions, trying to find a way to bring some peace and calmness to the area."

"Did they find a solution?"

The blood rushed from Brenna's head as she found the answer. She stood, swaying on her feet.

"Brenna?" Jake stepped forward. "What's wrong?"

Instead of answering, Brenna clutched the papers to her chest. She turned and climbed down the ladder before Jake could stop her.

"What is it?" he demanded, catching her arm before she could get out of the barn. "What did you find?"

She didn't want to tell. The solution her ancestors had reached shamed her. How could they have done this?

"Brenna." Jake took hold of her shoulders. "Tell me."

After all he had shared with her, there was no reason to hold back, she realized. "They decided the only way out was suicide."

"What?"

"One of the Connelly witches offered herself freely to the Woman in White. It worked. All the trouble in town subsided."

"No, let me see that." Jake took the papers and scanned them with a frown.

"See that?" Brenna pointed to the stark, underlined words in the middle of the page. "'The only way' is what they wrote. This was the only way."

Tears blurring her eyes, Brenna started to the cruiser. "I have to go. Get me out of here."

Jake caught her elbow and spun her around. "No," he said, his voice fierce. "Don't you even think about it, Brenna. Don't you dare."

Chapter 25

Brenna spent the rest of the morning trying to convince Jake she wouldn't take any impetuous action based on the new pages from *The Connelly Book of Magic*. The information had shaken her, but she wasn't ready to sacrifice herself as her ancestor had. She did want to talk about this with her family, so she asked for a coven meeting that evening.

Jake was called in just after noon. With the woods so dry, fires had broken out in a couple of remote areas of the county. He had to coordinate traffic detours.

Relieved to be alone, Brenna read the entire new section of the family book. In black and white, the words outlined what to do to protect New Mourne's humans and "other-natured residents." She had no doubt earlier history sections would reveal a similar pattern. However, why take this step? Instead of giving up, why not devote every day to finding the cause of the unrest and death that came once a generation?

She wanted answers tonight.

Everyone was in the dining room when she got back to the home place around seven. Coven members occupied their usual places, save for Doris, who was still in the hospital. Brenna noted her mother was there, but her father was not. That was fine with her. This was strictly coven business.

From the doorway to the kitchen, Marcus gave

Brenna a questioning look. His expression was grim, and his being upset filled her with sadness. Marcus had always been her champion. When he turned and walked out the back door, she took a deep breath to fortify herself and faced her family.

Sarah sat with arms folded, her face as solemn as her husband's. "You called this meeting, Brenna. What do you want?"

Brenna spread the newly discovered pages in front of her and related the morning's discovery in the barn.

Though Sarah's cheeks reddened, she didn't move.

Maggie began to cry. Eva Grace soothed her.

Lauren rolled her eyes. "Stop being so dramatic, Brenna, and tell us what you want us to know."

"Every time the Woman in White comes for her tribute, there's turmoil and unexplained events in New Mourne," Brenna said. "So it begs the question: why was it such a surprise to the elder generation that we've had all this upheaval in town?"

"Because of the Remember-Not spell," Frances said.

The ease of the explanation made Brenna groan. Why did the elders make them work so hard to understand their actions?

Sarah glared at her older sister. "We've never discussed the particulars of that spell with the younger ones."

Frances huffed. "Well, we have to now. They should know in case they need it, too."

"You deliberately chose to forget every time this happened?" Delia said, looking confused.

"Of course not," Sarah said. "I didn't forget my sister or Celia or the way the Woman took them. All of you have known about the curse since you were old enough to understand it. We never hid our history from each other. All we did with the spell was dull the pain a little."

"I told you it was collective amnesia," Brenna said to Fiona and Eva Grace. She could feel her temper stirring, however, as she turned back to Sarah and Frances. "What gave you the right to decide what should and shouldn't be remembered?"

"We protect this town." Sarah's gaze was hard as iron on Brenna's. "That's what our ancestors sacrificed for—so we would have power. Without that sacrifice, none of us would be witches. New Mourne would be just another place in the mountains instead of a haven."

"If the town survived at all," Frances added. "It could have crumbled under the usual human prejudices and petty disagreements unless we intervened from time to time. Witches would have been driven out, faeries burned, druids destroyed, and shifters and weres killed."

Delia frowned. "All that is true, but it seems to me that our family may have stretched the rules of the craft by dulling memories. We learn from the past."

"What if you wiped out some important memory?" Fiona's question surprised Brenna. It wasn't often her sister spoke up against Sarah.

"We were careful," Frances said.

"We did what we had to." Sarah glared at each witch, challenging them to disagree. "Besides, why would anyone want to remember unpleasantness?"

"Or why would we want every outsider to take away all of our secrets?" Frances added. "How do you think they killed all those European witches during the

Inquisition? Too many people knew their rituals and meeting places."

Sarah nodded. "We have always used Remember-Not spells as a precaution for those that stumble into our world without becoming a part of us."

"Of course," Delia said, "I know visitors to New Mourne don't leave with our secrets. I just didn't know that spell was used on us or our friends and allies."

"We choose the humans and supers who grow close to us with great care." Frances looked at Brenna. "Your sheriff wouldn't know as much as he does if he wasn't trustworthy."

"The only reason I allowed Fiona to embark on her Internet enterprise is because it focuses on her work as a medium," Sarah added. "There's no mention of the coven or Connelly secrets. That would not be safe."

"Yet our parents traveled the globe, lecturing about magic and becoming well-known as experts in the history and mythology of witchcraft," Brenna pointed out. "Wasn't that a breach of the coven's secrets?"

Color flooded Delia's cheeks. "I never betrayed this coven. Neither has your father. My interest in the roots of magic and mysticism came from who I am. Your father was already interested when we met. Our family's stories and history inspired him more. Our goal is simple: protect the craft. What Frances says about the Inquisition is all too true and could be repeated today. Too many humans want to destroy what they don't understand."

"Think of Fred Williams and his wife," Frances said, shuddering. "They both grew up here, and they know just enough to be dangerous. We can't let them know everything. They would wipe out all supers if they could. They're our enemies, and we treat them as such."

Brenna felt her anger drain. She also knew her history. In college, the subject of many of her required papers was witchcraft history. In Scotland, almost five thousand witches were executed during the sixteenth and seventeenth centuries. She supposed she understood why the coven might have chosen the Remember-Not spell to cope with what they faced.

However, it didn't solve her family's problems. She looked down at the pages in front of her again. "What I found today indicates the coven went even further than wiping out memories. During the Civil War, they decided they had to do something to appease the Woman in White, to end the discord in a town already wracked by war. One of the young witches chose death to save the town. She sacrificed herself."

Delia gasped. On either side of her, Aunt Diane and Aunt Estelle turned pale and took her hands.

Maggie's tears began again. "My husband and daughter need me. It can't be me."

"I'm not sacrificing anything," Lauren said. "I have too much to live for."

"It should be me," Eva Grace said quietly. "It's no secret that I'm the choice."

Fiona said, "As the youngest, maybe it's supposed to me. Maybe that's why I've always been connected to the dead."

"No," Delia said, reaching toward her daughter. "Not you, dear."

Fiona turned back to Brenna. "How did they choose the sacrifice? Was it a lottery?"

"She chose herself," Brenna explained. "Her

husband died in the war, her baby daughter passed as an infant. She was a very strong witch according to the family member who wrote the history, but they said she felt she had less to live for than the other coven members her age. She offered herself, and the Woman took her over the falls. The work of the demon stopped. The town and the rest of the family went on with their lives."

A hush fell around the table. There was no sound, even from Maggie.

"I think our sister Rose did the same," Frances murmured, looking troubled. "She was in love with that young criminal who ran moonshine and died on Bear Mountain."

"But you and Doris said you weren't sure of her feelings for him," Sarah protested.

Looking regretful, Frances said, "That's what we chose to say, and we started to believe it, probably because of the Remember-Not spell. She blamed our curse and his association with her for his death. In the end, she may have decided to join him."

Every head in the room swiveled back to Eva Grace. Brenna could sense them all wondering if Eva Grace would meet the same fate.

Eva Grace looked at Delia. "What about my mother? Did she want to die?"

Delia looked uncommonly fragile as she rubbed her forehead. "Your mother was depressed," she admitted. "She wouldn't tell anyone, even me, who your father was. None of us knew she was expecting a child. Her letters from Arizona were filled with school and work for six months, but she was pregnant before she left for school."

"But she may have chosen to die?" Eva Grace pressed. "You think it could be possible?"

Delia looked miserable. "I'm not sure. That day is so fuzzy in my mind."

"Because of the Remember-Not spell?" Brenna suggested, unable to keep the sharpness out of her tone.

Sarah and Frances glared at her.

"We won't let anyone sacrifice herself," Frances said.

"So we continue to wait?" Brenna asked.

"The trouble in town has ebbed since our encounter with the demon Tuesday night," Sarah pointed out.

"But he was back the next day, trying to get to Inez," Brenna reminded her.

"You prevented that," Sarah retorted. "Your power was strong enough to hold him."

Brenna was aghast. Her grandmother was choosing to ignore the obvious. "That was just a pause in the action. The demon is out there right now gathering strength. He and the Woman are sucking the very life out of the ground with this heat wave."

"It's been hot here before," Frances snapped.

"I can't believe all of you can't feel what's coming." Brenna saw fear and doubt in the faces around the table. "The Woman and the demon are hoping we'll give up, that one of us will decide to give in and make the ultimate sacrifice. The Woman doesn't take. She makes us give in."

"I have to get home to my family," Maggie said, standing abruptly. "I have to be with my daughter, to protect her." She darted out the door without a backward glance.

Diane stood as well, saying she should get to the

hospital and make sure Doris was okay. Her mouth set in grim lines, Lauren went with her.

Brenna was distressed to see them go. The coven was crumbling.

Maggie's vacated chair rocked forward, and then fell back with a crash to the floor. The papers on the table stirred.

"Stop it." Fiona addressed an unseen presence. "We don't need you playing your tricks."

The spirit ignored her command and knocked over the salt-and-pepper shakers on the table. A puff of dust blew out of the fireplace and a foul odor tinged the air.

"It's one of the ghosts I see all the time," Fiona said. "She's very upset."

"Even our ghosts are frightened," Brenna told the remaining coven members. "We need a plan of action."

Knowing the elders had no new possibilities to offer, Brenna reluctantly turned to her mother. "Any suggestions?"

"Your father and I have been studying the magic book," Delia said. "We're thinking we should try another spell at the falls in an attempt to draw out the Woman."

Brenna was uncertain. "By confronting her, wouldn't we be giving her what she wants?"

"Not necessarily." Eva Grace sat forward, clearly intrigued as she turned to Delia. "Are you thinking of making a show of force?"

"Go on the offensive?" Fiona also seemed interested.

"The demon was weak with Inez the other day," Delia pointed out. "Perhaps the Woman is weak, too. As Brenna said, it feels as if evil is gathering on the horizon like a storm. If we confront them now, we'll be prepared and armed. Our magic might be enough."

Doubt flooded Brenna. If they summoned this evil, would it infect all of them? Might someone impulsively sacrifice herself? She wished she could believe Eva Grace would not make that decision. Lauren and Maggie weren't likely to give up anything, much less their lives, but they weren't as strong in character. Fiona, on the other hand, was young and impulsive. The instinct to protect them all filled Brenna.

"We need to think this through," she offered to the group. "Didn't we go down this path the other night at the store?"

"Do you have another idea?" Delia asked. "We're open to suggestions if you do."

Brenna had nothing to offer, so she focused on her mother's idea. It could work. "We'd need everyone in the coven there. Even Doris."

"She's coming home tomorrow," Sarah said. "She'll stay here with us for a while."

"But is she up to magic?" Frances looked concerned.

"I'll help her," Eva Grace said. "And Diane will be there with her."

Fiona nodded to the two other empty chairs at the table. "What about Maggie and Lauren?"

"Leave them to me." Sarah said firmly. "They'll be there."

"We'll do it Monday night," Delia suggested. "That gives Doris more time to grow stronger."

And gives the demon and the Woman more time to do the same.

Brenna swallowed the impulse to point that out to

her relatives who were now so enthusiastic. Negativity would throw a pall over them all, and she had no viable alternative.

The back door slammed open, and Marcus's shout rang out. "Help me. The workshop is on fire."

Chapter 26

The fire spewed from the ground.

Jake ran down the driveway of the Connelly home place as geysers of flame rose from the earth and sprayed down on Marcus and Sarah's workshop. He'd heard the radio call as he was headed home, so he was first on scene. He had imagined the worst.

Brenna injured. Brenna needing his help.

But she was with the other Connelly witches, their hands linked, their voices rising in magical cadence over the roar of the blaze. No doubt they were trying to quell the fiery tentacles attacking their property.

He spied Marcus working a garden hose along with Dr. Burns as they tried to keep the fire from leaping to the nearby barn. The stream of water was inadequate. Jake heard sirens in the distance and knew the fire department was on the way, but what could their county volunteers do against this supernatural blast of heat?

"What the hell is this?" he shouted to the two men.

"Fire came up through the floor," Marcus shouted back. "Aiden and I barely got out before the whole place was engulfed."

"We need more water on it." Jake looked around for more hoses. Maybe they could run some from the kitchen somehow?

"It's demon fire," Dr. Burns yelled and jerked his head toward the witches. "They have to fight it."

A ball of light rose from the coven's circle and into the smoke. The fire pulsed.

Like a living thing, Jake thought, the flames reared and bucked against the magical force that sought to smother it.

He looked to the witches and saw Eva Grace's pale features, Fiona's fear and Brenna's determination. Only her mother's fierce concentration matched hers. Sarah, Frances and Estelle swayed with them and looked unsteady.

Again and again, they chanted, "Demon fire loosed from hell. Return to your maker, go back to your well. From this hell fire, set us free. As we will, so mote it be."

Like a giant damper, the ball of magic dropped over the fire. A brief plume of sparks rose from the ground and then disappeared.

The witches continued to chant. The ground belched one last blast of smoke. The smell of sulfur saturated the air.

The fire truck arrived, and Jake helped them maneuver down the drive to the workshop. The firemen quickly shot the contents of their tank into the building, and if anyone thought it odd that the Connellys had managed to almost put out the fire with one garden hose, they said nothing.

The coven broke the circle, and Jake urged everyone back away from the smoke of the smoldering workshop.

After a few steps, Sarah fell to her knees, sobbing. "Our work, Marcus!" she cried. "All of our work, gone."

Marcus knelt beside his wife and gathered her in

his arms. Tears streamed down his face. "That doesn't matter, Sarah darling. It doesn't matter. We're okay, that's what matters."

"But for how long?" she sobbed into his shoulder. "What will happen next?"

Fiona, Estelle and Eva Grace clutched each other while Dr. Burns drew Delia into his embrace.

Brenna backed away from them, one hand pressed to her mouth, looking horrified.

In two strides, Jake had her in his arms.

A tremor went through her body. Her voice choked with tears. "It took their art, what they pour themselves into. How could this happen right here? How could we allow it?"

Jake drew his hand through her hair. What could he say to soothe her?

"This has to end," she whispered. "I have to end it."

Alarmed, Jake drew back. "What do you mean?"

She looked glassy-eyed from shock, as if she didn't really see him.

"You can't do it alone," he told her, thinking of the information she had discovered that morning. "Brenna, you're not thinking—"

"Of course not," she said, her gaze sharpening. "But the coven has a plan."

"What—"

"I'll tell you later." Leaving Jake, she strode to Sarah and Marcus and dropped to her knees beside them. Silently, she wrapped her arms around them. Sarah turned into her granddaughter's arms, and they wept together.

In another hour, the firemen were gone. Marcus

had packed Sarah off to their room. Estelle and Frances left. Fiona and Eva Grace were staying the night, and Jake convinced Brenna she should come back to his house.

She said little on the drive home, but Jake sensed the wheels spinning in her head. Good, she was moving past this latest calamity and thinking about a solution.

Tasmin greeted her witch with a cry that sounded like relief to Jake. The cat padded off to supervise Brenna's shower. Jake pulled homemade soup from the freezer, nuked it to thaw and then put it in a pot on the stove. Brenna needed sustenance after the heartbreak and loss of this evening.

"Sit down and eat while I clean up," he told her when she emerged from her bath, hollow-eyed and pale.

The hearty soup restored Brenna's energy, and she sat with Jake as he ate a couple of bowls, as well. As they cleaned up, he asked about the coven meeting.

Brenna shrugged. "It was the usual. Tears from Maggie, frustration from all of us, more discussion."

"Did you do something?"

She looked confused.

"Did the fire start after a spell?"

Her laugh was mirthless. "Not at all. The fire came from the demon and the Woman. They're trying to destroy us, wear us all down." Brenna told him about the Remember-Not spell and Delia's plan for Monday night.

He was silent, wondering if any of it was wise. He was surprised Brenna was going along with the plan, especially since it came from her mother.

"I don't know what to do." She laid her head wearily on one hand. "It seems hopeless."

"You need some rest," Jake said. "You'll think better in the morning."

He got up and made his usual check of doors and windows. Brenna remained at the kitchen table. She studied him with an expression he didn't quite understand.

"What is it?"

"Look at you. Locking us in against demons and the like."

"Nothing is getting to you while you're with me."

"After tonight, I have to wonder if anywhere is safe."

"Come to bed." He put out his hand and drew her through the house to the bedroom, shutting off lights behind them.

He expected her to fall asleep immediately. Instead, she spooned against his naked body and kissed his neck. He turned to face her. "You have to sleep. You're exhausted."

"But I need you." The word was almost a plea. One he couldn't resist. "Especially tonight." She pressed her body to his, warm and fragrant, inviting.

There was only so much a male could resist, Jake thought as he framed her face with his hands. "Okay. I'm all yours."

Chapter 27

Brenna kissed his forehead, cheeks, lips and his chin. Her lips moved to both nipples and lingered there awhile. When he was breathless and fully aroused, she moved down to take him in her mouth.

Her magic was strong inside tonight. She felt it whirl through her body and infuse her lovemaking with an intensity she'd never felt before. According to the control Jake was exerting to hold his own release in check, he was experiencing the enhanced feelings, too.

Brenna knew the enhancement to her magic was her love for Jake. It moved through her into him like the slow spill of hot caramel.

That knowledge added heat to her climax, a thunder in her blood that was new for Brenna. Wave after wave of emotion collided inside her as Jake joined her in sweet release.

They lay entwined for a moment as pulses returned to normal. Then Brenna sent Jake to sleep with a wisp of magic. "I love you," she whispered before slipping out of bed.

There was work to be done, and she must do it.

He was deep into sleep by the time she dressed. She headed for the front door hoping her magic would keep him asleep till morning.

But she still had to get past her familiar. Tasmin barred the front door, spitting and arching her back.

Brenna stooped to stroke her. "You'll stay here with Jake and help him for me," she told the cat. "You know what I'm doing is the only way."

Tasmin's meow was disagreement in the most direct way possible. She even swiped out with her paws, raising a scratch on the back of Brenna's hand.

"Well, that's mean." With a flick of her wrist, Brenna moved the cat to the other side of the room and slipped out the door. Tasmin might well find another way to follow her, so she added a stay spell. She only hoped the cat's yowling didn't wake Jake.

As she stepped onto the front porch, the owl swooped down at her with a horrific screech that almost sent her back inside.

"Stop it," she ordered, but the owl followed her to her car, hissing like an ill-tempered snake.

Her journey to Mulligan Falls was accompanied by the disgruntled owl's swoops and bloodcurdling screams. Brenna counted it a minor miracle that she made it to the start of the back-end trail. As she parked the car and studied the angry bird sitting on the hood of the SUV, it dawned on her that the owl might have a reason to stop her. It was possible he wanted to protect her from what she was going to do.

And at last, she understood the owl's message…and the messenger.

"Garth. You couldn't leave with unfinished business, could you?"

The owl hissed and spread his wings, the noise rising to an ominous level that echoed through the woods.

"There's only one way to stop this. The fire tonight helped me see. The Woman in White demands tribute, and I'm prepared to save my family and this town with my life if necessary."

The bright yellow eyes of the bird burned with anger as he screamed at her again.

Brenna extended her hand and chanted, "The trees will soothe, the breeze will calm. The air contains a resting balm. My work is done as now you sleep. As I will, so mote it be."

The owl's big eyes blinked several times and then he tucked his wings in tightly before going to sleep.

Brenna opened the back door of the SUV and took out the royal blue cloak she sometimes wore for rituals.

Following the trail to Mulligan Falls, she was soon in the clearing. Water roared over the rocks, although if this heat wave continued without rain, the falls might dry up. The night air was hot and heavy as Brenna took off her clothes, donned the elegant cloak, and walked straight to the spot where Garth had died.

She raised her arms and summoned the wind. She was relieved when the trees rustled with a soft breeze that grew until the branches whipped and lashed.

"I'm a Connelly witch and proud of it. What you see is what you get, the witch with the strongest power of my generation. You want one of our clan. Here I am, a sacrifice offered freely for the Woman in White. Come and take me."

The wind continued its fury as Brenna waited. She wasn't afraid exactly, just not sure if this was the right thing to do. Could she stand here and die? She closed her eyes and forced herself to concentrate on the members of her family, her coven. She thought of the fire's devastation at the home place tonight. Reasons to die willingly. Then she thought of Jake. He was a reason to live happily. She knew this was the right thing, but she couldn't make herself enjoy giving up.

The seconds turned to minutes as Brenna waited in the clearing. The wind died and with it her hope of being the sacrifice the family needed. She was on the edge of despair when a female voice called her name.

Taking a deep breath, Brenna turned and faced the figure that melted into the clearing from the shadows. The Woman in White stepped toward her. Unlike the day that Garth died, the spirit looked more flesh and blood tonight. It was as if she lived and breathed.

The Woman began to laugh. Then her image wavered, shimmered and changed. Instead of the ghost she sought, Brenna found herself facing the old fae Willow.

She cackled at Brenna's startled cry.

Willow glided forward. "Did you really think it would be this easy to give yourself up?"

The faerie looked younger tonight. Her sequined dress sparkled in the moonlight and had a soft, magical glow.

Regaining her composure, Brenna asked, "Is there a way I'm supposed to do this? Why are you here and trying to trick me?"

"Gave you a good scare, didn't I?" Willow seemed pleased with herself.

Brenna knew the fae often used glamour illusions to mask their true nature, but she had never witnessed it before. A descendant of the House of Eiluned, the ancient Willow would be a master of illusions by now. No doubt her talent helped her marry and bury sixteen husbands and present herself as a younger version of herself to each succeeding generation in the community.

Brenna pulled her cloak around herself. “What are you hoping to gain by doing this to me?”

“I’m hoping this might help you come to your senses.”

“I just want this madness to stop.”

“Stupid girl,” Willow repeated with disdain. “You won’t end it just by calling to the evil spirits.”

“That’s what others of our family have done.”

“But they were willing, and you are not. The evil wants your surrender.”

Muttering an oath, Brenna turned back to the night and called, “I surrender. Take me.”

Once more Willow laughed. “You come here from your lover’s bed, glowing from his touch and expect them to believe you are willing to die? It doesn’t work that way.”

“But I will. I’ll do what I must for my family.”

“Then go with your strengths,” Willow said. “What you have at your fingertips is an unlimited resource if used properly.”

“I’m not feeling especially strong.”

“Don’t be modest. Even as you were offering yourself to the Woman in White, you were fighting. You couldn’t give in easily. You want her to show herself and face you.”

Brenna knew that was true.

“That’s your strength, and it’s why you’re wanted so badly by the truly evil.”

“Are you talking about the Woman or the demon that always comes with her? Aren’t both evil?”

“All I’m sure of is that they both want something from this place, and only the Connellys can stop them.”

Willow placed her hands on her hips. An unexpected smile came to her lips. "Look for help in an unlikely place. Your enemies, perhaps."

"Enemies?" Brenna frowned. "What do you mean?"

"Give it some thought, stupid girl."

"Don't the fae ever give a straightforward answer?" Brenna felt her anger rise. "What do you want me to do?"

Willow laughed, put a finger on her nose and disappeared just as a tiger leaped forward.

With a ferocious roar and flash of white fur, Jake filled the space Willow emptied. His fangs gleamed in the moonlight. One paw swung through the air, claws extended and caught in the edge of Brenna's cloak.

Brenna gasped and moved back as the garment was ripped from her. Naked, she cowered against a tree trunk before remembering this was Jake.

"Stop," she ordered the tiger. "It's me. It's Brenna, Jake. You don't want to hurt me."

The animal reared back, another roar tearing from deep inside. Then he fell, white fur retreating, muscles, bones and sinew twisting and turning as he morphed from tiger to human. When his change was complete, Jake was crouched, panting, looking up at Brenna with pain in his silver gray eyes that stung her heart.

Knowing his worst fear of hurting someone he cared about had almost just come true, Brenna reached out. "Jake, are you okay? What are you doing here?"

His movements slow, he straightened. "You were gone," he said. "I knew you were in danger, and I had to get here as fast as I could. I knew you were going to offer yourself. I had to stop you, but instead I—"

Hands going to his head, he turned away. Though thoroughly human now, he roared again. An agonizing cry.

The sound cut through Brenna. She had to make him see what was obvious to her. “You didn’t hurt me, Jake. You stopped yourself. It was just a mistake. You would never hurt me.”

He looked over his shoulder at her, and then in a shift of his body that was like lightning, he was a tiger again. He ran away without looking back, a pale blur in the dark woods.

Brenna wondered if he was running from her or from himself. She hadn’t wanted them to end this way. She hoped he would sleep and wake up with the memory of their lovemaking before he realized she was gone. Jake was good and decent, incapable of hurting her, but now he might never believe that.

Lifting her voice to the demon and the Woman, she screamed. “Why? Why did you do this?”

In a gust of wind, she thought she heard laughter.

Chapter 28

Jake ran for miles. Ran until his tiger's muscles trembled and his human cried out for rest. In the end he came home, dreading yet hoping Brenna would be there waiting. He was both disappointed and relieved when she wasn't. Despite her protests, maybe now she knew what he truly was. He fell into bed and slept, glad that his tired body could shut down his troubled mind.

The ringing of his cell phone woke him.

The display told him it was Fred Williams. He groaned but answered, greeted by Fred's wife's voice. "You need to get out to our house. Brenna Connelly is here trying to bewitch my husband."

She hung up without waiting for a reply. Jake redialed, but she didn't answer.

"Damn," he muttered, still groggy from sleep. "What's Brenna doing?"

At the foot of his bed, Tasmin meowed. Her green eyes were unblinking and clear, so like Brenna's. And faintly condemning, Jake imagined. How was he going to look at Brenna?

He turned away, tempted to call in for another deputy to go to Fred's house, but he couldn't do it. Fred and Ginny would make even more trouble for Brenna and her family if he didn't handle it himself.

He took a quick shower, not bothering to shave, pulled on a fresh uniform and headed for the door

Fred and Ginny lived just outside The Enclave in a big house with elaborate landscaping and a white-columned, broad front porch. Brenna's car was in the drive. Fred was on the front porch in pajamas and a white robe, his face spotted with shaving soap. Ginny was pointing a gun at Brenna.

A gun.

Blood running cold, Jake sounded his cruiser's siren one time to get everyone's attention. He was out of his cruiser almost before it stopped and advanced with caution toward the porch. Before seven o'clock in the morning, and Ginny was already in full Sunday dress with makeup and hair rigidly in place. Her face was red and her lips a thin line.

"Mrs. Williams, put the gun down and step out so I can see your hands."

The blonde tossed her head. "Oh, for goodness' sake. It's my husband's pellet gun. It wouldn't do more than sting. I'm just trying to get this evil trollop off my doorstep." She tossed the gun to the side.

Jake flinched at the metallic sound of the pistol hitting the heavy stone floor of the porch.

Fred reached out to placate his wife. "Calm down, Ginny. Brenna just wants to talk to me. If you'll be quiet, we can get through this and let her be on her way."

Jake stepped up on the porch between the two women, turning to Brenna. He was relieved she didn't back away from him. "Want to tell me what this is about?"

"I came to Fred for help," Brenna replied. "I thought he could provide some insight into our family's situation. Maybe his father dealt with the demon before."

Ginny drew her shoulders back. "I knew it. You witches brought a demon into our community again, just like you did the winter your aunt died."

"If you would stop screaming for a minute, maybe you'd understand that I came to your husband sincerely, looking to see if he could help us stop this madness," Brenna shot back at her.

"He's not going to do anything with you witches," Ginny spat out. "Not again."

Again? Jake sent a startled look toward Fred.

"Ginny, stop this." Fred reached for her again.

She slapped his hand away. "You're not helping this witch, Fred Williams. Not her or any other." She whirled back to Brenna. "We've dealt with your kind before, and we know what to do. I'd sooner sell my soul to the devil than deal with Connelly witches."

"Ginny." Though he only spoke her name, this time Fred put real command in his voice. "You need to stop. Brenna's out of the house, and the sheriff's here. Go back inside."

"You'll not be consorting with a witch, Fred Williams. You have a weakness for these people. It has hurt you before, and it will hurt you again."

"I heard you, Ginny," Fred replied through gritted teeth. "Now go on in and let me handle this."

Ginny disappeared into the house, slamming the heavy front door, her footsteps stomping away. Other doors banged inside.

Jake picked up the gun and frowned. He was sure the pellets would be more painful than Ginny thought. He handed it to Fred. "Maybe you should put this in a place where she can't get to it."

Fred dropped the pistol in the pocket of his terrycloth robe. “I’m sorry about that,” he said to Brenna. “Ginny has a tendency to overreact.”

“Forget her. You’ve got to help us, Fred,” Brenna said. “Willow Scanlan told me to look to our enemies for help.”

“Willow?” Fred shook his head. “We’re not your enemies, Brenna.”

“I never really thought of you that way until last night,” she agreed. “One of my aunts said something about enemies, then Willow said the same. At any rate, I need your help. It’s the curse, the same one that took my Aunt Celia. It’s coming again.”

“I thought as much given our recent troubles,” Fred said. “In fact, I tried to help Celia before she was taken. She wouldn’t listen.”

“So you don’t know anything to help us?” Brenna’s shoulders slumped.

“The only way to fight evil is with God.”

“Then help us fight,” Brenna said. “Gather with us and help.”

The horror on Fred’s face was almost comical. Jake had a sudden vision of him and Ginny in the clearing, joining hands with the coven.

“I don’t think I can do that,” Fred told Brenna.

“Can’t you just accept our differences in beliefs, and come help us?”

He shook his head. “There’s only one way, Brenna.”

“Your way?” Brenna’s tone was flat.

“I will pray to God that this evil leaves your family alone,” Fred replied. “But until you accept him, that’s all I can do. I believe God will always come down on the side of right."

Brenna turned and stalked down the steps onto the sidewalk toward her car.

Fred met Jake's eyes, his tone apologetic. "I'm sorry Ginny called you, but Brenna pushed her way into the house. Ginny felt threatened, although I knew that was nonsense. Brenna wasn't going to hurt either of us." He put out his hand. "It's good to know you'll come when we call."

Jake reluctantly shook the minister's hand. What he wanted to do was arrest Ginny, but Fred would round up the BOC and rain holy hell down on Jake's head. This wasn't the time, he thought as he went down the steps.

Besides, he still had to face Brenna. She stood beside her car, tapping her foot. He had blocked her in with his cruiser so she couldn't leave. That was good because he wanted to have a little chat. "Did you put a spell on me last night?"

She had the grace to blush. "Just a little one."

"Why?"

"I just wanted to be sure you'd sleep."

"While you offered yourself to the Woman in White?"

"I had to."

"What the hell is wrong with you?"

"Not a damn thing," she said angrily. "I'm trying to help my family."

"You frightened me out of my mind. I woke up and somehow I knew exactly what you were doing. I had to stop you. I was afraid I was too late. I saw you in the clearing, looking agitated, talking to someone. I feared the worst. Rage took hold of me, and I—" Jake had to steady himself against her car at the memory. "You know the rest."

She took a deep breath. "I know you believe you would have hurt me. But you wouldn't. I'm not sure what it will take for you to trust that you're not careless or mean like your father, but you're not."

He had known she would say this. It wasn't easy for Brenna to acknowledge that she was wrong. Last night, when Willow disappeared, he had almost hurt Brenna. He didn't want to argue about this.

"Why were you with Willow anyway? I thought you were arguing."

Brenna told him how the Woman and the demon had not responded to her and the faerie's explanation.

Jake was relieved. No matter what, he didn't believe Brenna would ever offer herself willingly to the spirits. So perhaps they would never take her.

"Willow said I needed to look for help from our enemies."

"So you thought of Fred."

He looked up at the minister's house. A movement caught his attention. Ginny was standing on the second-floor veranda. She was too far away for him to see her face, but her shoulders were rigid, her head flung back. It wasn't difficult to imagine she was still simmering with fury.

"Ginny could have shot you," Jake told Brenna. "She might not have killed you, but it would have hurt. Apparently she really hates the Connellys."

"I don't care about that." Brenna jerked open her car door. "I can't stand this much longer. I have to do something, even if it's the dangerous spell my mother is suggesting."

As he watched the play of emotions on her face, a vague memory came to Jake. Brenna leaning in, her breath caressing his face as she said, "I love you."

He drew back, the memory stilling his hands. She had told him she loved him last night. Just before she left him, she professed her love. She planned to die, even though she loved him. What a mess all of this was. Both he and Brenna were paying a price for pursuing their relationship.

He backed away from her, hands upheld. "All right. You won't listen to me about anything, so I'm done talking. You figure out your curse, and then we'll…" He swallowed the words. Then they would what?

He went to his cruiser and pulled out of the drive. Morning sun, hot already, glimmered on his rearview mirror as he watched Brenna turn her SUV in the opposite direction. He resisted the urge to follow her, to make sure she didn't go back to Mulligan Falls to offer herself again to the evil spirit who waited to claim a Connelly witch. He didn't know what to do.

Brenna wanted to die for her family.

Even though she loved him.

And he loved her.

Jake had never allowed himself to feel this deeply for any woman. He would have laid down his life for the men in his unit. He thought he would grieve for Garth for the rest of his life, but this need to protect Brenna, to save her, was the strongest emotion he had allowed himself to feel since his father ripped his mother out of his world.

Loving Brenna confirmed the most important lesson Jake had learned from his parents. Love wasn't enough. His mother's love had not saved his father. His father's love for her had not been enough to thwart his wild nature.

So what hope did Jake have of saving Brenna?

Not much. Not much at all.

Chapter 29

Brenna restrained herself from throwing one of Cousin Inez's journals across the bedroom.

After returning to the cabin from her encounter with the Williamses and Jake, she had called the home place to see how everyone was doing after the fire. Eva Grace said Sarah and Marcus were still asleep, and all was calm.

So Brenna caught a couple hours of fitful sleep. Waking still tired and groggy, she made coffee, ate cereal and settled back into bed with the journals, history books and her notes from *The Connelly Book of Magic*. Somewhere in all of this, there had to be answers, but where?

Brenna blew out an exhausted breath as Tasmin leapt onto the bed. The cat had avoided her for most of the morning, miffed over being left behind and sealed inside with magic last night.

Tasmin meowed as she settled on her haunches and regarded Brenna.

"I told you I was sorry. It couldn't be helped." Brenna reached out to stroke the cat, hoping their strong magical connection might spark a new thought about her problems. Her last feline familiar had often helped her focus on a spell, summon the elements or work through a dilemma. Scientists claimed that stroking an animal slowed the heart rate, reduced blood pressure and lowered stress.

Both her witch and human sides could use some calming right now.

"Who can help us?" she asked the cat.

Tasmin rolled on her back, paws outstretched, begging for a belly rub.

Brenna complied and let her thoughts wander. Who in New Mourne might know something to aid the coven? Brenna began to consider other supernaturals in town.

The most numerous were the werewolves. Maybe it wouldn't hurt to talk to the pack leaders. The druid county commissioner and his family were more secretive than the fae, so they might even refuse to discuss the current troubles with her. They also hadn't been in town more than a century, so they probably knew little about the Connelly curse.

The kitchen witch who ran the bakery had moved here in the last decade. Eva Grace had mentioned to Brenna a wizard who moved into the old farmhouse several miles up from Sarah's, but he was reputed to be cold and indifferent, preferring not to mix with his neighbors.

The shifters were an unorganized group that included some kinfolk of Garth's and loners like Jake. After discovering the peace and acceptance of New Mourne, they kept to themselves. She doubted they had anything to offer.

Among the humans, though, were those who married supers or coexisted with them for varying periods of time, some going back as far as the first group of settlers. There were farmers and owners of small businesses attracted to the county when Sarah opened the farm as a commune in the late 1960s. All would no doubt do what they could for the Connellys, but *what* could they do? Perhaps only be victimized further by the demon who had already affected them and their families.

Then there was The Enclave. The community built as an escape from Atlanta's metropolitan sprawl would be eager to put a stop to anything that ruffled their existence, but most of them belonged in Fred Williams' camp of ultra-conservatives. They were more likely to march onto the Connelly home place with pitchforks and burning torches, or their fully licensed automatic rifles, than come to the coven's aid.

The secret, Brenna still believed, lay in knowing more about the Woman in White. She turned to the history book with the sketch of the missionary's daughter who jumped to her death at Mulligan Falls. There was no doubt in Brenna's mind that this was the Woman in White. Had she truly been in love with a Native American? Did she go mad? Was that why her spirit still roamed here? Why had powerful witches bowed to her will for so long?

Brenna went back to Inez's journals. She finally located one that went into detail on some of the early Native Americans who lived in Mourne County. Inez had copied the "Ten Indian Commandments" in one of the books. Brenna was surprised how much those edicts matched the "Thirteen Goals Witches Strive to Achieve."

The Indian Commandments said, "Treat the Earth and all that dwell thereon with respect." The Witches' Goals included, "Attune with the cycles of the earth." Indians were encouraged to "remain close to the Great

Spirit," while witches were told to "honor the goddess and the god."

"We're so much alike," Brenna said as Tasmin carefully cleaned a paw. "But I guess that's what New Mourne is based on, isn't it? It's a place where people of different species, lifestyles, religions, beliefs—no matter what—are accepted and live in harmony. I guess Fred Williams and his group just missed that memo."

The look Tasmin gave her mistress told Brenna that nothing in New Mourne was harmonious right now.

"All right, I agree with you, but I believe we do work toward that harmony."

The cat placed her chin on her paws and shut her eyes.

Brenna closed the book and lay back on her pillows. No matter how much she read or learned about the Woman in White, it still came down to one point. There would be more suffering for family and friends until a Connelly died. Seeing the workshop burn last night had solidified what must be done. Brenna knew she had to offer herself again, this time with no hesitation.

Tasmin lifted her head and looked toward the window. Her ears pricked forward, and then she streaked off the bed. Not two seconds later, Brenna heard Jake's vehicle in the driveway.

Brenna sat up, wondering if it would be awkward between them now.

In a few moments, Jake entered the bedroom. He stood in the doorway and looked at her. "Are you okay?"

She nodded, feeling uncomfortable. "Sure."

"That's good."

"How are things in town?"

"Disturbing."

"Did something else happen?" Brenna asked, concerned. What if her attempt to sacrifice herself last night had stirred up trouble again?

"Downtown is jammed with people," he explained. "Every room in the inn is filled, and we've got day trippers galore in all the shops."

"Did you see someone suspicious?"

"No, but I feel like we're in a cauldron. There's something simmering. Literally about to boil. It's weird how hot it is. I've lived here for three years. The summer is always humid and uncomfortable, but not like now. It feels like the desert did when I was in service. Dry heat—"

"Like a furnace blast," Brenna completed for him.

"Yeah." He met her gaze, and then looked away. An uncomfortable silence settled as they avoided the big questions looming between them.

So Brenna asked, "Do you want me to leave, Jake?"

He hesitated, clearly torn. Then he nodded. "It would be for the best, I think. Don't you?"

Brenna didn't know what the best was, but this was Jake's home and she wasn't about to be here if he didn't want her.

She got up from the bed. "I need to get few things together, then Tasmin and I will leave. After what happened last night to the workshop, I should be with the family. We have to get ready if we're going to cast this spell tomorrow night."

Jake started to say something, and then

reconsidered. "I'll be out back," he told Brenna, but he stopped in the doorway and turned to her. "I've never cared about anyone the way I care about you, Brenna."

"I feel that way about you, too."

He seemed surprised at her admission.

She managed a tremulous smile. "I know. We were just going to be friends with benefits, but that's not working out too well. Not for you either, I think. I always thought when I fell in love it would be after I knew I was safe from the Woman in White. I thought it might be good thing. From your evident misery, you're not too pleased by these feeling, either."

"I never intended to love anyone." Jake leaned against the doorframe. "After what happened to my parents, can you blame me?"

She brushed that away, knowing her reassurances would fall on deaf ears. "And I've got other priorities right now."

"You're going to do something I won't like, aren't you?"

"If you want me to lie, I will." Tears gathered and slid down her cheeks.

Jake stepped back into the room and reached out brush her tears away. "You shouldn't have to die. None of you should have to die. There has to be a way out of this."

Brenna shook her head. "I've believed that, too, until now. At this point, we can only keep trying, but I'm not optimistic about winning." She stroked his cheek. "If it's me that's taken, you won't hurt for long, Jake. The coven will make it better for you."

"No, they won't." He pulled her close again, pressing his face against her neck, his voice choked with emotion. "Even magic couldn't make me forget you. Not ever."

He left then, and she heard his cruiser start up in the drive.

The stillness of the summer afternoon settled around Brenna as she gathered the few clothes she had brought with her. Despite everything, she didn't want to leave. She felt at home here. She understood now that running to Atlanta, the lack of focus in her career and her desertion of the coven were all excuses she used to avoid thoughts of the future.

She always wondered how Eva Grace and Maggie had moved on to making future plans with the curse to deal with. Maggie even had a child, a female child, knowing what the future might hold for her. Eva Grace made wedding plans. Loving Garth gave her hope, but hope wasn't evident in Brenna's life. Maybe it was all those years of hoping her parents would come home only to be disappointed.

Now she had a glimmer of understanding. She closed her eyes, imagining being with Jake five years from now, with children ten years from now, growing old together. She couldn't form the pictures. They just wouldn't come because Brenna couldn't see a future for herself. The present kept invading it.

She couldn't see past offering herself to the Woman in White. No matter what Jake said, she knew what her duty was—to her family, her coven, herself.

Duty called, and she must answer. Now, since she had so much to lose, maybe the Woman would oblige her and take it all away.

Chapter 30

Sweating in the fierce heat of the late afternoon, Jake walked down Main Street. He came to town rather than stay at the house while Brenna moved out.

New Mourne was as crowded as earlier in the day. A line waited outside Mary's Diner. The bakery was closed and had a "Sold out of bread" sign affixed to its front door, but other shops were still open and humming with business. The local snow cone vendor dispensed icy treats as fast as he could make them.

And no wonder, Jake thought as he glared overhead. The sun had bleached the color from the sky. Every flower and leaf within sight drooped. Nothing stirred except cars and people on the sidewalks.

There was no sign of trouble, however, as Jake turned a corner and headed to the back entrance of the courthouse. A man stood on the porch outside the sheriff's department. Legs planted apart, and hands opening and closing at his sides, he stared in Jake's direction.

Jake's hand moved toward his gun, though he didn't touch it.

"There ain't enough room in this town for both of us," the man said with an exaggerated Southern accent. "We're gonna have to shoot it out, sheriff."

"I'd be willing to do that, Dr. McGuire," Jake replied, "but I have hunted with you before, and I know you couldn't hit a pig in a barrel. That puts me at a distinct advantage."

"Well, hell," the man said and walked toward Jake. "Let's hug instead."

The rusty-haired man in rumpled khakis, white shirt and a navy blue blazer had Jake in a strong bear hug when the door to office opened and Gladys stepped out. "Everything okay out here, Jake?" Her eyes were wide as she took in Rodric McGuire, Ph.D. and supernatural investigator from Edinburgh, Scotland.

Jake noted with amusement that his trusty dispatcher was carrying a baseball bat. He also knew she would have used it. He quickly introduced her to Rodric.

His friend's Scottish accent was evident as he greeted the older woman. "So happy to meet you. I'm an old friend of Jake and Garth's."

Jake could see Gladys was as susceptible to Rodric as most females. Jake never quite understood the man's charm. He had a wiry build and was almost as tall as Jake, a bookish sort with his tortoise-shell glasses and an absent-minded air, but when he frequented bars with Jake and Garth, it was Rodric who never went home alone. Jake had often wondered what the true source of Rodric's appeal was.

"What brings you to New Mourne, Dr. McGuire?" Gladys asked.

"Studies of the paranormal. I hear you've had some interesting things going on, and I can't wait to start my own investigation."

Gladys's smile dimmed. "You may find more than you want to."

Jake turned to her in concern. "Has something

happened?”

“No, but there will be.” Gladys glared at the sky in the much the same way Jake had. “I can feel it.”

“Aren’t you supposed to be off tonight?” Jake said to her. She had been pulling double shifts most days since Garth’s death.

“I need to stay,” Gladys said. She nodded to Rodric again. “I hope you have some good luck with your studies, but I also hope we don’t live up to your expectations.” She went back into the office.

Rodric chuckled. “She’s just as you and Garth described her to be.” His expression turned serious as he looked at Jake. “Now tell me what’s happening. I tried to get here sooner, but I had quite a battle with a stubborn ghost in a tavern. Patrons were being driven away in droves, and I had to help the poor family save their business.”

“It was quiet here until last night,” Jake said and told Rodric about the fire that sprouted from the ground.

Rodric’s gaze sharpened when Jake explained that the Woman in White and demon had refused Brenna’s sacrifice. “Interesting that there is a spirit and a demon at work. Are they working together?”

“We assume so.”

“You should know yourself never to make assumptions about the paranormal.” His friend glanced toward Main Street. “It’s a charming town, but even I can tell there’s something wicked in the wind.”

“What wind?” Jake asked. The words were no sooner out of his mouth than a gust of super-heated air chased down the street.

“Very interesting.” Rodric studied the dying leaves

and debris that danced at their feet in the breeze.

Where earlier the sky had been so bright it hurt Jake's eyes, a film now lay over the town. He hoped the heat wave was breaking, but he didn't think it was that innocent or simple.

"I told Brenna's parents you were coming," he told Rodric. "You want to go meet them?"

"Lead the way."

Although he dreaded seeing Brenna, Jake knew that the entire family was gathering at the home place. Doris was coming home from the hospital, and despite the fire last night, the family still planned a welcome home party and celebration for the Summer Solstice. In addition to introducing Rodric to the Burns, Jake wanted to check on everything. The fire on Connelly land signaled a shift in action.

As they drove out of town, Rodric pointed toward the clouds that were lowering over the mountains. "The sun may leave us early." The sky was a strange color, a bilious green that Jake mistrusted.

"I'm very anxious to meet your Connelly women," Rodric continued. "It's incredible that Eva Grace is both a witch and an empath, and that Fiona is also a medium. I've watched some of her webcasts. She has an amazing ability."

"That has been inactive for the last four days. She's heard almost nothing from the town's spirits since the incident at Siren's Call."

Now Rodric looked worried. "That kind of silence is most unusual."

"It's extremely rare around here," Jake said, peering anxiously at the sky as they approached the turn-off to the Connelly's. "It looks like it could storm any minute, but I'm not hearing any thunder."

Lightning was playing over the peaks of the mountains. Bear Mountain and Big Frog were lit up in turn. Towering over them all at almost forty-seven hundred feet was Rabun Bald. According to Native American legend, Rabun was home to a fire-breathing dragon. The continuous stream of lightning gave credence to the name as the clouds glowed red, then yellow over the tall peaks.

"Quite a welcome you've rolled out for me," Rodric commented as they pulled to a stop behind the collection of Connelly cars.

Everyone was present for Doris and the Summer Solstice, including husbands and children. As they made their way across the broad front porch, Jake could see Rodric's eyes begin to glaze as he met the assorted cousins and uncles.

As usual, the Connelly witches were moving from the kitchen to the dining room, loading the sideboard and two other small tables with food. The table was set for the coven, with Doris already seated. The injured witch looked pale but strong, Jake thought as he greeted her and introduced Rodric. She was at last able to talk, albeit in a husky whisper. He didn't see Brenna, but spotted Dr. Burns immediately.

Jake introduced Rodric and the three of them drifted to a corner away from the traffic between kitchen and dining room.

A moment later Lauren sidled up to Rodric and held out a tall, frosted glass. "Have some peach tea." Her green-eyed gaze was avid with interest.

"Umm. Peach?" Rodric took the glass and studied it as if it was evidence of an ancient haunting.

"I think he would prefer a cup of hot tea," Jake said.

"Sugar and lemon, if it's no bother," Rodric added.

Lauren's emerald eyes flashed as she flipped back her hair. "I'll get that for you, Dr. McGuire. I'd be happy to help you with that or anything else."

"Call me Rodric, and you're most kind, Lauren. You live up to everything I've heard about Southern women."

She laughed and walked away to get his tea, her hips swaying.

Jake took the iced tea from his friend and enjoyed the bemused expression on Rodric's face. "I warned you about her," he reminded the Scot before taking a long drink.

Dr. Burns smiled at the interplay, but he brought the conversation back to where they had been heading. "I've heard a good deal about you from colleagues. I just read your study about weather conditions and how they relate to paranormal activity."

"Jake told me about the unusual storm that ushered in these events here in New Mourne."

Brenna's father frowned. "And now we've got this heat. Today we broke all temperature records, and it hasn't rained since Delia and I arrived."

"A storm's brewing now, I think," Jake said. "Clouds gathering over Rabun Bald."

"Strange, given that our storms usually boil up from the west and the Bald is east." Dr. Burns glanced toward the window. The outdoors was now a murky green. He moved off to speak to his wife while Jake finished introductions. Brenna wasn't with the others, and Jake looked around in concern and went into the kitchen.

Getting worried, he was about to search on the back porch when she came down the back stairs and into the kitchen.

He resisted the impulse to kiss her. “How are you doing?”

Her expression was serious. “There’s a storm on the way.”

He didn’t pretend not to understand what she meant. This storm wasn’t about rain, thunder and lightning. “Is it good or bad that you’re all together?”

“I’m not sure.”

Before they could continue, Sarah’s voice rang out from the dining room, calling the group to gather. Jake and Brenna slipped in, and she took her place at the coven’s table. The others in attendance crowded into the room as well.

Sarah looked pale and tired as could be expected after the shock of last evening. She stood tall and proud at the head of the table, however, and lifted a glass of iced tea to her oldest sister. “I’m delighted to say that Doris is, according to her doctor, doing quite well. With help from Eva Grace, she’s healing quickly and feeling better every day. She’ll be staying here with Marcus and me until she has recovered. Welcome home, Doris.”

A chorus of well wishes filled the room as drinks were lifted in salute.

Doris beamed while holding her daughter Diane’s hand. The entire coven clasped hands around the table. Jake felt the buzz of power that sprang to life in the room. Candles on the tables and mantel lit on their own. A shimmer of light drifted down from the ceiling and disappeared. The children giggled in delight.

Sarah glowed, smiling at the circle around her. "We're so grateful that we're all together, my sister witches and our families. We are whole." Her glance lingered on Brenna. "Despite the efforts of evil to burn us out, we are one."

Brenna nodded at her grandmother, and Jake was surprised at the real harmony he felt from them both. Out of the tragedy of last night, a truce had been called between the two.

Either that or Brenna had just given up.

The idea disturbed Jake as Sarah recognized him and Rodric. "We welcome our guests, as well. Now let's all eat, enjoy the bounty of the summer, and celebrate the good life we Connellys have made in New Mourne. May it continue forever."

In moments, the circle was broken, and everyone was moving around the room, filling plates, talking and laughing. Jake watched Brenna go into the hallway, toward the front door.

He followed her. "Aren't you hungry?"

She shook her head, looking sad.

Suspicious, he studied her. "What are you planning?"

"A good question," a voice said from behind.

Jake turned as Delia joined them.

Brenna glared at her mother. "I'm not going to spoil the party."

"The party is the least of my concerns," Delia replied. "You're up to something. I can always tell."

"Always?" Brenna laughed. "You don't know me well enough to know what I'm thinking or feeling or what I might do."

"You're enough like my sister and me to be easy to read." Delia's expression was grave. "Don't tempt evil, Brenna. Don't taunt it. It won't work."

Brenna looked puzzled. "What do you mean?"

Aiden came up beside Delia and put his arm around her shoulders. "Just listen to your mother's advice."

"What exactly is that advice?"

Delia took a deep breath before she spoke. "I've been remembering some details about the day Celia died. The truth is we went to call out the Woman in White. We each had a baby girl. We couldn't imagine losing you or Eva Grace, or dying before we could raise you. Like you, we wanted the curse to end. We were young and foolish and strong witches. We thought being twins made us invincible. We thought we could fight her."

She shook her head, her eyes filling with tears. "We fought, but at the last minute, Celia gave herself up. I think that's what she intended all along." Delia rubbed her forehead. "It's all been coming back to me, but I'm still not sure…"

Brenna looked stricken. "So first the Woman wanted a fight?"

The sudden flare in her eyes troubled Jake. "Your mother just said she's not clear on the details, Brenna. The Remember-Not spell could have clouded her thoughts."

"I think that spell is wearing off," Delia murmured.

Sarah appeared in the hallway. "What's going on out here?"

Jake expected Brenna to lash out at her grandmother in anger. She surprised him by simply shaking her head. "We're just talking." She turned, heading for the front door. "I think I'm going to get a little fresh air before I eat."

Jake followed her, wary of her calmness. From the look on Delia's face, she was equally worried.

Brenna opened the door to reveal Fred Williams on the front porch. His tailored suit was wrinkled and his tie askew. His normally smooth smile was absent, as well.

Jake stepped in front of Brenna. If this was about what happened this morning at Fred's house, Jake didn't want any unpleasantness spilling into the family gathering. "Surprised to see you here, Fred," he said as he held the door open.

The minister looked past Jake. "Sarah, do you mind if I come in for a moment and talk with you?"

"Of course not. Please come in." The coven leader moved forward to welcome the head of the largest Christian organization in the county. She led Fred to the dining room where the crowd of Connellys fell silent at the sight of him.

"Can I get you something?" Sarah asked the minister. "Sweet tea?"

"With lemon, if you've got it," Fred said and sat down in the chair Marcus vacated.

Jake introduced Fred to Rodric and studied the minister. The man was twitchy. Whatever Fred wanted to talk about was making him nervous. Marcus handed Fred a glass of tea. Fred gulped some down and then looked around at the group.

"I'm glad I found you together like this. I've known for many years that it's the Connelly family that keeps New Mourne safe and makes it a haven for anyone. My father explained all of that to me. He didn't agree with all of your practices, and neither do I, but…"

Fred turned to Brenna. "I'm sorry I couldn't say more this morning, but Ginny is not as open-minded."

Jake noticed as Fred sipped his tea again that his hand shook a little. Was he frightened by what he was saying or just frightened about being with the coven?

"We operate on different realms with our religious beliefs," Fred continued, setting his glass aside. "But I have wrestled with what to do about these problems a great deal lately. I've prayed and prayed for a solution or a way I might help."

He stood, hands out, palms up. "I believe something is about to happen, and I've got the prayer warriors in my congregation praying for all of you. I don't want anyone to die. Not any of you." His gaze locked with Delia's. "We go back to school days, you and me. Your sister was always kind to me."

Delia's smile was tremulous. "She was good to everyone."

"And was taken because of that, I think, because evil doesn't want goodness to live in this world." Expression hardening, Fred's gaze skipped to Eva Grace. Abruptly, he turned back to Sarah. "That's it, really. I just wanted you to know that I'm not against you. I can't be with you, but I do want this terrible time to be over for your family, for the tragedies of the past not to be repeated. "

Sarah rose and went to him, taking both his hands in hers. "Thank you, Fred, for your encouragement and your kind thoughts. It was good of you to come by and speak to us personally."

"There is one thing," he said and hesitated. "A

scripture keeps going through my mind. I feel a strong need to share it."

"Of course," Sarah said.

"It comes from the book of Esther, the story of a brave young queen who saved her people by telling her husband, the Persian king, that there was a plot to kill the Jews. Many scholars believe the Book of Esther shouldn't even be in the bible, but for Jewish people, she played a significant role with her willingness to put herself in harm's way to save them all."

He looked at the women around the room and smiled. "I think she might have felt right at home in this gathering of strong women. The verse that keeps coming to me is from chapter eight, verse six: 'For how can I endure to see the evil that shall come unto my people? Or how can I endure to see the destruction of my kindred?'"

The room was quiet as the words sank in. Jake glanced at Brenna. Her expression was thoughtful.

Fred walked to the door and turned for a last goodbye. "I wish I could stop whatever is about to happen. I believe my prayers and those of the faithful in my church will help, but I think only the Connellys have the power to stop this. I truly hope you can."

Thunder rumbled over the house, and Jake's radio squawked, the first call he'd had in days.

Gladys's voice tumbled out, calm and steady, but with a thread of urgency. "Robbery at the County Line Market. All units. Report to County Line Market. Suspect is armed."

Brian pulled out his cell phone and moved toward the door.

Jake glanced at Brenna. "Looks like the crime

draught has broken. Let's hope it's just a regular, run-of-the-mill incident."

"No such luck." Brian looked troubled. "I just spoke to Dispatch to get the details. Several people on cell phones are calling from the market and the suspect is being identified as Commissioner Harry Chambers. They say he has a gun on the owner and a couple of other people. The story is that he's drunk and pulled the gun when they wouldn't sell him beer."

Fred muttered. "That must be a mistake. Harry doesn't even drink."

"Multiple accounts say he does tonight," Brian stated. "Jake, we'd better get up there."

Jake didn't want to leave Brenna. "Are you going to be okay here?"

"Of course."

"But—"

"Go do your job," she murmured. "Take care of yourself, shifter."

He wanted with all of his heart to stay, to be sure that what he suspected wasn't true. He wanted Brenna to follow her mother's advice.

"Jake," Brian said again, "are you coming?"

He gave Brenna one last warning look before he left.

Chapter 31

Watching Jake leave broke Brenna's heart. She didn't want to believe this could be the last time she saw him or her family, but wasn't her path clear? The message in the verse Fred had shared spoke directly to her need to be the sacrifice for her family. Who'd ever think a sign for a witch could come from a fundamentalist preacher and the Bible?

As Jake's cruiser turned out of the driveway and the pleasant noise of family drifted through the evening air, Brenna recalled that verse. "For how can I endure to see the evil that shall come unto my people? Or how can I endure to see the destruction of my kindred?"

According to Fred, Esther willingly put herself in danger to protect those she loved.

Willow's words drifted through her mind. "The help you will need will be found in an unlikely place."

There was no more unlikely place for a witch to seek help than the Holy Bible. Brenna knew there was hope for the future, but only if she was able to change the present.

She went to her car for her cloak, and then around the house and into the woods. A hot wind was rising. Although thunder boomed and lightning danced off the hills and mountains, no rain fell. The heat was almost as intense as during the day. Like air from a blacksmith's bellows, Brenna thought.

The Summer Solstice moon peeked in and out of the clouds that streamed in the darkened sky. Clouds heading west, she noted, opposite the normal flow. Her father and Dr. McGuire had commented on the strangeness of this weather.

But this was no real storm. And it was waiting for Brenna.

She plunged forward, thinking about the coven. She believed her Aunt Celia had brought Fiona a message, and there was a traitor in their midst. The traitor had planted the evil flower, caused Aunt Doris's injury, and allowed the demon in last night to belch fire from the ground. Brenna didn't blame the traitor for her actions. The demon or the Woman in White or perhaps both entities were influencing the choices being made.

The thought of choices made her think of Jake again. Her choice was going to hurt him, and that filled her with regret, but she was certain the incident he was going to at the market was just the beginning. The demon was loose in the county again, wreaking havoc.

"This needs to be finished," she said into the wind. Brenna was going to call the Woman in White again. She was ready to give herself as she had been last night.

She chanted under her breath, gathering her magic around her and building its strength until she reached the clearing at the top of falls.

The familiar circle felt warm and inviting as Brenna stepped inside. She waved her hands across the rim of candles. They lit and the flames stood strong in spite of the wind.

She lifted her hands and began her spell.

"I light these candles in the presence of the gods and goddesses. In the name of the four mighty elements, please gather within this circle and let the power descend to this place. Gather now and hear my plea. As I will, so mote it be."

The magic swirled around her in a twist of light and sound. Brenna basked in the warmth. Last night, her offer of sacrifice had been dulled by defiance. Her mother warned her tonight not to taunt the Woman. Maybe Delia provided the last piece of advice Brenna needed from an unexpected source. Tonight she faced the Woman feeling like an equal.

She remained calm and spoke with confidence. "I summon the Woman in White. Standing here in power and light, I offer myself as a sacrifice."

The wind settled. A fine mist fell, cold against Brenna skin, seeping through her cloak. She waited and took deep breaths so her power remained steady and flowing. Something was coming. She could sense motion beyond the circle.

To her surprise, her cousin Maggie stepped out of the trees. It was Maggie, but different. Her hair was alive with electricity, moving like Medusa's. Her face was white, stark against the darkness around them. Her movements were jerky and robotic, as if she didn't have control over her own limbs.

As she came closer to the light, Brenna saw a black mass swoop in and out of Maggie's body, moving from her head to her toes and back again. A sick feeling started in Brenna's stomach.

"Maggie, what are you doing here?"

It wasn't Maggie's voice that roared at her through the mist. The voice was deep and hollow, echoing through the clearing like the rumble of doom. "I've made my own way, and because I've been strong enough to do this, my husband, my baby and I are safe from the Woman in White."

Brenna began to tremble, fear momentarily overwhelming her. "Maggie, what have you done?"

"I let the demon inside me." Maggie's laughter was maniacal. "He knocked on my door. You said demons don't knock on doors, but he did. He promised me I would be safe. He said as long as he could use me, the Woman in White couldn't touch me. He wants New Mourne. To take it, he knows he needs you. He couldn't get to you on his own. Even last night, when you tried to offer yourself, we couldn't reach you with that old fae in the way. But tonight he has me, and we're all alone."

Brenna's heart pounded as answers fell into place. "You put the plant that attacked me in Aunt Frances's garden?"

Maggie's head moved up and down like a puppet's.

"And you hurt Aunt Doris?"

The thing that was inside Maggie laughed again.

"Did you kill Sandy?"

Tears replaced the laughter. Brenna could see her cousin's true features through the demon's twisting veil. "He came out of me in front of her," she cried in her real voice. "Sandy was so frightened. She fell to floor. I don't know what happened after that."

Other parts of the puzzle clicked into place in Brenna's mind. She thought she saw Lauren in town when the demonic troubles began and again before the plant attacked her, but it must have been Maggie. Then there was Maggie's odd appearance the night at the shop. From the beginning, Maggie had an overpowering fear about being taken from her husband

and child. That made her weak and susceptible to the demon's offer.

"But why does he do this?" Brenna cried. "We saw the Woman in White kill Garth. We know she's waiting for one of us. Why does the demon torture the town, too?"

The answer was an unholy roar that shook the ground. "She thinks she won," the demon shrieked, the words crawling along Brenna's skin. "She thinks she has all the power, but I can show her. I can *be* her."

The blackness in Maggie morphed into the Woman in White. This time, Brenna wasn't fooled. She knew this was the demon, trying to trick her into believing he was the entity she had been seeking.

Brenna fell back, terrified but wanting to appear strong. Maggie dropped to the ground and began to crawl toward the path. "I'll get help," she sobbed to Brenna. "I promise I'll get help."

The wraith with the beautiful face wavered and then flashed back into Maggie's body. She straightened and moved forward with a jerk. Brenna could see her cousin was fighting the evil with all of her might.

"Now I have you where I want you," the demon rumbled at Brenna. "You're the one I want, the strongest, most powerful Connelly witch of your generation. With your power, I can banish the Woman forever. This land and this town will be mine."

The demon couldn't penetrate the circle, but he pushed Maggie's body as close as possible. Her eyes glowed as she screamed, "You are mine. You can't get away from me now."

Brenna raised her arms and stood firm, focusing her whole being on summoning help. "I call on the gods and goddesses to come to me, to ride within me, to help me dispel the evil in this place."

The air cracked with power as a light streaked down and passed through Brenna's hand into her body. When she pushed her hands out in front of her, a stream of radiance shot out and pushed Maggie to the ground.

"Brenna!" The sound of her mother calling her name shocked Brenna, and her magic wavered.

Delia stepped out of the trees. Brenna shouted a warning. "The demon has Maggie. Get away from here and get help."

Maggie stood and roared again, this time at Brenna's mother.

"Please, Mother, get the others."

"Please, Mommy," the demon mocked and threw fire at Delia.

The other witch was prepared, however, and she deflected the black magic flame so that it went back toward Maggie. Brenna pushed out another wave of light at the same time, sending Maggie to the ground again.

Instead of fleeing, Delia set her feet and began chanting. Light and magic filled the clearing. The demon struggled to bring Maggie to her feet while the wind rose, moaning through the trees.

Brenna let Delia's voice penetrate her mind. She picked up the chant as well. She felt the same power she experienced at the shop with Sarah—an unbreakable connection.

For a moment, Brenna felt hope. She thought they might defeat this evil.

Chapter 32

Jake barreled through the night in his cruiser. The situation at the market was now under control, and he was eager to check on Brenna. She didn't answer, and so he was headed back to the Connellys'. He had been hasty in saying she should leave his house today. At least until they found a way out of this curse, she should be with him.

As he rounded a curve in the road, a huge shape swept in front of him. He hit the brakes, fishtailing onto the shoulder. He jumped out of the car and turned round and round, trying to see what had he had almost hit.

A voice stopped him. A very familiar voice. "Garth?" Jake whispered into the night.

A low hiss sounded from above, and the owl swooped down and landed on the road.

"Jake," a voice said. The voice was strained, as if the words were spoken with great effort, but Jake knew it was definitely the voice of the shifter he trusted above all others.

The owl spoke in Garth's voice again, clearly struggling to communicate. "Help Brenna. You know where she is."

At the falls, Jake thought. Of course she would go again to offer herself. It was what she planned all along.

"Go," the owl hissed.

There was only one way to get to her quickly. Jake

threw himself forward, allowing his muscles to shift into tiger form in one seamless motion. His big paws gripped the ground, and he streaked toward Connelly land with the stealth and ease of a jungle cat.

He slowed as he approached Mulligan Falls, heard the sounds of battle and smelled the burnt ozone of magic. Through the foliage, he saw Brenna and Delia battling with Maggie. The quiet little wife and mother looked like a madwoman.

Without thought, Jake jumped at Maggie. She turned on him with inhuman speed, a huge sound coming from deep in her throat. She wasn't human, he realized. She wasn't even Maggie. He roared at her again, his teeth bared and his jaw wide. She collapsed to the ground, and the black spirit inside her whipped up, lingered in the air a moment, and then jumped into Jake.

"Kill Brenna," the demon whispered to Jake's tiger. "Take her for me."

Jake pulled back, resisting with all of his might. The part of him that Brenna said was not like his father fought the demon. The tiger prowled and growled, its eyes narrowed, its fangs dripping saliva. Infected by evil, he trembled with a need to kill, to tear tender flesh and rip the helpless human body into pieces.

He burned with the desire to go for Brenna's throat, to taste her warm, sweet blood. He would kill her, take her power and control the town. It would be his—New Mourne ruled by a demon. Jake could feel frustration, rage and a desire for vengeance. The demon wanted to prove his dominance.

All Jake had to do was kill Brenna. Killing was his legacy, wasn't it? He was his father's son, and he had killed before. How hard could it be to kill her? She had magic, but he had pure strength. He weighed more than four hundred pounds. All he had to do was pounce and she was his.

Lifting his head, Jake roared. The air vibrated with his rage. He stalked toward Brenna, his head low. She stood firm, though he could smell her fear. It was a delicious odor that made him even hungrier for her blood. Soft, sweet Brenna. She would be his. He knew she could not stop him.

But even as his tiger prepared to spring, Jake fought. For the memory of his mother's love. For the person Brenna believed he could be. In atonement for all he had done wrong in the past. He fought the evil. He pushed it away.

The black spirit slid out of him, rising to become a grotesque monster covered with a thick, black liquid that oozed on its skin and rippled like a repugnant black marsh. The smell of sulfur filled the air along with the putrid odor of rotting flesh.

"Damn you!" the demon screamed at Jake.

Jake prepared for a fresh attack just as Connelly witches appeared from the darkness, chanting as they moved toward the altar where Brenna and Delia stood. They were all together. Even Doris was there, supported by Fiona and Eva Grace. As their circle closed, the Gaelic chanting became louder. Jake felt the power grow as the women united.

White magic washed over him. It was rich and sweet and filled his senses, blocking the demon's pull. Supported by magic, his human pushed through.

The demon shrieked and spun in the air above the circle of witches, and then leapt back into Maggie.

Her body sat up with a jerk, and she looked at the tiger. “Come and get me,” she taunted him. “Kill me the way you want to.”

Blind rage seized Jake again.

As the monster had known she would, Brenna broke the circle and ran forward, putting herself between Maggie and the demon. “Jake, no. Don’t.”

Jake roared and prepared to spring, ready to kill Maggie if that’s what it took to defeat the demon.

Sarah called out. Brenna turned. The Connelly wand flew, end over end, across the clearing. For long, horrible seconds it hung in the air, and the monster reached out of Maggie. Long, black fingers inched toward the wand…reaching, stretching.

But the wand rose, caught in an air current, and fell into Brenna’s hand. The carved wood glowed like fire as Brenna caught it.

The demon retreated toward the edge of the cliff. Brenna lifted the wand. “In the names of the gods and goddesses, I send you back to the darkness. Back to the hellfire from whence you came. Away from our world. Be gone.”

The demon laughed and streaked out of Maggie, straight toward Brenna. Fire shot out of the wand and into the demon. It writhed and moaned but kept coming.

Jake rose on his hind feet beside Brenna and roared. The witches gathered behind Jake and Brenna, their bodies touching, magic sizzling in the air. Advancing toward it, they pushed the demon nearer to the edge of the cliff.

“Be gone,” they chanted. “Be gone.”

A blaze of light unlike any Jake had ever seen

spewed from the wand and touched the demon. A fire lit inside the creature. Screams of pure agony filled the very air they breathed. In an explosion of light and sound, the demon stumbled and fell over the cliff. Arms outstretched, the flames withered and screams faded while it tumbled into the valley below.

Jake stood at the edge with Brenna as only a tiny flicker remained in the air below them. Then that, too, was gone.

Rain came then. Not a driving storm, but a warm, sweet summer rain. The big drops washed through the air, cleansing it and bringing the fresh smell of pine trees, wildflowers and wet earth.

Jake turned his face to the sky, gratitude flooding his form. Brenna went to him without any fear of his tiger.

Under her gentle touch, he shifted. Then he caught her in his arms. For a moment, they simply held onto each other.

"Do you believe in yourself now?" Brenna asked him. "You beat him."

"Because of you," Jake said. "With you, I have all the strength I need."

She smiled and then turned to the coven. The witches were tending Maggie, who was dirty and dazed. She cried against Sarah's shoulder, begging forgiveness for her betrayal while Eva Grace held her hand. Everyone else appeared fine. They had weathered this attack without injuries.

Brenna reached out to her mother. "Thank you for following me."

"I told you I knew you were up to something," Delia replied as she grasped her daughter's hand. She motioned for Fiona and pulled both her daughters close.

Fiona stared over the cliff. “Do you think he’s gone?”

Delia answered. “We can only hope.”

“And what about the Woman?”

Jake felt Brenna’s shiver and slipped an arm around her. This battle was over but had they won it all? He wasn’t sure. The demon was tied to the Woman in some way, but vanquishing one didn’t mean the other was gone, as well.

As if by magic, which Jake didn’t doubt it was, the rain tapered off and the big Solstice moon glowed above them. Sarah stepped forward and lit the bonfire laid earlier. The coven joined hands again and chanted praise to the gods and goddesses for the good fortune of the harvest and the blessings of the night.

When the elder aunts and Maggie were gone, Brenna, Jake and the others made sure the fire was out.

“Let’s get out of here,” Lauren suggested. “It’s getting chilly.”

Reveling in the coolness, Jake pulled Brenna to his side again. “Lauren has the right idea,” he told Brenna before he kissed her. “Let’s go home.”

Brenna smiled up at him and peace like he had never known before settled in Jake’s bones. He was home, he realized as he walked through the woods with his new family. No matter what came next to New Mourne, this was where he belonged forever. With Brenna.

Chapter 33

Brenna and the rest of the coven stood back as Eva Grace stroked the barn owl perched on a stump near the altar. Candles added light to the evening shadows. Brenna saw the owl look at Eva Grace with adoring eyes.

Fiona came up beside Brenna. “It’s almost time for Garth to go.”

“Yes, she’s been with him for a while.” Brenna put an arm around her sister. “Are you feeling better since everything has settled down?”

“Not all the ghosts are back in their places,” Fiona noted with a frown. “I’m not sure why.”

The rest of the family stood beyond Fiona and Brenna. There had been a great deal of celebration and rejoicing during the past three days. Maggie was back to normal. Her daughter was in her husband’s arms. Maggie held the hand of her niece, her older brother’s four-year-old daughter.

The next generation, Brenna thought, as she watched both green-eyed girls study Eva Grace and the owl. They were young, but it was right that they were here along with everyone else.

Lauren stood not far away, looking voluptuous in a blue silk dress. Sarah and Marcus talked quietly with Delia, Rodric, Jake and Aiden were deep in conversation. The elder aunts, flanked by Estelle and

Diane, were intent on Eva Grace, who was saying goodbye to her love.

"I'm still not sure I understand why Garth's spirit didn't just come to you," Brenna murmured to Fiona as Eva Grace stroked the owl again.

Her sister sighed. "Even I don't fully understand the ways of the spirits. Garth was weak from being killed by the demon. The owl took him in. The strength and magical power of the bird were a boon to him, but he was also constrained by the owl's limitations. He couldn't just tell you what was happening. Speaking to Jake took a lot of strength."

"But why wouldn't he go to Eva Grace instead of me?"

"You needed Garth more," Fiona said. "The demon wanted you from the start."

"And the demon knew that by making me think the Woman in White was hurting my family, I would end up sacrificing myself. In the end, he was sure I would give myself to him. Instead, I fought. We all fought."

Fiona hugged Brenna. "You were brave to offer yourself. Twice you came here to the Woman."

Brenna shivered. "She never answered me. She didn't kill Garth. She didn't come to the shop, either. The demon only wanted us to think it was her. He tricked us."

"He said he wants to banish the Woman." Fiona frowned. "I wonder why?"

"We'll only know when we find her true story." There were still too many questions, Brenna thought. No matter that everyone felt strong and confident after banishing the demon, there was much they didn't understand.

And now when she had so very many reasons to want to live, she wanted more than ever to find the answers.

"I just wish I'd had more time to think about the spell I used to send the demon over the cliff," Brenna fretted. "I wanted him destroyed, and I'm not sure I did that."

The owl spread his wings. The beautiful brown and gold of his feathers glimmered in the light from the candles while the compassion of the man inside him seemed to reach out to Brenna from his snowy face.

Eva Grace smiled through her tears. "How can I ever love another when I've known love from you?"

A sparkling light descended nearby. For a moment the owl sat very still. Then his wings unfurled and a glow lifted from his body. Tears slid down Eva Grace's cheeks as the two glimmering spots of light merged into one. She blew a kiss, and the radiant orb melted into the night. Garth's spirit was gone. Eva Grace gently touched the owl once more before it took flight.

Fiona and Brenna joined Eva Grace and watched the owl soar above the falls before disappearing.

"Are you all right?" Fiona asked their cousin.

"Fine." Eva Grace wiped her eyes and gave her cousins quick hugs. "I'm really fine. I'm glad Garth is at peace."

"Maybe we can all have some peace now," Fiona said. "Let's form the circle and complete the ceremony."

As her sister and cousin headed for the altar, Brenna had a prickly sensation of being watched. She glanced to the trees beyond, but saw nothing.

Jake came up beside her and leaned in for a kiss.

"Hello, my bewitching beauty."

The touch of his lips and the sound of his voice drove Brenna's paranoid feelings away. She loved this shifter. She was his. No curse was going to end what they were beginning.

Brenna kissed Jake back with enthusiasm. "How have things been in town today?"

"Quiet and peaceful. Just the way this sheriff likes them."

"I'm so glad," Brenna said. "It's wonderful to have New Mourne back to normal." When Jake grinned, she added, "Well, at least normal for us."

They joined the others as Brenna tried to remain hopeful. Maybe the Woman in White would leave the Connellys alone and let her start her new life with Jake.

A cold, mocking laughter filled the clearing. The members of the coven looked at one another in apprehension. Maggie gathered the children to her. Sarah, the elder aunts, and the women surrounded them. Jake, Brenna and the others closed ranks as well, as if in battle formation.

Jake took Brenna's hand.

Though his presence was warm and comforting, she shivered as the laughter faded. It wasn't over.

The Woman in White was still coming for one of them.

Epilogue

She strolled among the trees as the witches gathered in their circle while their men and their children watched. In her full-skirted dress, she glided through the woods without disturbing the bushes or moving a leaf.

They were so ridiculous with their little candles and silly rituals.

"They never learn," she said as the witches began to chant. "Every generation thinks they can subvert me and keep me from getting what is my due. They want to be happy and live in peace, but they must pay the price, just as I did."

Her time for tribute would be soon.

She was pleased they had defeated the demon. Time and again, their triumph over him aided her. Each time they sent him away, they reminded her how it felt to dominate him. She had never known real power until she defeated him. She had drawn that triumph into her spirit. While her sins and losses meant she could never move on from this place, she was content to know that *he* suffered, fretted and plotted to rise again. And the Connellys would always fight him for her. When they did, it only increased her power over him.

The witches chanted, voices lifting in praise to the gods and goddesses. The Woman in White listened, knowing they would soon know the pain of sacrifice.

She had decided long ago that they had to suffer, to give up what was most precious, just as she had.

That was the deal Sarah Connelly had made, a deal honored through the centuries. As long as she suffered and remained tethered to this place, the Connellys must suffer as well.

Forever.

Once more, she allowed her laughter to ring out like the bells of doom.

A word about the author…

Neely Powell is the pseudonym for co-writers Leigh Neely and Jan Hamilton Powell. They are the authors of *TRUE NATURE*, also from The Wild Rose Press, about a shapeshifting lawyer and a dysfunctional psychic, as well as *AWAKENING MAGIC*, about the witches of New Mourne.

The best friends met when they both worked at a rock 'n roll radio station in Chattanooga. Though they wrote fiction together, they first found success on separate paths.

Writing as Celeste Hamilton, Jan published 24 romance novels. Her books appeared on numerous bestseller lists before she left fiction for a career in corporate communications. Leigh became a successful nonfiction writer and editor of newspapers and magazines.

Their fiction collaboration resumed when they focused on the paranormal world. Now Neely Powell writes about shifters, witches, werewolves, faeries, and ghosts, mixing in shades of mystery, romance, and thrillers—the kinds of books they both enjoy reading.